Murder on the Front Nine

A Grand Strand Mystery/Thriller

A work of fiction

Steve McMillen

This book is a work of fiction. Names, characters, places and incidents are either products of the author's imagination or are used fictitiously and are not to be construed as real. Any resemblance to actual events, locales or persons, living or dead, is entirely coincidental.

ISBN: 1-4699-1228-7
ISBN-13: 9781469912288

Dedication

This book is dedicated, first, to my lovely bride Beverly and to my family. Also to old friends, new friends, old neighbors, new neighbors and to my brother Tim, who never got a chance to read the book.

PROLOGUE

Trever Byers is on his way to catch the 6:00 ferry from Southport for the twenty-minute boat ride to Bald Head Island for his weekly early morning golf game. It is late spring along the Carolina coast and the forecast is for another beautiful Chamber of Commerce day.

Trever, a retired ATF agent, is currently an advisor and consultant to United States Senator R. Gene Brazile of North Carolina. He is also a freelance underwater self-proclaimed salvage junkie. He likes to catch the first ferry out of Southport, a quaint little resort town along the North Carolina coast, so he can get his round in before lunch and catch the 12:30 ferry back to the mainland. Today he plans to meet his friend and fellow salvage junkie, retired Federal Judge Thomas Allen Cadium, for a business lunch before leaving the island.

He always enjoys playing golf at the Bald Head Island Club. The 18-hole seaside golf course winds its way over dunes, around lagoons, along the ocean, and through a maritime forest. The course designer left much of the terrain the way he found it, creating a course of almost unparalleled wild beauty. Many of the holes are undisturbed, bordered by the still lively natural habitats of herons, egrets, foxes and alligators. It is unspoiled, quiet, and very few golfers play this early in the day. He can already smell the salt air and he can hardly wait to see the fine, clear rooster tail of water that his traversing golf ball leaves on the fairway from the early morning dew. He usually plays alone, walking with a pull cart. A normal round of golf for him is under four hours.

What a beautiful day, he is thinking as he readies himself to tee off on number 1. He does several minutes of stretching exercises as soft white clouds chase one another, like tumbleweeds, across the clear, blue sky. He was told by Justin, the golf pro, that someone who he thinks is staying on the island teed off about fifteen minutes before him and if Trever hurries he can catch up to him and play as a twosome.

Justin told Trever he tried to start a conversation with the guy but all of his answers were one or two syllable words," yeah, no, uh-huh". Justin said he was truly a strange person.

Justin said he did not know the man's name, but he rented a golf cart and clubs and bought a dozen golf balls. He paid for everything in cash. The pro said he had a case with him, which the man said, in as few words as possible, contained a telescope so that he could do some bird watching while playing.

Trever thinks the whole thing is a little strange because he did not see any other golf carts in the parking lot. There are no automobiles on Bald Head Island. Transportation on the island is limited to golf carts, bikes, skates, and well-worn walking shoes.... an accurate reflection of the slower, more relaxed island attitude. The pro said the man would be easy to spot; he had on dark glasses, a beard, moustache, and a wide-brimmed Panama hat. He said he truly looked more like a bird watcher than a golfer.

Trever plays the first hole in one over par and then he pars number 2 and number 3. His day is going well. Number 4 is a slight dogleg left and he begins to think he is good, so of course he ends up with a double bogey on the hole. He comes back to reality, stops thinking and begins just playing golf again. He misses a birdie putt by inches on number 5 and ends up with a par. As he walks to the tee box on number 6, which also just happens to be as far away from the clubhouse and as close to the 10,000-acre tidal creek preserve as you can get, he is only three over par.

A disconcerting thought enters his mind. He has not seen anything of the bird-watching golfer who teed off ahead of him, although he did see occasional cart tire tracks zigzagging across the fairway in the early morning dew. Little does he know that the bird watcher is seeing a lot of him, in fact, he has him right in his sights. The bird watcher visually checks the area with his scope.

He sees nothing but a majestic view of a beautiful golf course with a light mist hovering above the lakes and ponds. He finds no one else within sight.

Trever places the ball on the tee, takes a practice swing and addresses the ball. There is the slight, quiet, thud sound of a silencer and Trever's round of golf ends at three over par and so does his life. He is dead, shot through the heart.

The assassin checks the area again for traffic before going to Trever's body. He feels for and finds no pulse. He searches and discovers what he is looking for in Trever's golf bag. He hurriedly rolls the body onto a plastic drop cloth he brought with him, cleans up what little blood is on the ground and drags the body, along with the pull cart into the trees. He folds up his rifle, places it back in the carrying case, takes off his beard and hat but leaves on the moustache. He puts everything in a green garbage bag. He leaves the rental clubs but takes the dozen golf balls; after all, they are Pro V1's. He drives the golf cart back through the trees toward the tidal creek for about one-quarter mile where his rented boat is moored to a dilapidated old wooden boat dock, waiting to take him back to the mainland. By the time the authorities discover Trever's body, the assassin is well on his way to the Wilmington Airport and home.

⮞⮜

Earlier that day, before dawn, the assassin took his luggage, to the boat he had stashed on the tidal creek. He did not have to check out of the condo because he paid in full under an assumed name when he checked in. He bought food when he first arrived and had all of his meals in the condo. The fewer people who see him, the better. He cleaned and wiped down the condo the night before and that morning he wore gloves. The condo was probably cleaner when he left than when he arrived.

He checked the area around the sixth tee box several times while riding his golf cart and looking for birds. He knew exactly where he was going. He had gone over repeatedly in his mind every step of the attack. He received an e-mail before he left home about the golfing habits of Trever Byers and they were the same each week. Trever was a creature of habit. The assassin cleaned his weapon several times and calibrated his scope. He probably did not need the scope but he decided to use it anyway. When you are a hired assassin, still alive and not in jail, you make sure you have everything right or you will not live free to a ripe old age. He drove his cart back to the condo, wiped it down and walked the short distance to the clubhouse.

ॐ

The assassin arrived at the Wilmington Airport about two hours after he left Bald Head Island. He boarded a private plane and arrived home mid-afternoon.

After a shower, he called a pre-determined number and left a message, "The birdie putt fell and I have the scorecard with me as proof. Bring your clubs and meet me at the course tomorrow at noon."

He arrived at the exchange point about an hour ahead of the scheduled meeting to look around and make sure that it was not a trap. A master of disguise, he was dressed in khaki shorts, orange t-shirt, brown ball cap, and a carefully applied goatee. He had the scorecard in a brown paper bag along with his lunch and a .38 revolver.

The exchange point was a large city park full of benches, playground equipment, and screaming kids. There were trees, mounds of lush green grass, and carefully cleaned sidewalks where the kids rode their skateboards and the parents took their walks. It was wide open with several escape routes. His rule has always been do not go in unless you know how you are going to get out. He did reconnaissance at the park several times for escape routes before he left on his trip to Wilmington and then on to Bald Head Island. He plans to be very careful because this client was a referral. They already wired the first twenty-five thousand to his numbered Singapore bank account. He has done the job. If he has to walk away without the other twenty-five thousand, so be it. He would still have the scorecard, his life and his freedom. He could always collect later.

He brought with him a unique electronic device which he had plugged into his ear. The device allowed him to know if anyone was trying to bug him and it scanned for radio transmissions in the area. He sat on a bench almost one hundred yards away from the designated pick-up point and began eating his lunch, which consisted of a sandwich with pastrami, Swiss cheese, and onion on a rye bun. He brought along a Diet Pepsi to wash it all down. All the time he was enjoying his lunch, he was also listening. Soon his attention to the sounds around him paid off. The park became crowded and extremely noisy. And all of the noise did not come from screaming kids. Someone was planning to kill him.

The usual smile on his face turned into a frown, his eyes slit lizard like against the desert sun. He reached for his gun and almost said aloud, *who do they think they are dealing with, an amateur?* However, he kept quiet, stayed calm, and he did not panic. He finished his lunch, got up and left with the scorecard still in his brown paper lunch bag. He would collect later.

Chapter 1: Mickke D

I sluggishly and slowly pull myself out of bed around 7:00am. It's Saturday morning and I heard my overnight guest leave about 6:30. She told me last night she had to be at work by 7:00 at some resort on the ocean. She was a cute, well put together young thing with freckles, I'm guessing in her mid-twenties. I must have really made a big impression on her because she did not even say good-bye. She did leave me a note which read, *Mickke D, been fun but my boyfriend will be back in town tomorrow. See ya "pops".*

She never mentioned she had a boyfriend and what is this "pops" bit? Oh, well, there are quite a few available women in Myrtle Beach. Of course, sometimes I feel as if I have been married to most of them.

I walk into the bathroom and with blurry eyes gaze soulfully into the mirror. Staring back at me is a 45 year-old single again male about 6'1" 190 pounds with sandy blond hair. He looks to be in good shape when he pulls his stomach in and throws his shoulders back. Maybe not the buff, ex-Green Beret he was after mustering out of the army fifteen years ago, but certainly not a "pops."

Maybe the bright red boxers he is wearing made her think of Santa Clause. Maybe that was what Paula Ann did not like. My third wife hated them also but I thought it was just because I told her my second wife gave them to me. Gee, maybe I need to buy new underwear and all of my women problems will disappear.

Still looking in the mirror, I check out my butt in the reflection of the mirrors on the door of my walk-in closet. One of my ex-wives once told me my butt was as nice as Freddie Couples' backside. Since I am not into checking out pro-golfers posteriors, I took for granted that it was a compliment but it just looks like a rear end to me.

I throw on some shorts, a t-shirt, and flip-flops before going out to retrieve the morning paper. I smile as the warm, balmy, salt air hits my face. Looks and feels like it is going to be another perfect day at the beach. I may even try to play golf today and forget about my rather mundane way of life here in Myrtle Beach.

However, do you know what? My life wasn't always boring. Paula Ann spent most of the evening talking about herself. If "pops" could have gotten a word in edgewise, I would have told her that after graduating from Ohio State with a degree in landscape architecture and four years of ROTC I went directly into the Army. I spent time in Colombia and Panama training troops and chasing bad guys around. I finished my tour of duty at Fort Bragg as an Investigative Officer for Army Jag. Nothing dull about those times.

As I reach into the newspaper box, I hear a gushing noise as all of a sudden my neighbor's sprinkler system heads pop-up out of the ground as if flowers were being born instantly. I get my morning shower outside instead of in. I move away from the path of the water and return to my rather cookie-cutter, three-bedroom, two-bath ranch. It is a poster home for golf course living along the Grand Strand. I make it back to the safe confines of my house. I am drenched. Fifteen years ago I would have been quick enough to avoid the water barrage altogether. My God, maybe Paula Ann was right. I am getting old. Of course, she did not mention anything about "pops" being old in bed last night.

Just as I get back inside, my phone rings. It is my neighbor. As I dry my hands and stand dripping water on my tiled kitchen floor, he says with a chuckle that he saw me outside and is sorry about the sprinkler going off and soaking me. He also tells me to be sure and read in the paper about the golfer who died at the Bald Head Island Golf Course. He and I played there not too long ago.

I throw the paper on the table, towel off and get ready to prepare my usual Saturday morning breakfast of orange juice, two eggs over easy, nice piece of ham steak, a blueberry bagel with honey and a cup of decaffeinated green tea. The other six days of the week, I listen to my doctor, who seems to think my cholesterol is too high. Those days I have orange juice and oatmeal. Actually, I was hoping to have breakfast with Paula Ann at one of the local pancake houses so I, the middle-aged bachelor, could show off my young, trophy girlfriend. So much for that idea, "pops."

I get breakfast prepared and I sit down to enjoy it along with the morning paper. I see the article my neighbor was referring to. The headline reads, "Golfer killed in North Carolina". The report says that a man was shot and killed at the Bald Head Island golf course Friday morning and the local police are calling it a homicide. The article goes on to say the man killed was a retired government employee who was working as a consultant to United States Senator R. Gene Brazile of North Carolina.

I think what the world is coming to if you cannot feel safe on a golf course? My mind wanders back to dangerous Army times when golf was a welcome relief from the everyday stress of Army life.

My playing partners were fellow officers back then who were looking to fill out their weekend foursome.

There was "By the Book" Barry Green, a first lieutenant from Port Clinton, Ohio. We called him that because he was always quoting some Army regulation. Our second member was Second Lieutenant Bill "Tank" Cutter from Greenville, South Carolina. He acquired that nickname because he said he always wanted to drive a tank but no one would let him. The third member was Second Lieutenant Ted "The Reverend" DeShort from Orlando, Florida. He got that name because he had transferred from the Chaplin Service to the Infantry. He never told me why and I never asked. Bill invited me to join the group and I became the fourth, First Lieutenant Mickke David MacCandlish from Lancaster, Ohio. You're right, that's why my nickname has always been Mickke D.

I became good friends with my golf partners while at Fort Bragg and after their tour of duty was over, Barry, Bill, and Ted started a "Spook" business called SIL (Special Investigations Limited). That business would eventually involve me.

I don't seem to have the time to play golf now. Why is that? Aside from the fact that I have been married, divorced, and broke three times, I run a landscape business, have my own real estate company, and teach golf on the side. No wonder I have no time to play golf. I work too hard. All three of my ex-wives said the same thing in court. I spent more time working than paying attention to them. I need to re-align my priority list. I need to add some excitement and fun to my life. I need new underwear and a new girlfriend.

I should have remembered that old saying, *be careful what you wish.*

స్థ్

How did I end up in the Myrtle Beach area? It was the perfect storm. I was just recently divorced from my first wife and I wanted to get away from the Ohio winters, especially the snow and ice; I loved to play golf and liked the thought of the beach with lots of girls in bikinis. In addition, I had a job offer from a landscape company in North Myrtle Beach. They needed someone to manage the landscaping of a new golf course. It was a no-brainer decision on my part.

స్థ్

Myrtle Beach, aka the Grand Strand, runs from Brunswick County, North Carolina to Georgetown, South Carolina. It is sixty miles of beaches, golf courses and restaurants.

Many have called the area the golf mecca of the world. One hundred plus golf courses and you can play golf three hundred sixty-five days a year. Need I say more about golf?

The beaches are wide and have easy access routes for parking or walking. There are also many fishing piers dotting the horizon if you're into that form of recreation. In addition, the great part is that the beaches are only crowded with tourists in those little bikinis for about three months out of the year. The remaining months, it is like having your own private beach. It's empty.

There are more than fifteen hundred restaurants along the Grand Strand and they provide some of the best seafood along the Mid-Atlantic

Coast. You can have seafood, a steak, Carolina barbecue, or an old-fashioned hamburger. The choice is yours.

ॐॐ

So why did I relocate to Myrtle Beach? It was all of the above. It had everything I ever wanted or needed and I had a great job waiting for me. There was golf, girls, the beach, and a job. It doesn't get any better than this.

Chapter 2: The Army Buddies

Allow me to tell you what my three amigos told me about SIL. They started SIL because there were some cases and investigations that the CIA, NSA, and other covert organizations wanted information on but could not or would not get officially involved. They needed some other entity to do the down and dirty work and keep them out of the headlines. These organizations would hire SIL as an independent contractor to gather the information, report their findings, offer suggestions and keep the big boys out of the public eye. Barry, Bill, and Ted usually did the legwork themselves but occasionally a case would come along which required a special type of operative.

I suppose that is why I get this off-the-wall phone call. "Hey old buddy, it's Bill. How are you and how is your golf game these days?"

"Hey Tank, good to hear your voice, game's not very good because I never get a chance to play or practice, how's yours?"

I have not heard from any of my old Army buddies in almost fifteen years, so Bill's call really comes from out of the blue.

He answers, "My golf game is about the same Mickke D, not very good. Say, Barry, Ted, and I will be in the Myrtle Beach area next week and we are hoping to get together with you, play some golf, drink a few beers, and check on your new lifestyle."

Then all of a sudden, "Sorry guy, I've got another call; I'll get back to you in a few days."

He hangs up! I am speechless. I don't know what to think. How do they know I am living in Myrtle Beach and how did they get my cell phone number?

ॐ॰ॐ

Monday evening I receive another call from Bill. "Hey Mickke D, how about picking us up at the airport on Friday evening. We'll be leaving Sunday morning and can we camp out at your place?"

"Sounds great," I reply, "should I make a tee time for Saturday morning?"

"You bet, and be sure to bring your A game because Barry says he is going to kick your ass, Mr. Golf Teaching Pro."

I ask him what airline they will be flying and what time they will be arriving.

There is hesitation on the other end of the line and finally he comes back, "We will be coming in on a private plane and we will call you when we get close."

"Are you coming into Myrtle Beach International?"

Again silence, finally he says, "No we're flying into the Grand Strand Airport. Do you know where it is located?"

"Yes, I do, and tell Barry not to forget his clubs; I don't want to hear any excuses at the end of the day."

After we hang up I start thinking, private plane, no definite time, and how do they know I am a teaching pro? That happened several years after the last time I had seen any of them. I had been improving my own golf game by reading books and listening to golf tapes and then I began to help some of my friends who were willing to try my new methods and ideas.

One of my friends said one day after a lesson, "Mickke D, you should become a teaching pro." I took his advice, enrolled in a golf teaching school in Florida, passed the course and began teaching on a part-time basis. The rest is history.

ॐॐ

My military training begins to click in. What are these guys up to? I decide to pull in a favor and get the down and dirty on my old friends and SIL.

My next-door neighbor, Jimmy Bolin, the same one who drenched me with his sprinkler system, is a retired FBI staff special agent and I have given him several golf lessons at no charge. He said that if I ever needed anything, be sure and let him know. I call him Tuesday morning and tell him I need some background information on a company called Special Investigation Limited located in Culpepper, Virginia.

He asks what specific information I am looking for and I answer, "I would like to know the current status of the main principals, Barry, Bill, and Ted, and if there are any bad rumors going around about them. Also I would like to know the financial status of the company."

He replies, "I'll see what I can do, how soon do you need this?"

I tell him I need whatever he can find out by midday Friday.

❧❦

Thursday evening around 7:30 my doorbell rings. I look out the side window and see Jimmy. He comes in with a folder, which does not seem to have a whole lot of material in it. After some small talk about his golf game and a beer, we get down to business. He tells me that information on SIL is very limited and very hush-hush. They have worked for the CIA, NSA, FBI, and several other "spook" organizations.

It is rumored they may have even done some work directly for the White House, hanging chads in Florida. The story is that they gathered intelligence on the main parties making the decisions in Florida and found enough dirt to make sure the White House got the proper outcome for the election. If this is true, they know people in high places, about as high as you can go.

As far as the principals are concerned, they are not much more than ex-Special Forces officers who found a niche for themselves. They are not married, have nice condos, and nice cars. The company owns a Gulfstream airplane and a helicopter, which they use regularly. They stay out of the limelight and don't seem to be in any trouble financially. Jimmy also states that without his contacts at the Bureau, none of this information would have been available. They definitely know someone high up the ladder.

I decide to fill Jimmy in with what little information I have about the upcoming weekend just in case I need him later. He is a big, strong, tough, smart guy, in his mid-fifties who has done some things that if I told you about them... well you know.

He cautions me to be careful. From what he has gathered, SIL usually gets the dirtiest and sometimes strangest cases. I tell him I am probably just building a mountain out of a molehill and that they are just coming down to play golf and talk about old times. Yeah, right.

Chapter 3: Mickke D

Friday morning I make a 10:00 tee time for Saturday at River Hills. I clean up the two spare bedrooms and clean my golf clubs. The clubs are not very dirty because they never get used. I even get out my gun, a shiny, chrome-plated Colt .45 and clean it. In the afternoon, I go to the store, pick up some rib-eye steaks, salad mixings, and beer and then stop by my office to see if I have any messages.

I seem to spend a lot of time in my office these days but I don't seem to accomplish much. When I first moved to Myrtle Beach, I was doing commercial and residential landscaping. That was the period when real estate was going crazy so I decided to get my sales agent license and later on I got my brokers license and started my own company. Therefore, my office is a landscape and real estate office all in one.

At one time, I had a large office with several employees but that became too much of a hassle and then the real estate business went to hell in a hand basket, so now it is just me in one room, which I rent from a local plumbing contractor. His receptionist, who is also his wife, answers my phone when I'm not there.

I paid off my house (I did real well in real estate), paid off my Trailblazer and even paid off my third ex-wife. I also have a free and clear 1981 Black Corvette in the garage, so I am virtually debt free. When I am working as a landscape architect consultant to several local golf design companies, I charge three hundred a day plus expenses. Life is good although not very exciting.

None of the messages are pressing except I did get a 911 call from Robert, one of my golf students. His once-straight drives have turned into a terrible duck hook. He is close to a meltdown. He wants to know if I can meet him sometime to work out his problem. I call and tell him I will meet him at Harbor View Driving Range around 3:00 today. He sounds better already.

I figure I have until at least 6:00 before my group arrives so I meet Robert and within twenty minutes we have replaced the duck hook with a gentle draw and some very straight shots. He had gone back to gripping the club too tightly and was hitting the ball instead of swinging the club head and just letting the ball get in the way. Life is now good for Robert.

I usually charge thirty dollars for a lesson but Robert gives me a fifty and tells me to keep the change. I decide to go home and wait for the guys to call since I am only fifteen minutes from the airport.

While I am waiting, I search through a junk drawer and find an old photo of the four of us standing on the first tee at a local charity golf tournament. I start thinking, what do I really know about my old golfing friends?

Barry was a martial arts instructor and a computer whiz kid. Bill taught survival training, small weapons, and sniper skills. Ted was a computer geek and an explosive expert. The three of them were always together when they were not training or teaching. Bill told me the three of them met at Officers Candidate School at Fort Benning, Georgia and have been good friends ever since. They always took their vacations at the same time. They never said where they went, and I never asked. They didn't smoke, didn't drink too much, and as far as I knew, absolutely no drugs. Of course, I haven't seen them in more than fifteen years. Things may have changed.

They tried several times to bring me into their tightly knit group as a permanent member but I knew I would be the fifth wheel. (They were always talking about pirates and sunken treasure. They were like kids in a candy store when anyone mentioned old shipwrecks and buried treasure). I did not think I would fit into their little club. Barry and I did not always see eye to eye on a lot of things when we were together. They even offered to make me a part of SIL but I said thanks but no thanks. They never brought up the subject again. Our relationship remained simply a weekend golf foursome.

Chapter 4: The Reunion

I am starting to become concerned, it is now past 7:30pm and no word from the group. I go out on my deck, which overlooks the 16th fairway at River Hills and wait for their call to go to the airport. I have always thought the 16th at River Hills is the most eye-appealing hole on the course. It is a tree-lined short par 4 but the green is surrounded by water on three sides plus a sand trap. An errant tee shot or approach shot can lead to a big number on the hole.

River Hills is a very nice, laid-back golf community in Little River. It is located just over the Intercoastal Waterway from North Myrtle Beach, with around 370 single-family homes. It is off the beaten path and usually very quiet. Residents take their dogs out for walks and if there were sidewalks, they would fold up about 8:00 in the evening and unfold around 9:00 the next morning.

I am watching the last group of golfers for the day come through; I know that because they have a red flag on their cart. It is still light and I figure they will be finished before dark with no problem.

I can hear the distant sound of a helicopter heading my way, probably bound for Myrtle Beach International, the Grand Strand Airport, or maybe continuing down the coast.

As the chopper noise gets louder and closer, my phone rings. It's Barry. "Hey old buddy, are you ready to pick us up?"

I reply casually, "I don't know. Are you close?"

He laughs, "Well in about two minutes we'll be in your back yard, is there anyone coming down the fairway?"

Oh, my God, they are in that chopper I hear and they are going to land in the fairway behind my house.

Barry comes back, "We are running a little late so I told the pilot to just drop us off at your place. Don't worry, you know us, we'll be in and out in thirty seconds or have you forgotten all of your training?"

In shock, I wonder if the HOA has a covenant about choppers landing in my back yard. If not, you can bet there will be one after tonight. How am I going to explain this?

I guess I have grown soft and passive after all these years while my Army buddies still have that zest and flair for adventure in their lives. Where did I go wrong?

Oh yeah, I remember. Married, divorced, and broke three times. Let's not even talk about the bright red boxers. My old friends are the ones who have missed all the joys of life, not me.

I am waiting to hear sirens coming down the streets of River Hills. They will come, arrest all of us, and take us off to jail or worse yet, call out the Marines, thinking this is an invasion.

I am glad I don't see Jimmy's car next door. I am not sure what he may do. All I can do is stand on the deck and stare as this helicopter sits down in the fairway behind my house. Three people jump out, each carrying a small hand-held bag and one large golf bag. Barry was right, it took about thirty seconds and the chopper was up, up, and away. Maybe my neighbors will just think this is a new golf package deal thought up by some innovative golf director here in town.

As my old Army buddies come up the back stairs of my deck I give them a good looking over to see if any drastic changes have taken place in the last fifteen years.

They are each wearing kakis, a denim shirt with a light sport coat, and no ties. After handshakes and hugs (real men do sometimes hug), I notice Barry, who I always thought looked like Billy Mayfair on the PGA Tour, has less hair and has put on about fifteen pounds.

Bill looks the same, a lean, mean, fighting machine; except his blond hair is now silver gray (must be the spook thing).

Ted has put on some weight, lost some hair, and is wearing glasses, but overall they look good and in good shape. Of course one thing I couldn't miss, they are all packing weapons.

I ask the group as a whole, "Is there an invasion coming or do you always carry guns on a golf weekend?"

"Sorry guy, occupational hazard. We'll stick them in our bags," Barry quickly replies and they stash their weapons.

After getting their bags stowed in their rooms, I suggest we go get a sandwich and a beer at a local place called Crab Catchers. The restaurant and bar is located on the Intercoastal Waterway, a string of both man-made and natural channels that periodically dump into the Atlantic Ocean. It is a 3,000-mile highway for pleasure boats and barge traffic. The fellows lose their sport coats and put on golf shirts. We get into the Trailblazer and head into Little River. Funny thing is, I hear no sirens or see no Marines coming our way and it has been almost forty-five minutes since they made their grand entrance.

On the way to dinner, I amuse them by giving the local Chamber of Commerce story on Little River.

"It has been written that in 1791, President George Washington dined in Little River on his southern tour."

They smirk as I imitate a tour guide and continue. "He is one of the first in a long line of travelers who have visited this tiny village to savor the fresh seafood caught by a fleet of local fisherman. (And yes, we've remained a tiny village because every time incorporation comes up on the ballot, it is voted down)."

Barry only smiles but Bill and Ted laugh hysterically and ask for more.

I continue, "Over the years, plenty of other northerners have found their way south. In fact, for a while the village got the name Yankee Town because of all the New Englanders who had moved here during the early days of the United States. Some of the folks in Little River swear that if you listen closely, you can detect a hint of British, Massachusetts, or perhaps Connecticut accent in the chatter of the fishermen down on the docks. Others believe the village's unique personality comes from the combination of pirates, Indians, Spanish explorers, and shipwrecked sailors who founded the place back in the 1500s."

"Has any sunken treasure been found, Mr. Tour Guide?" Ted chides.

Barry frowns and I ignore them. "And of course Little River's real claim to fame is the annual Blue Crab Festival. Thousands of people come to the waterfront each spring to partake of Blue Crab and live music at the yearly weekend party."

Thank goodness, the restaurant comes into view. I can tell the guys have lost interest in the local history and their tour guide.

∾∾

We arrive at Crab Catchers and get a table out on the deck next to the waterway. Our waitress is Dee, a pretty, middle-aged, platinum blonde. She is trying to be helpful and take our order but she keeps looking back at a table in the middle of the deck where four loud mouths, maybe golfers, are sitting.

"Sorry guys, I'll be right back, I need to quiet someone down," she says as she turns and moves toward the loud table.

When she arrives, she says in a very soft voice and with a smile, "Gentlemen, if you could keep your voices down to a soft roar I would really appreciate it. I have several tables of people who are here for a nice quiet evening on the deck with a few drinks and some good food."

I have a feeling some of the possible golfers had a bad day on the course and are letting off steam because of how poorly they played.

One of them, let's call him Bozo 1 slams his hand on the table and says to Dee, who jumps back from the table, "Listen here lady, our money is as good as anyone's money here and if they don't like our conservation, then they can just leave. Now just do your job and get out of my face."

I think to myself, *I really wish he had not said that because I have known Dee, as a waitress at Crab Catchers, for a long time and she seems like a nice lady.* Bozo 1 has just really pissed me off.

Before I can get up, Barry gets up from the table and says, "I'll be right back, order me the fish sandwich with fries and coleslaw."

All I can do is shake my head, I have been coming here for years and I have never seen any problems with noisy guests. Why do they have to show up on the one night when the Cavalry is in town? One good thing, at least my guys left their guns at home.

Bill puts his hand on my shoulder, "Easy Mickke D, you know Barry, he will take care of the problem."

Barry walks over to the rowdy table and says in a very calm but sincere voice, "Fellows I would really like to enjoy my sandwich and beer in this lovely little restaurant, so if you could keep the noise down, that would be great. If you can't, maybe you should just leave."

Barry returns to our table with a smile. Again, I just shake my head because I know along with everyone else at our table that Barry is just baiting Bozo 1.

Bozo 1 is dumbfounded. He cannot believe what he has just heard, that someone is actually asking him to leave. He then makes a big mistake. He gets up from the table, but instead of leaving, he comes over to our table. Big, big mistake. He walks up to Barry and gets right in his face, which is not a good idea and very poor judgment.

Problem #1 for Bozo 1. You should always keep some space between you and your adversary. He says to Barry in a sort of slurred voice, "No one tells me to leave, I paid my money and I plan to stay and yell as much as I want, so screw you."

Problem #2 for Bozo 1. He takes a roundhouse swing at Barry's head. Barry easily grabs his wrist with his left hand because he can see the punch coming a mile away.

Problem #3 for Bozo 1. Never fight a sober man let alone a martial arts expert if you're drunk. With his right hand, Barry delivers a short, sharp straight blow with the knuckles of his fore finger and middle finger to his solar plexus and he is down on his knees gasping for air.

Now here comes Bozo 2, who really should have known better after what he had just observed. Instead he yells out, "Why you no good son of a bitch, I'll kick your ass."

As he gets to our table, Bill's leg comes up and out and catches him in the side of his knee. He is also on the ground, writhing in pain. Bill did not kick him hard enough to break anything but it definitely got his attention.

Now for Bozos 3 and 4. They are looking at their two friends, one gasping for air and the other one writhing in pain. They had just got their butts kicked by a couple of guys who never got up from their chairs. Let us just say they sobered up in a hurry and decide it would behoove them to get their friends out of here and cut their losses.

They apologize to us, to Dee, and everyone on the outside deck. They quickly pay their bill, leave Dee a big tip and walk out, dragging 1 and 2 with their tails between their legs. As they leave, everyone out on the deck stands up, faces us, and applauds. We get up and take a short bow and our dinner is on the house. After our new friends send over the third round of beers, we decide it is time to go.

On the way out, Larry McHerron, the general manager and chef at Crab Catchers, thanks us and tells me he called the cops but they didn't show up, which is strange because they are usually very prompt when summoned. I found out later that the police called back about fifteen minutes after we left and said they were behind on calls. It's a three-man police force and they are backed up by North Myrtle Beach and Horry County. They asked if there was still a problem. Larry told them everything was okay, that some of his guests had taken care of the situation. I'm starting to believe Jimmy's statement more and more every minute I'm around these guys. They do know people in high places but I did not know they knew so many people in Little River. There have been two major incidents within the last two hours, no police, and no Marines.

We all laugh on the way back to my house and Bill and Ted say they haven't had this much fun since they left Fort Bragg. Somehow I don't believe that statement is true for them, but I don't want to know about all of their fun-filled moments because... oh well, you know.

We decide to go to bed early because the big golf match is tomorrow morning and God only knows what may happen on the golf course. One thing is for sure, if it's bad, neither the police nor the Marines will show up.

Before going to bed, I ask, "Am I supposed to take you to the airport on Sunday morning or is the chopper picking you up in the fairway?"

They all laugh and Barry says I will need to take them to the airport unless there is an unexpected emergency.

I am still wondering why they are here. Something tells me they are not here to visit me and play golf.

Chapter 5: The Golf Match

The next morning we are up by 7:00am and I take them to The Shack on Sea Mountain Highway for breakfast. I ask them to behave because after they leave, I still have to work and live here. They assure me that they will be on their best behavior.

We get back to the house around 8:30 without any confrontations. We decide to go up to the course to hit some balls before we play. Everyone seems excited about playing today. We load up our clubs, head to the clubhouse, pay our fees and go to the range. It is another beautiful day in Myrtle Beach, seventy-two degrees, a slight breeze and lots of sunshine.

While we are at the range, I give everyone a few tips on their swing and then we head for the putting green for a few putting tips. Everyone seems relaxed and enjoying the beautiful day.

We decide to play partners where you partner-up with each player for six holes. You get a point for low individual score on the hole and a point for best low team score on the hole. Each point is worth five dollars so no one is going to go broke. Ted is the lucky one because he draws me as a partner for the first six holes and I begin par, birdie, par. We take six of the possible twelve points available with four points ending in a tie. Barry and Bill get two.

The day was actually uneventful on the course, although Barry did answer a couple of cell phone calls during my putting stroke. There were no fights and no shootings. I made sure they left their weapons at the house.

At the end of the day Barry did not kick my ass, in fact, I was low man with a 79. Barry had 82 with a birdie on 17, the number one handicap hole. Ted had 86 while making a forty-foot par putt on 10. Bill shot 88 and almost had a hole in one on number 6. The ball hit the flagstick and landed three feet away. He missed the birdie putt.

After we finish playing, we go into the clubhouse for a beer and while we are there, Jimmy, my neighbor, comes in and I introduce him to the fellows. Jimmy's foursome just completed nine holes and he tells me he is having a bad day. He just got some new clubs and they are driving him crazy. I do not introduce Jimmy as an ex-FBI agent but it is as if the guys know he is one of them (spooks). Barry does ask me what Jimmy's last name is so I figure he is going to check him out as soon as possible. As we leave, I introduce the guys to Mr. Harris, the general manager and golf director at River Hills. They compliment him on the layout and condition of the course.

कॄॼक

We get back to the house around 4:00pm and Bill asks me where I am taking them for dinner since I am the big winner. I tell him twenty dollars won't get us much and that I have steaks in the fridge and plenty of beer on hand. I suggest we just stay here, grill the steaks and not get into any trouble.

I hear Ted say, "You're no fun."

I laugh and reply, "I had enough fun last night to last me for another year."

Barry goes outside on the deck to make some phone calls, probably checking up on Jimmy, while I get out a deck of cards to play some Euchre before dinner.

We play cards for about two hours for a quarter a point and Ted ends up winning three dollars. About 6:30, I put the steaks on and Bill whips up a big salad. The steaks are perfect, the salad is great and the beer is cold. It doesn't get any better than this.

Just as we finish eating, Barry says to me, "How's business these days? Are you making any money?"

I think to myself, *here it comes.* "Well, let's see, real estate is down, my landscape business is down because real estate is down, and the economy is in the tank. Right now, I am not making a lot of money. Do you guys want to give me an interest free loan?"

They all laugh and Barry says, "No, but we may have a small job for you if you're interested."

Barry's offer sounds short, sweet, and easy. "SIL would like to hire you to do some leg work for us on a per diem basis. We will pay you three hundred a day plus all your expenses and fifty cents per mile to cover your transportation costs."

I sarcastically reply, "Do I have to shoot anyone?"

"Of course not, we just need you to find someone for us and we will take it from there."

"Who do I have to find and will they shoot me?" I reply with a smile on my face, "And why can't SIL find them?"

Barry knows that I will want details, so he continues, "Do you remember reading about a man who was killed on Bald Head Island a month or so ago?"

"Yes I remember reading that in the paper. I've played that course, it is gorgeous."

"The man who was shot was a consultant to Senator R. Gene Brazile from North Carolina, who chairs some very influential committees in Washington." Then he adds, "You do realize everything I tell you is confidential, don't you?"

"Of course, I know the drill."

He continues, "One of the programs Trever Byers, the man who was shot, was looking into was offshore drilling along the Carolina coast for an energy committee. Some people in Washington want us to look into the possibility that this may have been why he died. Since the local police and Feds have come up empty, they want us to see if we can identify the killer."

"And what did you find?" I ask before he has a chance to continue.

"Mickke D, it is rather embarrassing. We thought we had the guy, but he slipped through our fingers as we were about to apprehend him."

Bill interjects, "The guy is not an amateur Mickke D, he is a real pro, so be careful."

It's as if I have already accepted the job, which I have not.

"Who's the guy?" I ask.

This time Ted answers, "We're not sure but we have it narrowed down to six suspects who were all in the general area when the assassination took place."

Barry jumps in, "We'll give you bios of the possible shooters when you take the job."

"Why do you need me?"

"Because all of the suspects are avid golfers and gamblers. We believe they will all be coming to play in the World Amateur in Myrtle Beach in a couple of weeks. Since you are into the golf scene here, we think you may be able to get close to these guys and maybe pinpoint the shooter for us without putting yourself or anyone else in danger."

One thing is for certain, the guys have done their homework. They know what my fees are and that I probably could use some walking around cash. I'm just not sure I want to go after a killer. But then again, the thought of getting back into the investigative business and trying to find the enemy does raise my excitement level.

I tell them I will sleep on it and let them know in the morning. Barry says we need to be at the airport around 8:00 unless I want them picked up in the fairway. I tell him we will be there by 7:30.

While getting ready for bed I notice the red boxers lying on my bathroom floor. I think about throwing them in the trash can but I change my mind and put them in the laundry pile. Hey, Paula Ann is gone so maybe I'll get a second opinion from another lovely young lady before I get rid of them.

Chapter 6: The Judge and The Coins

(The day of Trever's death)

Thomas Allen Cadium, aka TC, drives up from Pawleys Island to Southport and catches the 10:00am ferry to Bald Head Island. This is his first visit to Bald Head and he is not disappointed. Trever had told him about this place and he was not wrong. He stops in the Information Center and finds out that although the pace of life on the island encourages rest and reflection, there is no shortage of recreational options for every age. You can play golf or climb up North Carolina's oldest lighthouse, Old Baldy, first commissioned by Thomas Jefferson. You can explore the islands protected creeks and maritime forest through programs offered by the Bald Head Island Conservancy. TC's mind is already planning a day trip here on his boat in the near future.

TC rents a golf cart at the Information Center and gets to the golf course clubhouse about 10:45. He is meeting Trever, his friend and business partner, for lunch to discuss a possible salvage project, which TC mailed to him.

TC is a retired federal judge, 52 years old and a widower. He is 6'2" tall, 175 pounds and in good shape for a man his age who has spent most of his life sitting on a bench. He picked up the nickname TC years before becoming a lawyer and judge and it has followed him throughout his entire career. He now spends most of his time as a salvage junkie looking for ship-wrecks and sunken treasure. He has a 46-foot boat outfitted with the latest technology and he is a certified diver. He and Trever are always trying to find the big one but up to this point, they have only found small pockets of treasure, very small. But hey, TC has a great pension from the government, he loves the beach scene, and he really enjoys being out on the ocean in his boat.

As 11:30 comes and goes, he begins to get a little concerned about Trever who told him that he would be finished playing golf around 11:00 and that he would meet him in the restaurant around 11:15. He tries calling him on his cell phone but gets no answer. At 11:45, he walks over to the pro shop and asks if anyone has seen Trever Byers this morning.

Justin, the head pro, tells him that Trever teed off about 7:15 and he did not see Trever make the turn. Of course, he may have just missed seeing him for one reason or another. He gets on his radio and calls one of his course rangers. He asks him to take a ride out on the course to see if he can spot Trever.

About 12:30, Justin comes running into the restaurant, with a look of both excitement and sadness on his face. He tells TC that they have found Trever. That is the good news. The bad news is that Trever is dead. Someone shot him!

TC just sits there with a blank look on his face. A twinge of sorrow pierces through his anger and fear. Why would anyone want to kill Trever? How could this have happened and why has this happened? He hears sirens coming towards the clubhouse and before long, an EMS vehicle and the police chief pull up. They have the only gas-powered vehicles on the island.

As TC watches, the police chief, Marty Vette, and the EMS people take several golf carts and maintenance vehicles out on the golf course. In about 45 minutes, they return with a covered body, a pull cart with clubs and another set of clubs. Justin tells Chief Vette that TC was supposed to meet Trever for lunch. The chief wants to interview TC before he leaves for the mainland with the body.

Justin also tells the chief about the strange man who teed off ahead of Trever and that the other set of clubs they had found belonged to the pro shop. Justin had rented them to the man along with a golf cart and a dozen golf balls. They did not find the golf cart or golf balls. Chief Vette gets ready to interview TC while Justin and his assistant pro go looking for the missing golf cart.

ॐℯ

Even though TC has been an officer of the court for many years and he knows it is wrong to give false information to a police officer, he is not sure that as the interview begins, if he will tell Chief Vette about the map. After all, only he and Trever knew about the map, or so he thinks, and maybe the map is still on Trever or in his golf bag.

He makes a major decision. He is not going to tell Chief Vette about the map.

"Mr. Cadium, what was your relationship with Trever Byers?" Chief Vette asks.

"He is, or now I guess I should say, he was a good friend of mine who I have known for about two years."

"Why were you meeting him for lunch today?"

"Trever called and said he had found a book which he thought I might enjoy reading. If I would come up today we could have lunch and he would give me the book. By the way, did you find a book on him?"

"What is the name of the book?" Vette asks.

TC replies without skipping a beat, "I think he said the name was *Life along the Carolina Coast* (spur of the moment title but not bad) but I'm really not sure."

"I did not find a book on his person or in his golf bag, but I did notice that all of the zippers on his golf bag were open."

TC thinks to himself, *this tells me something. Whoever killed Trever took the map. But why, it's only a hand drawn map of a possible wreck off the coast of Pawleys Island.*

He uses the word *possible* because it could just as easily be nothing. TC and Trever have found quite a few nothings.

TC and Chief Vette exchange business cards, "Oh, so you are a federal judge. Thanks for staying around and answering my questions judge."

"Retired judge," TC replies, "I hope you find whoever killed Trever. If you need anything more, please give me a call."

As the chief is about to leave, Justin comes in and says they found the missing golf cart. It was located about one-half mile from the course next to the tidal creek, which bounds Bald Head on the west. Of course, Justin has contaminated the crime scene because he drove the cart back to the clubhouse. (CSI would have been livid.) Chief Vette did not seem that concerned. He did ask Justin to take him out to where he had found the cart.

TC just sits in the restaurant after the chief and Justin leave. He tries to figure out what is going on and if he could be in any danger. Did the killer know that he had sent the map to Trever and that he had the original? In addition, he is still not sure why he lied to Chief Vette.

On the drive back to Pawleys Island, he is much more observant of his surroundings than he was on the drive up to Southport this morning. He is constantly watching for anyone who he thinks is watching him. He is also thinking about how he first learned about the possible shipwreck.

ಹಿ~ಆ

He had been walking on the beach at Pawleys Island and afterward he stopped to have a cup of coffee at his favorite little restaurant along the beach, Nibils, which was located at the end of the fishing pier. The restaurant is full as an older gentleman walks in, looks around and sees there are no empty seats. As he starts to leave, TC tells him he can share his table. The old man sits down and they begin to talk.

As the old man takes his seat across from him, he judges the man to be in his mid-seventies and he looks as if he is in good health. The man tells him he has been walking on the beach with his metal detector and has come in for a cup of coffee. He thanks TC for allowing him to share his table.

TC asks him if he had any luck and the old man replies, "Well I'm not really sure. I found some strange coins on the beach but I have no idea what they are."

This, of course, gets TC's attention. He says, "I've done some metal detecting myself over the years. Do you have them with you?"

"Oh yeah, I've got them right here in my pocket, let me show you."

The old man smiles and takes out a folded Kleenex and lays it on the table. He carefully unfolds the Kleenex and shows him the four coins.

TC can hardly hold back a grin from ear to ear. The man has found two 1600s Atocha Silver Eight Grade coins worth about 4,000 dollars each and two very rare 1715 Fleet Gold Escudo with Fisher Certificate worth around 13,000 dollars each. This old man has just found four coins worth around 35,000 thousand dollars walking on the beach with a fifty-dollar metal detector. He and Trever have not found that much in the last two years out in the ocean with a 750,000 dollar boat filled with thousands of dollars of equipment. Go figure!

He has to make a decision. Should he tell the old man what the coins are worth or take another path? The salvage junkie, treasure-hunting demon inside him wins the battle and he decides on the other path, at least for the time being.

He says to the old man, "Where did you find them, if you don't mind me asking?"

"Oh, not at all, do you know where they were doing the beach renourishment last week? I found them right there and I searched all around the area for more but I came up with nothing."

This gives TC exactly what he is looking for, an area to search with the boat. He is guessing that the barge digging up sand in the ocean had picked them up from an old wreck and sprayed them on the beach with the new sand.

He gets back to the old man, "Do you have a computer at home?"

The old man laughs and says, "Nope, wouldn't know what to do with it if I did."

"Would you like me to look your coins up on my computer and let you know what they are worth?"

The old man's eyes get big and he gives TC a toothy grin, "You mean they could be worth something? I've found a few rings and regular coins before but shoot they weren't worth much."

"I can't promise you they are worth anything but you just don't know," he replies, "let me make some drawings of the coins and I'll see what I can find out for you. Write your phone number on the back of my card and I'll call you when I find out something."

The old man looks at the card and then looks back at him. He says, "Mr. Cadium, my name is Rusty and why don't you just take the coins with you. I trust you. You're a federal judge and an attorney."

He can't believe his ears, someone actually trusts an attorney.

He thinks for a minute and then says, "Rusty, I'll tell you what I'll do. I'll take two of the coins and give you a receipt for them."

"Sounds fair to me," Rusty replies.

He takes one of each of the different coins. He writes and signs a receipt for Rusty on the back of one of his cards and gives him that card along with another unblemished card. Rusty puts the other two coins back in the Kleenex and into his pocket. He thanks TC again and leaves the restaurant.

TC just sits there and stares. He is thinking to himself, *I can't believe I just did that. Unreal.*

Chapter 7: The Failed Attack

(Earlier)

As the assassin leaves the park, he is not a happy camper. He heard three voices on his listening device setting up an ambush and he spotted two of them. Who do these people think they are? He did not try to cheat them, he did the job he contracted to do and now they're trying to kill him.

He decides his clients are either wacky or the hand-drawn crude map he has in the brown paper bag is worth a lot more than the 25,000 dollars they owe him. Why not just pay him and take the map? He thinks there is probably more to this than just the map. This could become a very expensive screw-up for them. Maybe he will just sell the map to the highest bidder.

ॐ∾

Barry, Bill and Ted are also not happy. They did not take the assassin serious enough. Their plan was flawed. They must have made mistakes. Either he did not show up or he spotted them. Twenty-five thousand dollars is a lot of money to leave on the table. Several things are very clear: They do not have the map, the assassin is not dead, and one of the only links back to them is still alive.

They are now afraid that he knows more about them than they know about him. Somehow, they need to determine who he is, find him, get the map, and eliminate him, the sooner the better. The biggest problem they are going to have is that he will probably put the map in a safe place and even if they do find him and kill him, they may not get the map. So now the questions are: Where is the map, how many maps are there, who might have another copy of the map, and the big question - who drew the map?

Barry found out about the map from a low-grade operative who knew they were into old shipwrecks and sunken treasure. For a small nominal fee of five hundred dollars, he told them about an old man in Pawleys Island who was bragging about finding some rare old coins along the beach. The old man said a friend of his had a map and knew where to search for the treasure. Before the operative could find the old man and ask politely for his friends name, the old man was killed by a hit and run driver while crossing the street in Murrells Inlet.

Of course, the part about the map was false. Rusty had made that up. However, while Barry was doing his research on Trever Byers, he discovered he spent a lot of time in Pawleys Island. Maybe he knew the old man. Trever's hobby was salvage work with Judge Cadium; maybe they both knew the old man.

When Barry made his contract with the assassin, he asked him, if possible, to search for a map. That way he could have Trever Byers killed and possibly end up with a treasure map. He was thrilled and considered himself lucky when the assassin called and said he had the *scorecard*.

Chapter 8: The Suspects

We roll out of bed around 6:00am Sunday morning. The fellows enjoyed The Shack so we go back there for breakfast. As a precaution, I talk them into leaving their weapons in their bags, at the house, while we eat.

We get a table out on the enclosed porch and after we order, Barry says, "Well buddy boy before I ask you what your decision is, I want to add a little icing to the cake. If you find this guy for us, there will be a five thousand dollar bonus in it for you. So have you made your mind up yet?"

I was thinking about the offer all night and I didn't get a whole lot of sleep. The pay seems fair enough, especially now with the bonus at the end. If I take the job, I believe I will find the killer if he shows up at the World Am. What do I have to lose? I'll get a chance to see if my old investigative skills come back to me. Probably like riding a bike. My biggest problem will be keeping the inside demons away. Sometimes ghosts are better left alone. I sucked a deep breath and steeled my nerves. I also fought a spasm of panic. I decided I really needed to do this.

I look at Barry and give him my answer, "Gentlemen, I will take the job but I do have some questions. First of all, who are my suspects, how do I get in touch with you, and how much support can I expect from you?"

Barry looks at Ted and says, "Let me have the suspect list."

Ted pulls a folded sheet of paper from his sport coat and hands it to Barry.

Barry takes the paper and hands it to me. "Here you are my man, six very possible killers and whatever background information we could find on them."

છ~જ

The Suspect List

Ken (the player) Bellinger—hometown Richmond, Virginia—Age 42—Army brat—traveled all over the world before settling down in Vegas—loves golf and gambling—always looking for a game—has bet $1000 on which way the tee would go on the tee box—usually wins—works part-time as a financial advisor but everyone thinks he is a bookie

Dave (the police) Prendels—hometown Lexington, Kentucky—Age 46—former city police officer—resigned after being accused of taking bribes from call girls and bookies, never indicted—loves to gamble—plays golf and bowls for money—always in a pot game somewhere—spends most of his time in Florida and Vegas—works part-time as a security officer

Andy (the farmer) Bottier—hometown Saugatuck, Michigan—Age 42—grew up on a farm with dairy cows and blueberries—spent ten years in the Army as a Gunnery Sergeant—went home to farm but gambling got the best of him and he lost the farm—loves golf—will wager something on every hole—spends most of his time in Vegas and Florida selling timeshares

Paul (the mechanic) Hills—hometown Canton, Ohio—Age 50—can fix anything—always tinkering with his golf clubs and sometimes with his opponents—once changed the lie of his opponents wedge and five iron—won the match—spends time in South Carolina, Florida and Vegas—loves to gamble—usually does well

Steve (the signman) Griggs—hometown Phoenix, Arizona—Age 40—loves golf—big gambler on basketball—was a college referee but was fired for possibly fixing games—never proven and never indicted—travels all over the country for skins games and Calcutta's—works as a part time sales consultant for a major sign company in Vegas

Stan (the man) Hutchinson—hometown Orange County, California—age 43—spent six years in the Navy—Navy Seal—after the Navy got a degree in Nuclear Engineering—was vice-president of Nuclear Parts Company but resigned because he was accused of allegedly selling nuclear information and parts to North Korea and Iran—the investigation was dropped by the Justice Department because two of the main witnesses would not testify—dropped out of Corporate America and became a golf bum—will travel anywhere for a golf game—has his own, one person, Computer Sales & Service Company located in Vegas—does websites and troubleshooting (This guy is our main suspect but we have been unable to find him)

Note: None of the above work full time, they are always on the move. We believe all of them were within 100 miles of Bald Head Island on the day of the shooting. In addition, they were all in the general vicinity of three other previous murder/assassinations.

I study the list of suspects for a few minutes and notice one thing they all have in common besides being golf junkies. They all spend time in Vegas. I say to Barry, "I'm guessing you missed catching the guy in Vegas?"

Barry laughs and says to Bill and Ted, "I told you he would figure that out right away, you both owe me fifty. Good catch Mickke D, so do you know who did the deed?"

"The butler did it, in the study, with a wrench," I say loudly and they all laugh.

Barry gives me his personal cell phone number along with Bill's and Ted's. He tells me they will all be available 24/7 and that their Intel Support Team will be available.

We finish our breakfast and stop by the house to pick up their clubs and bags. We arrive at the airport about 7:30 and I don't see a chopper on the tarmac. I do see a twin engine Gulfstream ready and waiting. I ask Barry where the chopper is and he tells me they sent the company plane to pick them up.

Barry asks Ted to go out to the plane to see when the pilot will be ready to leave. We sit down in the little waiting area and get a cup of coffee out of the vending machine. We watch as Ted enters the plane and then in the blink of an eye, all hell breaks loose.

A huge explosion sends a ball of fire one hundred feet into the air. SIL has just lost their plane and I no longer need Ted's cell phone number. There is no way he could have survived the explosion.

≈•≈

The concussion of the explosion rocks the building and shatters all of the windows in our small waiting area. We are thrown to the floor like rag dolls. The heat from the blast feels like a 100-degree day on the beach with no wind or ocean breeze. We hear parts of the plane hitting the metal roof above us. Within a couple of seconds, the sounds on the roof and the heat are gone. The only sound we hear is that of a roaring fire. We try to get up but are not very successful. Bill receives a cut on the forehead from flying glass but Barry and I remain intact.

Finally, we are able to get our bearings and slowly venture out toward where the plane had been. The searing heat from the burning plane keeps us almost fifty yards away. It was just serviced and full of aviation fuel. We can't do anything but just watch it burn. We hear a voice yelling at us from the direction of one of the maintenance buildings. It is the pilot of Barry's plane, Rob Logan, and he is running in our direction.

"What the hell happened?" he exclaimed, "Are you guys alright?"

Rob is a tall, thin man who looks more like a basketball player than a pilot. However, he must be good if he is flying for SIL.

Barry answers, "Why were you over there and not on the plane?"

"I got a call on my radio saying I was needed in Building C for some pre-flight weather information," he replies and then asks, "Where is Ted?"

There is silence and finally Bill says, "He just stepped into the plane when the explosion occurred, I'm pretty sure he's gone."

Barry looks at Rob, "Who did you see in Building C?"

"That's the strange part, there was no one there. The building was empty. I was looking for someone when I heard the explosion."

After talking with the pilot, Barry determines this was a personal attack on SIL. It has to be the assassin. He takes the pilot out of harm's way and then destroys the plane along with Ted.

He walks away and makes a call on his cell phone. He comes back and tells us the chopper will be here to pick them up in about two hours. They will return to get Ted's remains later. Bill comments that Ted's choice of burial was cremation. He got his wish.

After Barry tells me the chopper is coming to get them, I walk over to the Trailblazer, which is still warm from the blast, and get my camera. At least there was no damage to my SUV. I figure this is not an accident so I take some quick pictures of the people standing around gawking at the burning debris of the plane. Sometimes bad guys like to admire their work from up close and personal.

The police, fire trucks and EMS trucks are pulling into the tarmac area. Barry and Bill meet with the police for about thirty minutes and then come out to where I am standing. Barry tells me he has told the police it was probably a mechanical problem, which caused the explosion, but he does not think they believe him. I wonder why? Barry also tells me not to be alarmed, that if it was a hit, they were the targets and not me. Now that makes me feel all warm and fuzzy inside.

જાૹ

My time with the police also lasts about thirty minutes. They ask me a lot of questions. I tell them what I saw but I do not tell them what I think happened. The chopper arrives about one hour later. Barry and Bill are ready to depart back to Virginia. The Coroner's Office tells Barry they will contact him about picking up Ted's remains.

Before he leaves, Barry says, "Mickke D., I hope you can help us find this guy. Keep us advised, keep your head down, and watch your back."

"I'll let you know as soon as I know anything. I'm real sorry about Ted. He was a good man."

Barry and Bill just shake their heads and proceed to the chopper. I stay around until they are on board and on their way just in case something else tragic happens. They get away with no problems.

There are newspaper cars, TV cars, police cars, fire trucks and lots of people milling around but I feel like someone is watching me. I can't wait to get my pictures developed and see if anyone looks guilty. On the way home, I stop at a local drugstore to have the photos developed.

After I have the pictures and am on my way home, I begin thinking about the weekend with my old Army buddies. First, they land a helicopter in my back yard on the golf course. They beat up a couple of bozos at my favorite eating place and now their plane is blown up and Ted gets his cremation wish much sooner than he had expected. They come back into my life after all of these years and I have to watch one of them die.

So much for a nice quiet weekend, I think to myself. In addition, what makes this whole thing even worse: I have agreed to try to find a cold-blooded killer for them. That was probably not too smart on my part. Those demons inside me are beginning to churn and just aching to be turned loose.

၁⁓၁

The assassin is smiling. He is across the street from the airport standing with a group of onlookers. He had made entry to the plane disguised as a maintenance worker and planted the explosives. Small airports have very lax security. He had no beef with the pilot, so he made a call to get him off the plane. His plan was to just blow up and destroy the plane. He did not see Ted enter the plane until it was too late. He had already dialed the number of the detonator cell phone. Oh well, collateral damage happens sometimes. He bets now they wish they had just left the money, picked up the map, and gone on their merry way.

Chapter 9: Mickke D

Since I didn't receive photos of my suspects from SIL, I opt to give my neighbor a call to see if the Bureau has any pictures of these guys. I call Jimmy Sunday night and ask him if he has a few minutes to spare. He says to come on over, the front door is open. I start by telling him about my weekend, from the chopper to the explosion.

He just keeps saying, "You're kidding, you have to be kidding me. Wow, that's exciting."

He says he thought he heard an explosion while he was on the golf course Sunday morning but he wasn't sure. I ask him if he can check with the Bureau to see if they have any pictures of my suspects. He says he will see what he can dig up on them. I also tell him I may need his help at some point in time but that it may be dangerous. He smiles, rubs his hands together and tells me no problem. I can call him any time. I think Jimmy is playing way too much golf and is looking for something else to do on the side. I think he misses police work. Personally, I never thought playing golf every day would be boring. I could just never afford to do it. I leave him a copy of the suspect list and ask him to get back to me when he has something.

I go home and begin to put together my plan of action for the upcoming World Am. I need to be ready when the bell rings. The first thing I need is someone on the inside at The World Am, someone who can get me inside information when and if I need it. I opt to call in a favor from an old golf student of mine, Bob McClellan.

Bob is a retired journalist with the local newspaper who still writes a weekly column for the paper. He has covered the World Am for the last ten years. He is on the advisory board and works with handicap adjustments.

I used to enjoy Bob's daily column when I first moved to Myrtle Beach and after reading about his not so great golf game,

I tried for years to get him to allow me to help him with his game. I guess it was an act of desperation (his game was in the toilet) on his part, but he finally called me to set up a lesson. I offered to give him free lessons, but he said he would only agree if he could pay me. We finally compromised by me agreeing to be paid only if he thought the lessons improved his game. I did help his game (of course) and then he asked me what he owed me. I told him that he owed me a favor and that someday I will call and want paid (almost sounds like an old TV show, doesn't it). Although I did not receive payment at the time, Bob has sent me several students who have paid, so it worked out great. Bob will be receiving a call from me real soon.

I also need a weapon, not just my .45, which will be very hard to hide, even though it will knock a man down just by hitting him in the finger. I should also go to a shooting range and practice. I haven't fired my .45 in years. I look through my war closet footlocker and find a .25-caliber revolver complete with an ankle holster. This will work great with long pants, but at the beach in the middle of summer, not very *kosher*. I also dig out my Army Jag Investigator License and stick it in my wallet. A quick flash and no one will question my authority to ask questions and gather information.

తోళ

I receive a call from Jimmy on Tuesday morning. He tells me he has some photos for me, sent by over night courier. I wish the rest of the mail in and out of Myrtle Beach moved that quickly.

I go directly over to his house and open the envelope sent to him by the Bureau. Of the six possible suspects, he has received four photos, *the police, the farmer, the sign man, and Stan the man. The police* of course had to have his photo taken because he was in law enforcement, *the farmer* was in the Army and *Stan the man* was in the Navy, so photos were available of them. There was a mug shot of *the sign man*. The police arrested him. However, they never brought him to trial. The Bureau could not find any pictures of the other two. So at least I know what four of my suspects look like unless they are wearing a disguise.

I thank Jimmy for his help and go back to the house where I make my phone call to my former golf student and hopefully my inside person at the World Am.

Bob answers the phone and once he learns who is calling says, "Mickke D, I suppose someone told you my game was back in the tank again."

"No, not really Bob," I answer and laugh, "I'm calling to tell you I need to collect that favor you owe me. I'll bet you never thought I would try to collect, did you?"

He replies, "Oh, I'm glad you called. Now I can get together with you for another lesson and not feel bad because you won't accept payment. What kind of a favor can I do for you?"

I tell him I need information on a few of the players who will be playing in the upcoming World Am this year. He conveys to me that this will not be a problem. I tell Bob I will e-mail him the names and information I need. Before he can ask why I need the information, I lie and tell him I have had a request to check on some guys when they get in town. They may be possible golf students or real estate clients. I think it will be safer for Bob if he knows as little as possible.

Chapter 10: The Search

(Earlier)

TC feels bad about what he did in the restaurant. Is he so hung up on finding a treasure buried at sea that he would try to screw an old man out of his coins? Probably not. However, the longer he thinks about the old coins the more those negative thoughts begin to mellow. He does commit to one thing, if he finds something; he will see to it that Rusty is compensated.

He has the information he needs from Rusty; where he found the coins. He now needs to take the boat out and run sweeps in the area where he thinks the wreck may be, if there really is a wreck. Moreover, even if there is a wreck, are there any coins left or has someone already made the discovery, confiscated the treasure and the only thing left is the old wreck and the four coins Rusty found on the beach?

Since Trever is busy and not available, he calls a friend of his, Freddy Rioz, to help him on the boat. He met Freddy at a local restaurant, River City Café, in Murrells Inlet where he was waiting tables. He had taken a liking to him right away. Freddy is in his mid-thirties and just one of those nice guys. He is tall, dark, and handsome and has a great accent. He learned that Freddy was born in Chile but moved to the beach from Upper Michigan. He is a great artist and is very good with anything made of glass. However, his real love is the sea and he moved to the beach to try to find a way to get his own fishing boat and because it was too damn cold in Upper Michigan. He is a certified diver and TC pays him to help when Trever is busy.

The day he picks to go is a lousy day on the water to dive, so he lets Freddy know that they will just do some sweeps and if they find anything, they will come back on a better dive day to see what they may have found.

This is fine with Freddy because he receives a hundred dollars a day whether he dives or not. He is great with boats; it is like driving a car for him. He just has the knack for it. He also has another nice skill. He is a great cook. TC will give him money to buy groceries and he will show up with a cooler full of food, beer and sodas. Even if they do not find anything, they always eat and drink well.

They leave the dock in Murrells Inlet around 7:30am. It is an overcast day along the Carolina coast. The temperature is 68 degrees, the sky is cloudy and the wind is coming out of the southwest at around 15 to 20 knots.

Murrells Inlet was a haven for pirates back in the early days of the Americas. Pirates like Blackbeard and others would bring their ships into the many coves around Murrells Inlet and hide from the British or they would use the coves as a launching point to attack an unsuspecting ship laden with treasure traveling up or down the coast.

It is written and rumored that chests filled with treasure abound in this area but no proof of that exists. However, since they do not dig basements here, because of the sandy soil and the fact that the water table is so high, you could actually build a house or a condo building right on top of buried treasure and never know it. This is good because this means that there is probably a better chance of finding treasure in the ocean on an old shipwreck than buried in the ground on land. This is all the better for TC and Freddy.

Freddy has his cooler full of food and drinks for their day trip, but he will keep the contents a surprise until the time comes to have lunch. TC hands over the controls of his boat to Freddy as soon as they leave the dock in Murrells Inlet. He tells Freddy to head south, that he wants to check out an area around Pawleys Island. He has chosen not to tell Freddy about the coins until he checks with Trever. That is another reason they are not going to dive today.

TC has his CRS (Close Radar Sonar) ready to go. The CRS is great at picking up small or large areas of metals hidden under the sand. It will penetrate almost ten feet of sand. These areas may contain coins, jewelry, metal bowls, cannons, cannon balls, other weapons, nails, and even barrel hoops. Once you locate an area, you dive to see what you may have found.

TC will need to find his search area by line of sight. He has a good idea of where the barge was digging sand to spread on the beach but it is also a guessing game in a very big ocean. However, there is no rush; they are not on a timetable to find treasure. One thing he has learned since moving to South Carolina, everything is slower here and that is not all bad. Actually, he is enjoying his new, unhurried way of life.

He has Freddy go about a half mile from shore at a place which looks like where the barge may have been working. He probably should sight the location from shore because that is where he had seen the barge. Things always look different from the shore rather than looking from the boat toward the shore.

They begin their sweeps around 9:00. If they pick up an echo, they will note the location and then they will retrace their route from another direction and see if they pick up the echo again. If they get the echo again, TC will plot the location on his map and return at another time to dive and investigate.

By noon, they completed multiple sweeps, burned a lot of gas, drank a few sodas, but didn't hear the first *ping*. They elect to anchor and have a bite to eat. Lunch turns out to be a Ruben sandwich, a dill pickle, chips, and a cold beer. Freddy pulls out a mint chocolate cheesecake from the bottom of the cooler, probably made by him, for dessert. What a feast. They soon forget about their lack of *pings*.

Their bellies are full so they opt to fish for a while before starting another sweep. They both cast their rods and lures into the blue Atlantic and of course, Freddy has to say his fishing prayer. "Dear Lord, will the fishy, fishy in the brook, come and jump on Freddy's hook."

The sad part about it is that Freddy always catches fish. TC thinks what's wrong with this picture? The next time he goes fishing without Freddy, he is going to try the same prayer, just change the name to protect the innocent.

They continue fishing for about an hour and of course, Freddy catches a fish, a medium-size yellow fin tuna. His catch will be dinner tonight at the River City Café. The owner always allows Freddy to fix his catch of the day for employees and friends. TC can hardly wait. There is never a dull moment at the beach.

The afternoon sweeps go much better. They find an area which seems to have a lot of activity somewhere close to where TC saw the barge digging sand. He plots and draws a crude map. They proceed back to Murrells Inlet with a cold beer in hand. TC mails the map to Trever Byers the following morning. *The die has been cast.*

Chapter 11: Barry & Dean

The trip back to Culpepper from Myrtle Beach is very quiet. The chopper is noisy but the conversation on board is null and void. Neither Barry nor Bill say much of anything the entire trip, mainly because the pilot of the destroyed plane has hitched a ride back with them and he is pretty shaken up. If he had not received that phone call, he would have been on the plane when it exploded. He still has no idea who made the call.

Once they arrive in Culpepper, they pick up the company Jeep at the airport and drive the four miles to the office. Barry tells Rob to take some time off and chill out. He will call him later in the week.

Once inside his office, Barry checks his e-mails and opens the mail on his desk while Bill just sits and stares.

Finally, Bill says, "Ted was the only one of us who did not want to go after the assassin and yet he is the one who died."

Barry replies, "I know, but we can't think about what might have been. The question now is what do we do? The plane is insured and will be replaced but how do we deal with Ted's death?"

There are several minutes of silence and then Bill says, "I don't think we should make any decisions at this point in time. We should go home, get a good night's sleep, and make plans tomorrow."

"You're right, let's get together tomorrow and discuss our options. I'll call Ted's family in Florida and give them the bad news. After that, I'm out of here."

"Do you want me to stick around while you make the call?" Bill asks with a very somber sigh.

"No, you go ahead. I'll see you in the morning and by the way, be careful; we may be next on his list."

Bill leaves and as Barry sits at his desk contemplating the phone call he needs to make, he thinks back to the events that got them into this mess.

Barry answered the phone. The call was from Dean Rutland, chief aide to Senator R. Gene Brazile of North Carolina. SIL had done some small jobs for Dean in the past. He lived just outside Culpepper and he said he wanted to meet Barry about a very private matter. Barry figured this had to be big if Dean did not want to discuss it on the phone. They agreed on a 12:00 lunch meeting for the next day at a local park in Culpepper. Dean said he would provide lunch.

Barry and Dean both arrived at about the same time and sat down on a secluded bench near the entrance. Dean Rutland was in his early forties. He was divorced, tall with a muscular build and had a head full of dark, wavy hair. In Washington circles, he was referred to as a ladies man. He had brought roast beef sandwiches and Diet Pepsis for lunch.

Barry complimented Dean on the menu then asked, "Why all the secrecy, Dean?"

Dean finished swallowing what he had in his mouth and then answered, "Barry, I have a job for you if you want it, but don't feel obligated to answer today."

"That sounds fair, what is the job?"

"I need someone eliminated," Dean said in a very subdued voice.

Barry's eyes widened. "You want what?" he said in a very loud voice.

They both looked around to see if anyone had heard the uplifted reply from Barry.

No one seemed to notice or they just didn't care so Barry continued. "Are you out of your freaking mind? SIL does not do assassinations and what would make you think we did?"

Dean quickly replied in a whispered tone of voice, "Barry, you don't have to do the job yourself but I figure you may know someone who can."

Barry stared at Dean for a minute and then said, "Well, just for the sake of conversation, what are you talking about?"

Dean continued, "I need a person eliminated and I'm willing to provide one hundred thousand dollars for the completion of the project, fifty up front and the other fifty when the job is done. I don't care where you do it or how you do it, as long as it happens soon."

They finished their lunch without speaking but Barry's mind is doing several calculations. Finally, he broke the silence, "I'll get back to you."

When Barry returned from his meeting, he called Bill and Ted into his office and told them about his lunch with Dean. Neither of them said anything; then finally Barry asked, "Well, tell me what you think, but before you do let me say two things. One, I don't expect any one of us to assassinate anyone and two, right now we can use some cash flow."

Bill replied, "You're right on both things but if we don't do it, who will?"

Ted decided to chime in, "Hey guys, we have done a lot of low things but I do not see us as hired assassins, do you?"

"Of course not," Barry said, "but I may know of a way to get this done and still have us end up with some cash flow. Let me make a call and see what I can find out."

As soon as Bill and Ted left the office, Barry called a friend of his, an ex-CIA agent, Glenn Griffin. He had been able to help Barry on a couple of other deals. Griff was now operating on his own and seemed to know where to go and who to see about anything and everything.

"Griff, if I needed a hit man, where would I go?"

Glenn replied, "Why don't you beat around the bush a little bit and tell me what you really want Barry?"

"Oh no, it's not for me. I need the information for a report I'm doing for a client."

"Yeah right. Well if I were looking for a person to fulfill a contract, here's what I would do."

Barry interrupted, "Can you e-mail me the information?"

"I don't think so. Do you want an electronic trail out there somewhere even if it is just information for a client?"

"You're right. Tell me what I should do but first let me grab a pen."

"First of all, I would take out a classified ad in the following cities under Sales Position: Las Vegas, Atlanta, Denver, New Orleans, Chicago, LA, New York and Dallas. Sales position open, no benefits, post resume. Wait three days and then get a copy of each paper and read the Classified under Jobs Wanted. If you see Resume Ready for Sales Position, then just follow the instructions. Oh by the way, don't screw up. You will need a referral."

"Thanks Griff, I owe you one."

"Don't thank me yet; remember these people play for keeps."

Barry did as he was instructed and three days later, in each of the papers, he found: Resume ready, e-mail salary and location to <u>www.chatroominfo@infocape.com</u>. Barry, being a computer whiz kid, decided to check out the web site and discovered that each of the cities on his list was connected to that web site. He could not trace the site back to a specific city or location. This person was good. He sent the following information to the web site: 50k in Carolinas. Three days later, he received an e-mail from the assassin asking for a description, the exact location of the contract and a referral name.

Before he went any further, he got back to Bill and Ted. He did not give them details, just that everything was in place. They both agreed that as long as they did not have to do the killing, they would go along with the plan.

Barry, Bill, and Ted had just taken their shovels out of the garage and started digging a deep and treacherous hole with no way out.

Chapter 12: The Oil Company

(Earlier)

Gary Sherman is president and CEO of Derrick Oil Drilling & Production Company in Houston, Texas. He is fifty years old with graying red hair, in good shape, and most people would guess he was maybe forty. If you met him at the mall, you would probably think he was a schoolteacher instead of the president and CEO of a Texas Oil Company. Derrick does mainly offshore drilling in the Gulf of Mexico but they are planning to expand their operations to the East Coast.

Gary has been funneling thousands of dollars to North Carolina Senator R. Gene Brazile's re-election campaign fund because Senator Brazile heads the sub-committee in Washington that is about to decide on whether or not to allow offshore drilling off the coast of the Carolinas. He wants to keep the senator in office.

He has moved these illegal funds through Dean Rutland, the senator's right-hand man. Dean is being paid thousands of dollars to get the money into the fund without a trail of where or from whom the money came. Therefore, the Senator's closest associate is in the back pocket of Derrick Oil. Gary has a built-in lobbyist.

Derrick Oil owns several lease blocks off the North Carolina and South Carolina coasts. Each of these blocks are four miles long by four miles wide and consist of sixteen square miles of offshore drilling potential. Derrick invested several million dollars before bidding on these lease blocks by running sonar and seismic geological tests to try to determine where the best possible areas may be to drill along the coast. They then had to submit a onetime sealed bid to the federal government and hope that they were the highest bidder. They got six of the nine blocks for which they bid. These lease blocks cost them four hundred thousand, non-refundable dollars each and the lease is good for two years. At the end of the two years, the government has the right to renew the lease to Derrick for another two years for the same amount. They can also decide to have another bidding process or they can just discontinue the entire program. Offshore drilling is very costly and very risky. It is not for the faint of heart.

Gary has learned from some of his friends along the Carolina coast that the main consultant for Senator Brazile, Trever Byers, may come back with a negative report for offshore drilling. Trever may believe that offshore drilling can cause harm to the plant and fish environment along the coast as well as tourism. If this happens, Gary could lose his lease blocks and the entire amount of money he has invested so far. We're talking millions of dollars. However, if the committee approves offshore drilling and Derrick is successful in its search for oil and gas, they stand to make billions.

Gary calls Dean, "Dean, I am looking at a big problem with our lease blocks if Trever Byers' report comes back negative for the oil companies. What have you heard?"

"I haven't heard anything definite, but I think Trever is leaning toward a *no* vote," Dean replies with a small sense of unrest in his voice.

Gary continues, "Well, what can we do to change his mind?"

"I'm afraid there's not much we can do, Trever is a pretty straight shooter and I don't think he will change his report, although I am not positive what his report will say."

Dean knows that if he offers Trever any type of financial incentive to bring back a positive report, he will go directly to the senator and the Feds. That would not be good for anyone involved.

Gary is silent for more than a few seconds and Dean is starting to get nervous.

Finally, Gary says, "Dean, I can't take any chances with a bad report and if I end up losing millions of dollars, a lot of heads will roll and yours may be the first. Now I am willing to invest some more money, let's say one hundred thousand dollars, to make sure we do not get a negative report. Do you understand what I'm talking about?"

This time Dean is silent for a long time, "Yes sir, I understand. I will make sure your lease block interest and drill sites are secure."

The next call Dean makes is to Barry Green at SIL.

Chapter 13: The Contract

(Earlier)

The assassin accepts the contract. He directs Barry where to wire one-half of the fifty thousand dollar contract fee and he wants specific information about the target. Barry agrees to get him the information.

Before he goes any further, it is time for a board meeting. Barry, Bill, and Ted have a very important sit-down meeting before making any final decision, although Barry has already made up his mind. The meeting is just a formality.

The big problem with Trever Byers is that he is a rather high profile target. In other words, many important people know him and that he is working with Senator Brazile as a consultant. Therefore, what the guys have to decide is whether there will ever be a way to link the hit back to SIL.

Barry makes a suggestion. "I have a problem with actually killing a non-enemy person for money, which of course we are not going to do. I do not have a problem getting rid of a murderer, or in this case, a known assassin who can possibly black-mail us at a later date."

Bill replies, "So if I understand what you're saying, is that we hire an assassin to kill Trever Byers and then we kill the assassin to cover up our tracks. And since he's a hired killer, it's okay."

Ted then comes back with, "So what about your contact person who got you in touch with the assassin? And what about Dean Rutland, do we kill them also?"

Barry thinks for a minute and then says, "I would not rule out any of what you just said Ted, they would be the only two people who could ever trace the hit back to us."

Bill jumps in, "Now I know you know how to find Dean and your contact person but how will we ever track down the assassin?"

Barry does not know the answer to that question but he is sure there is a way.

He continues, "For right now, let's make a decision on hiring the assassin, okay? We can worry about the other part later. I don't believe my contact person or Dean wants to go to jail. They will keep their mouths shut. How do you guys vote? I vote to order the hit."

Bill thinks for a minute and then says, "I'll go along with hiring the assassin." He figures Barry is going to do this with or without their approval.

Ted looks at Barry and Bill and says, "Since my vote means nothing, I vote no."

The vote is two to one for the hit so Barry gathers the information about Trever, e-mails it to the address he received and wires the twenty-five thousand to a Singapore account.

The plan is in motion and irreversible. The e-mail address disappeared the same day the assassin received the information and confirmed the wire deposit. There is no way to trace anything back to him. He is a ghost.

Now Barry has to figure out a way to find the assassin after the hit and solve one-third of his problem. The other two-thirds will not be difficult. He knows where to find Dean and Griff. They can easily have a fatal accident with no problem. Barry is not concerned about killing any of these three people. Then there is only Bill and Ted.

હ≫ન્≈

Barry's plan is for the hit to take place in an area where the police are not as sophisticated as in a big city. After researching Trever Byers habits, he makes a trip to Bald Head Island and likes what he finds there. He selects the island because it has a one-man police department and there has not been a murder there for as long as anyone can remember. The worse crime anyone can ever remember on Bald Head is someone once stole a golf bag off the ferry, or it was misplaced. The company found it and returned to its rightful owner the next day.

Chapter 14: SIL Receives Payment

(Earlier)

The local police department and the Feds are drawing a blank on the murder of Trever Byers. The assassin did a great job of not leaving any evidence around for anyone to discover. The condo was clean, the murder area was clean and the drawing of the bird watcher doesn't match anyone in anybody's mug file. It is fast becoming an acute cold case.

Judge Cadium is the only connection to Trever Byers that day but his whereabouts are verifiable and after all, he is a retired federal judge. Any leads are few and far between. Everyone involved with the case thinks it has to do with politics and big oil, but thinking and proving are two different things

The day after the killing of Trever Byers hits the papers, Barry calls Dean. "Let's get together in the park again and since you did such a good job with the menu the last time, you can bring lunch. And by the way, don't forget to bring my dessert."

Dean replies, "I figured you'd be calling so dessert is ready. Same place, same time tomorrow?"

"Sounds good to me, see you then."

Barry is starting to become paranoid because after hanging up he thinks to himself, *maybe I should bring lunch in case Dean tries to poison me.* Then he decides Dean is not the killer type or he would have taken care of Trever Byers himself.

Barry meets Dean at the appointed place at the appointed time the following day. After a few pleasantries and lunch, Dean thanks Barry for taking care of his problem and tells him dessert is in the canvas bag. Dean leaves first while Barry sits on the bench and takes in the park scenery for a few minutes. He does not touch the bag in case this is a trap. Nothing looks out of place in the park. He picks up the bag, walks out of the park, and gets into his SUV. Instead of going directly back to the office, he follows Dean back to his house, which just happens to be in the Culpepper area.

Barry has to make some major decisions: Can he afford to allow Dean to live since he is one of only two people who can trace the killing of Trever Byers back to SIL? Barry doesn't include Glenn Griffin. He doesn't think Griff will put together the murder of Trever Byers with their conversation about hiring a hit man unless the assassin actually did contact Griff as a reference. If that has happened, Griff will have to go also. He will have to consider all options.

Barry does not believe Trever's murder was Dean's idea alone. Someone else had to have ordered Dean to get rid of Trever. However, since Dean is no dummy, he doubts that he would have told that person about SIL. Moreover, that person probably does not want to know anyway.

Barry does a quick review of the property where Dean lives and draws a small map for future reference. His death will be tricky because one person dying within an organization is bad enough but if two people are killed, the police and the Feds start digging deeper and more intently into the case. For now, Barry elects to let things cool down a little bit and see what happens.

ॐॐ

About a week after the assassin realizes he has been set up in the Vegas park, he calls Glenn Griffin, "Glenn, this is Mr. Smith."

"Mr. Smith, what can I do for you?"

"I'm calling to tell you that you owe me $25,000."

"Why would I owe you money?" Glenn asks in a rather irritated, direct tone of voice.

"Because the last client you referred to me tried to kill me and of course I did not get paid."

"What do you mean, they tried to kill you?"

Mr. Smith goes into detail about the attempt on his life and when he finishes he says, "Now you both pay me and eliminate the problem or I will eliminate the problem and then I'll start looking for you. You know the rules, they have to go."

Glenn Griffin is still holding his phone to his ear and staring into a blank world. However, there is no one on the other end. Mr. Smith has hung up. He remembers giving Barry a warning when he said, "Don't screw up, these guys play for keeps."

Chapter 15: The Suspects Arrive

(Present)

All of the suspects get into town on Sunday except for the assassin who is already here. He came a few days early to blow up an airplane. They all check into different condos or resorts. They are all here for the same reason, to play in the World Am. They all plan to practice, play golf, and most likely gamble. They will be looking for a sucker or two on the golf course and probably a poker game.

There is casino boat gambling out of Little River and I will venture to say they will try to take an afternoon or evening cruise at least once while they are in town. It's a five-hour gambling cruise. It takes the boat about an hour to get out beyond the three-mile limit, you gamble for three hours and then another one-hour trip back to port. It's not Vegas, but it's about as close as they are going to get to Vegas while being in Myrtle Beach.

I am planning to play a lot of golf the week prior to the World Am and I hope I run into several of my suspects along the way. I now have photos of four of them; also, it's an expense so SIL will be paying the bill for my golf. Life is good.

❧❦

Kenney (the player) Bellinger checks into The Villas at The Legends Resort just off 501 in Myrtle Beach. The villas where he is staying reminds him of a Scottish village complete with a Scottish pub, The Ailsa Pub. He has stayed here before. He really enjoys the resort and especially the location. He actually took a lesson from Matt, the head pro, once and was very pleased with the outcome. There are three golf courses here, The Heathland, The Moorland and The Parkland, all beautiful courses. There is also a 30-acre lighted practice facility, which he probably won't use much, except for chipping and putting, because of his bad knees. Maybe he'll get Matt to help him with his short game this time around. He is planning to play golf every day this week and hopes he can find out which courses he will be playing so he can practice on those courses. He always enjoys coming to Myrtle Beach. The weather is always good, the food is great, and the golf courses are fantastic.

He is looking forward to playing in the World Am because he has heard about it but has never made the effort to establish a handicap and participate.

As he unpacks his bags, he makes sure the snub nose .38 special he carries with him on all trips is fully loaded and then puts it back in his bag. In his line of work, one can't be too careful.

ॐॐ

Andrew (the farmer) Bottier checks into Sea Trails Golf Resort located in Sunset Beach, North Carolina. He rents a villa at Sea Trails because it's away from the hustle and bustle of the beach scene in Myrtle Beach. It is almost a rural setting, which reminds him more of his farm and log home in Michigan.

Sunset Beach is located just outside of Calabash, North Carolina. Calabash got its name for a style of preparing fried food, usually seafood. Andy plans to eat in Calabash every chance he gets.

Sea Trails is a beautiful resort with three beautiful golf courses; The Maples, The Jones, and The Byrd, all named after the architect who designed them. There are two clubhouses, a lighted driving range, and a Golf Learning Center on site. Everything Andy needs to get ready for the World Am is here. His only problem is going to be playing it straight during the tourney. He has been working on that and plans to play several practice rounds without betting while playing. It won't be easy.

Andy checks on his .25-caliber pistol. Twice people tried to rob him because they thought he was carrying large sums of cash.

Neither attempt was successful. One of the bodies is still missing. Andy is capable of taking care of himself and he comes prepared for the worse.

❧❦

Steve (the sign man) Griggs checks into a condo at Myrtle Beach National just outside of Conway. He knows the golf director at Myrtle Beach National, A.J., so he always gets a good deal when he comes to town. He stays at Myrtle Beach National because of one thing; Kings North.

Kings North is an Arnold Palmer-designed golf course and Steve thinks it is one of the greatest courses in the country. It has one of the finest golf holes ever built. *The Gambler* is a par-5 with water everywhere. It has an island landing area for the brave and not so faint of heart. It's the ultimate risk-reward golf shot ever. Hit a perfect drive to the end of the island landing area and you have a mid-to long-iron over water into the green which is wide but not very deep. Take the conventional way around and it is a three-shot hole.

There are two other great courses at Myrtle Beach National but Steve will only play Kings North.

Actually, this will be Steve's second attempt in the World Am. He played three years ago but it rained all week and he is not a mudder. He hopes the weather will be better this year because he plans to win. He loves the Myrtle Beach area, the food, the golf, the casino boats, and the shows. He will attempt to take it all in while he is here.

The only weapon Steve has with him in the room is a six-inch switchblade knife. He leaves it in his room where he can get to it if need be. He keeps his gun locked in the trunk of his car. Steve likes to keep a low profile when he is out on the road. He does not enjoy drawing attention to himself. He has never had a problem but several of his fellow gamblers have, so he also is prepared.

❧❦

Stan (the man) Hutchinson checks into a condo at Tidewater Resort in North Myrtle Beach. Tidewater is an up-scale gated community with a beautiful golf course and a great practice facility. It is quiet and out of the way. He feels safe and secure here. It fits well with his solitary lifestyle. He wants to be able to come and go without drawing attention to himself. He found Tidewater because Keith, the marketing director, e-mailed him about his computer service. He decided this was the place for him. He can play and practice without being disturbed or threatened.

He brings several laptops with him when he is out on the golf circuit. He can actually run his computer business from his condo and this provides cash flow to take care of his golf habit. He also can keep abreast of world news and the local police reports. He has been planning a trip to the World Am for years and everything just sort of fell into place this year. Now that he's here, his goal is to win.

Stan has several weapons in the condo with him; a 9mm Glock and a sawed-off shotgun, which fits in his duffel bag. He has other weapons locked in his trunk. Being an ex-Seal, he enjoys having weapons at his disposal.

He is looking forward to his stay in Myrtle Beach. He has some business to take care of and a lot of golf to play.

&⋆&

Dave (the police) Prendels checks into the Prince Resort in Cherry Grove. He is looking forward to the next two weeks in Myrtle Beach. He is planning to play golf every day this week to get ready for the big tournament. He can always find a little action somewhere in the Myrtle Beach area, whether it is golf, bowling, poker, or the casino boat. He has been to Myrtle Beach several times and it is just a great place to kick back, relax and play.

He has never stayed at the Prince Resort, but from what he has seen so far, he is impressed. The condo suite he is staying in is a very beautiful two-bedroom, two-bath unit overlooking the ocean. He is directly above the pool so he can check out the girls and there is a fishing pier just out from the resort.

He is hoping for some rest and relaxation along with playing a lot of golf. He is planning on a good card game or two and possibly some time on the casino boat. If it has to do with wine, women, golf, and gambling, he is all for it.

Once in his condo, he gets his .357 revolver out of his bag and places it under his pillow. He will sleep better knowing it is within reach.

తింక

Paul (the mechanic) Hills checks into the North Towers at Barefoot Resort in North Myrtle Beach. Barefoot is one of the premier resorts in the Myrtle Beach area. His seventh-floor three-bedroom, three-bath condo overlooks a huge pool and the Intercoastal Waterway. There are four great golf courses to play at the resort, The Fazio, The Love, The Norman, and the private Dye course. There is also a beautiful new learning center and driving range. He can't wait to get over there and hit some balls. He is planning to play golf every day plus practice to get ready for the World Am. He has plans to visit the casino boat in Little River and he plans to spend a little time at the beach checking out the girls.

After he gets into his room, he checks to make sure his 9mm Luger is loaded. He came prepared for any problem, which may arise although he does not foresee any problems here. He just wants some privacy, to relax, have some fun and play golf.

తింక

All of the suspects have at one time or another played golf together or gambled together. None of them had any idea they would all be in the Myrtle Beach area at the same time to play golf in the World Am and that all of them would be suspects in a murder investigation.

తింక

The World Amateur is celebrating twenty-seven years in Myrtle Beach. That's a long time. It gives the amateur golfer a chance to play against other amateurs and stays fair by using the USGA handicap system. It is the amateurs' chance to play in a four-round tournament. They now have an opportunity to see what tournament golf is all about, the ups, the downs, and most of all, the pressure. They will now know what it's like to have to hit a tee-shot in the fairway, over a waste area or to sink a three-foot birdie putt to make it into the finals.. They also have a lot of fun and a large percentage of them bring their families along as well.

The World Am has grown from a few hundred to more than five thousand golfers one year. Golfers from all fifty states and twenty different countries have participated in the World Am.

There are six divisions and forty-five flights. They play seventy-two holes of golf and then the winners and ties from all of the flights play for the Championship on the final day. Handicaps range from 0 to 30 and they must have a USGA handicap to enter.

There are more than seventy courses used for the tourney and each golfer plays a different course each day. They usually play the final championship round at the Dunes Club.

There is over $130,000 in gift certificates won and given away each year. At the end of each day, everyone gets together at the world's largest 19th hole, The Myrtle Beach Convention Center, where the hosts provide food, drinks, and live entertainment.

Quite a few women play each year along with the men and the last two years have produced a woman champion on the final day. You go girls!

This year may be another first. A suspected cold-blooded killer may be playing. Now all I have to do is find that killer among 4,000 golfers and make sure he doesn't kill again.

Chapter 16: The Plan

I opt to call Bob McClellan and see if he can tell me what courses my suspects will be playing during the tournament. I feel that if they come into town early, they will want to practice on the courses they will be playing. I know for sure one of them is in town. He has already made an appearance at the airport.

I get Bob on the phone. "Bob, Mickke D here. How are you?"

"Well Mickke D, my game is still in the toilet so I hope you need your favor so I can get another lesson, the sooner the better."

"I think we can work that out and as for the favor, if I give you some names, can you let me know what courses they will be playing during the tournament?"

"Give me the names and I will get back to you within the hour."

I give him my home fax number and tell him I really appreciate this. About forty-five minutes later, I get a fax with my suspect's entire schedules for the week. Ken (the player)—Sandpiper Bay, The Pearl, Arcadian Shores, and Possum Trot; Dave (the police)—Tidewater, Kings North, Possum Trot, and River Hills; Andy (the farmer)—Thistle, Beachwood, Crow Creek, and Possum Trot; Paul (the mechanic)—Indigo Creek, Tradition, Possum Trot, and Long Bay; Steve (the sign man)—Meadowlands, Black Bear, Possum Trot, and Prestwick; Stan (the man)—Glen Dornoch, Farmstead, Possum Trot, and The Witch.

After looking over the list of courses, I decide Possum Trot will probably be my best bet to see some of my suspects. All six of them are playing that course during the World Am. In fact, four of them will be playing Possum Trot on Wednesday while the other two will be playing on Thursday. It has a great practice facility and my suspects may go there to practice and play.

I call my neighbor Jimmy and ask if he is available to play golf or practice and that it will be on me (actually, SIL will be paying the bill). He says, "Count me in. Should I bring my gun?"

I tell him this will be a feeling-out process and I do not think we need to be armed.

After I finish speaking with Jimmy, I get in the Corvette, which needs to be driven, and go down to Possum Trot. I ask to see Dane Minehart, the general manager and golf director. I have met and played golf with him through The Grand Strand Golf Directors Association. I ask him if we can speak in private and he takes me into his office. I get out my Army ID and flash it towards him. I am quick enough that he does not have time to read it but it probably looks official to him.

I say to Dane, "I don't want you to be alarmed but I will be conducting an undercover operation at your course this week. I am doing it this week so as not to interfere with the World Am next week. I need you to keep this to yourself and please don't tell your employees."

Dane looks confused, "Are we in any danger?"

"No, everyone will be fine. I just want to give you a heads up about why you will be seeing me and my neighbor, Jimmy Bolin, around here a lot this week."

I tell him I will talk with him tomorrow. As I'm leaving Possum Trot, I call Jimmy and leave a message that I will pick him up at 7:30 in the morning and that he should plan to spend the entire day at the golf course.

෨෧

The next morning, I load my clubs into the Trailblazer and at the last minute, I elect to take my .25 caliber, along with three extra clips. I just purchased a new Ohio State golf bag and it has so many extra pockets in it that I can easily stash my small weapon in a zippered pocket with no problem. I drive next door to Jimmy's house and of course, he is waiting for me.

I say to him, "I know I told you no weapons will be needed, but I decided to bring mine at the last minute. If you want to bring a weapon, just be sure you keep it in your golf bag out of sight. I don't want to start a firefight with this guy in the middle of a busy golf course. However, he is extremely dangerous and cunning so I guess we should go prepared."

"Since you have yours, I'll leave mine at home. Besides, it is too big to hide in my golf bag."

Jimmy is laughing as we depart for Possum Trot. When we arrive at the golf course, I find Dane and introduce him to Jimmy. We go into Dane's office and he asks, "Mickke D, how did you get from real estate broker and golf teaching pro to private eye or whatever it is that you are doing?"

I try to answer as evasively as I can. "Dane, I have already told you more about this operation than I should have. I have been hired to look into a small problem and I'll be finished before you knew I was ever here. I will keep you advised on a need to know basis and no one is going to get hurt. I would like to see your tee time sheets for today and tomorrow."

Dane, looking confused and somewhat irritated, leaves and returns in about five minutes with a copy for both of us. I then say to him, "Can you call over to the driving range and tell the manager that I may be walking the tee line and talking to some of the people practicing and not to be concerned?"

I do this because sometimes the golf pro or manager gets their feathers ruffled if they think someone is trying to pick up a lesson at *their* range without permission. I always like to get permission ahead of time. I don't want to upset anyone but I do want the opportunity to make conversation with my possible suspects. Dane says he will make the call. Just as he starts to ask another question, I motion to Jimmy that we are leaving.

We depart with Dane shaking his head and wondering if he has learned anything more than what he learned yesterday. Jimmy and I go back to the Trailblazer to look over the names on the tee sheet. We only have four photos but we do have a list of names. Three of the names we have are on the tee sheet for today and the other three have tee times for tomorrow.

A cold chill goes up and down the back of my neck. All of a sudden, I realize this is for real and it is happening right now. I had better not screw this up or one or both of us might die. I need to control the demons and remember my training. Be in control.

Suddenly I am concerned about Jimmy. "Are you sure you want to get involved in this?"

"Oh hell yes, this is the most fun I've had since I retired. Now, how do you want to handle it?"

The three suspects who are playing today are Ken (the player) Ballinger, Steve (the sign man) Griggs, and Stan (the man) Hutchinson. Tomorrow it is Dave (the police) Prendels, Andy (the farmer) Bottier, and Paul (the mechanic) Hills. I need to plan today and tomorrow so we will get to see all six of them.

I also need to format my own mental and physical plan if things go bad. I don't want to end up in the jungles of Colombia again.

Chapter 17: The Failed Ambush

(Earlier)

After they agree to the contract, Barry e-mails the assassin with the information on Trever Byers and Bald Head Island. He also asks the assassin to check for a map, which Trever may have on him. His last request is to have a drop location where he can leave the payment and pick up the map, if there is one.

The assassin does not like meeting with clients but since this will not be a one-on-one meeting, he agrees to make the exchange in a park in Las Vegas. He can then control what goes on and where. He has checked with Glenn Griffin and received a good referral report on SIL. He gets a phone number from Barry and says he will call him when the contract is completed.

When Barry gets the call that the hit has taken place and that there is indeed a map, he calls a meeting with Bill and Ted.

"Gentlemen, the deed is done and there is a map."

"You're kidding, there really is a map. Now what do we do?" Bill asks.

"Well, to start with, we need to get to Vegas and deal with the hit man but not until we have the map in hand," Barry replies.

They put together a plan to set up an ambush and eliminate the assassin. They need to be in Vegas early tomorrow morning so they need to get their gear together and ready to go. The plan is to allow the assassin to pick up the money and leave the map. Barry will then go to the pick-up point and check that the map is there. He will radio Bill and Ted and tell them to proceed. The assassin is not to get out of the park alive. If possible, get the twenty-five thousand but that is not a priority. They will have pistols and several rifles available, all with silencers.

They take park maintenance worker uniforms with them. This makes it easier to hide weapons. Bill and Ted position themselves so that whoever has a clear field of fire will take the shot. They will strip off their uniforms, throw them into a trash barrel along with the weapons, which are untraceable, keep the silencers and be on their way. They are three ex-special forces against one assassin. It really doesn't seem fair. If only they had known this was not your normal run-of-the-mill assassin.

They arrive in Vegas aboard the company plane around 7:00am Vegas time. This gives them plenty of time to check out the park where the exchange is to take place. They rent a van using fake ID's, pay with cash and do their recon work before they go to breakfast. They do a radio check in the park at their assigned positions and everything works according to plan. They will make one more radio check just before the exchange is to take place. This will be the radio check that breaks the Camel's back.

About an hour before the planned exchange, they enter the park with their brooms and weapons. They go to their assigned areas, make their last radio check and start looking for the assassin. As they look around, they stay in radio contact with each other. Barry takes the twenty-five thousand, which also is in a brown paper bag, and places it at the end of the predetermined bench. The plan is to exchange one bag for another. The only flaw in their plan is that the assassin has arrived first and he is watching and listening to them. The exchange never takes place.

At 12:30pm, Barry calls off the operation and picks up the brown paper bag. The assassin is still alive, they do not have the map but they do have seventy-five thousand in new cash flow. They all agree they would rather have the map.

Chapter 18: Ken, Steve & Stan

Jimmy and I get lucky. Three of our suspects will be at Possum Trot on Wednesday and the other three will be there on Thursday. The Wednesday morning group plan to play about the same time. We elect to try to catch all three of the suspects at the driving range. I stop by the range office and pick up a large bucket of balls and go over to the grass tees. We are set up on the far left hand side of the range and I am working with Jimmy and his wedge. It is not long before our day begins to get exciting.

We have all of the photos with us and I recognize Steve (the sign man) Griggs right away. He is about 5'10" and wearing glasses. He looks in good shape although he does have gray hair. He does not look our way and sets up in about the middle of the range. As he is getting his clubs arranged, I hear someone say to him. "Hey Sign Man, what are you doing down here?"

"Well, hey yourself Player, I could ask you the same thing."

Ken (the player) Ballinger has also arrived. He is about 6'1" and a little bit on the heavy side. I can tell by the way he is moving that his knees are not in good shape. He doesn't look agile enough to be an assassin, where the Sign Man is thin and looks in good shape.

So now, I have the Sign Man and the Player side-by-side not more than fifty yards away from us. All of a sudden, I actually feel a little nervous about the whole situation but the feeling quickly passes. I was hoping to catch them one on one and not together. It will be more difficult to see any type of a split-second hint of recognition this way.

Just as I am about to walk their way, I notice the third suspect of the day coming our way. I turn my back as Stan (the man) Hutchinson walks past us and sets up between us and the other two suspects.

Steve and Ken acknowledge Stan with a nod of their heads. Stan looks their way, glares and does not nod back. Steve and Ken pick up their clubs and go further down toward the far end of the range. I get the idea that they are not real good friends with Stan.

I wait until Stan starts hitting shots, then go up, and sit on a bench behind him. He has a very nice golf swing. He is about 6' tall, thinning hair, and looks as if he could run a marathon tomorrow. He finally feels me watching him and turns around. As I glance into his eyes, the intensity is scary. He stares back at me with cold, dark eyes and assumes an expression that conveys not the slightest hint of what he is thinking, but I can see the disgust in his eyes. He drops his club on the ground and walks over to where I am sitting.

"I don't like people watching me so why don't you go down to the far end of the range and watch those two losers down there," He points to where Steve and Ken have gone.

"I'm sorry. I was just admiring your golf swing. I teach golf and I always enjoy watching people with good swings."

"Well take your sorry golf teaching ass somewhere else. I don't need any lessons."

What an arrogant thing to say. I tried the being a nice guy approach and that didn't work so I stand up and look him directly in the eyes. "Excuse me friend, I think this is a public driving range and if I want to sit on this bench and watch you hit balls then that is exactly what I am going to do. Now do you have a problem with that?"

I can tell my rebuttal baffles him. We stare at each other like two gladiators poised for battle but no one speaks. We are like two caged animals that have just been freed. The testosterone levels are almost to the point of boiling over and exploding.

I can tell he is thinking but he doesn't want to be the one to blink first and then finally he replies, "Let me guess, Army Special Forces.

He blinked first and I never lose eye contact. "Right, and you, Navy Seal?"

We are both surprised at each other's remarks and think, *how did he know that?* However, in the heat of the moment, the thought quickly disappears.

Without him acknowledging the question, I say, "Well, Mr. Seal, you have a piss-poor attitude. Sorry if I bothered you."

Now is not the time for a confrontation. My job is to discover the identity of the assassin, not to engage. I turn and move back to where Jimmy is standing. He seems to have a concerned look on his face. My sense of hearing intensifies just in case Stan decides to jump me from behind. I am also watching Jimmy for any sign of upcoming danger, but he turns and starts hitting balls again. I also hear Stan make contact with a ball.

In the Army, I trained to be ready for all situations but this guy Stan is one scary dude. He has been down some unmarked channels in his life.

I return to where Jimmy is going through *our* large bucket of range balls like *Machine Gun Kelly*. I have asked him many times to take his time and think about each shot.

Jimmy looks back at me and says, "I thought you two were going to get into it over there. What did he say?"

"He did not like me watching him. He seems paranoid to me and somehow he knew I was Special Forces.

"Do you think he's the one?"

"Jimmy, that guy is one frightening person. I think my army buddies were correct to put him at the top of their list."

Stan finishes his small bucket of balls and walks toward us. Just before he turns and goes over to the golf course he stops. He does have balls and I don't mean golf balls.

"Hey army, watch your back. And that goes for your friend also."

Jimmy starts to move forward but I put my arm out to stop him. I don't think he likes being threatened.

"No problem Seal, we're covered. Who's watching your back?"

Stan's face doesn't change expression. He turns and walks away.

After a few minutes, our adrenalin slows down and Jimmy's face comes back to its natural color. He goes back to taking out his frustrations on the range balls and I proceed up the tee line toward Steve and Ken.

Before I leave, I say to Jimmy, "Keep your eyes open, big guy."

"No problem, I've got you covered."

I stop along the way and talk to several other people on the tee line just to keep my golf teacher image intact. As I near Steve and Ken's location, they both turn and look at me at about the same time. I don't believe either one of them recognize me.

Steve says, "I saw you talking to that guy. Be careful, he's about three fries short of a happy meal."

"He did seem to have an attitude problem, so you know him?"

"Oh we both know him. His name is Stan Hutchinson. Hey, I'm Steve and this is Ken."

"Nice to meet you, I'm Mickke D."

Ken laughs, "I guess you know all about happy meals."

"Yeah, right. Tell me more about Stan."

All of a sudden, they both get defensive and Steve says, "Why do you want to know? Are you writing a book?"

I answer, "You could say that. No I just thought he was a strange guy."

Ken looks at Steve and says, "Nice talking to you Mickke D, but we need to get back to practicing."

I pull a couple of real estate business cards out of my pocket and give one to each of them. "If you're ever in the market for a place at the beach give me a call. And by the way, good luck in the World Am next week." I walk away.

I hear Ken say softly to Steve, "How does he know we're playing next week?"

I just smile to myself and continue down the tee line to where Jimmy has almost run out of range balls.

He asks, "So what do you think about those two guys at the end of the range?

I reply, "No way, they just do not have an assassin profile or mentality. I think we can eliminate them. They're just gamblers and hustlers."

"So we're back to your Seal friend," he says sarcastically.

"So far, but we don't know if any of the six is the assassin. Let's see what happens tomorrow."

Chapter 19: Dave, Andy & Paul

Thursday morning, after thinking about and discussing a plan of action, we decide to try to catch Andy and Dave at the driving range and then I hope we can play with Paul in the afternoon since I sort of promised Jimmy we would be playing golf. I hope today goes better than yesterday. We go to the Possum Trot clubhouse to find Dane.

"Dane, can you change some tee times around for us so that we can play with Paul Hills and Lee Donaldson at 12:06?"

Dane replies, "Let me check with Karen. She is in charge of the check-in desk."

Dane leaves and goes out to the front desk. When he returns he says, "No problem, you are playing with Paul and Lee."

So far, so good. We thank Dane and move over to the practice range to get ready for Andy and Dave.

I go inside, ask for a large bucket of balls and tell the young woman behind the desk, Rita, who is different from the person who was working yesterday, that Dane sent me over.

All of a sudden from behind the counter, a medium size, blond dog puts its paws up on the counter. It looks like a mix between a lab and a pit bull.

As I reach over to pet the dog, Rita says to me, "Don't touch her, she doesn't like strangers, she may bite you."

"What's her name?"

"Bogey."

"Well Bogey, you don't look that mean to me."

I reach over and pet her head. She jumps back down and runs into the back room and in a split second returns with a tennis ball in her mouth. She lays the ball on the counter.

"Bogey, I wish I had time to play with you. Maybe I'll come back later and we can play."

Rita is dumbfounded. "I have never seen her act that way with a stranger. It's as if she knows you."

"Oh, I just have a way with dogs. Too bad it doesn't work the same way with women."

She blushes and then says that Dane called and said to comp me for any practice balls, which means I don't have to pay for them. She wants to know what I have on Dane for him to do that. I tell her, with a smile, that it is top secret and that if I tell her I will have to hunt her down and kill her.

Rita takes a step backward and stares at me with a strange frown on her face. She starts to say something. I laugh; tell her that Dane is an old friend and that I was just *yanking her chain.* I thank her, say good-bye to Bogey, and proceed out to the tee line.

Possum Trot has a great practice facility: huge chipping and putting green, a large grass tee area, sand bunkers, and a great separate pitching area. We set up on the far left side of the grass tees so I can observe everyone on the tee area and unless they are left-handed, they will not be looking back at me watching them. It is around 8:30am and it doesn't take long for our first suspect to show up.

Dave (the police) Prendels walks out to the grass tees with a medium bucket of balls. He sets up about five stations away from us. He is a big dude, at least six foot and probably weighs 230 to 240 pounds with a military haircut. The way he walks, his knees are probably as bad as Ken Ballinger's. I always try to notice any weaknesses in the enemy before I confront them. He is big but slow so I can probably outrun him in a race and out maneuver him in a fight even though he outweighs me by fifty pounds. I do not notice any weapons on his person. He does some stretching exercises before getting several clubs out of his bag.

I hear him say to the fellow hitting balls next to him, "Hey I have not hit a ball yet but I will bet you twenty bucks that I can put this first ball on that 50-yard practice green over there."

The man smiles, shrugs his shoulders, and replies, "You've got a bet young man, one ball only," and pulls a twenty out of his pocket.

Dave gets a twenty, takes the other twenty and places them under a club on the ground.

I smile to myself because I'm pretty sure I know what is coming next. I use to do the same scam during my youth when I worked part-time at Lincoln Lanes back in Lancaster. I would bet some unsuspecting customer that I could bowl over 250 before I had ever warmed up. If they took my bet, I would take a score sheet, (yes back then they still had score sheets,) turn it over and write in big, bold numbers 250. Then I would place the score sheet on the lane at the foul line and roll my bowling ball over the sheet with 250 written on it. I had just bowled over 250.

I was right; Dave walks out in front of the tee line and holds up his arms to stop everyone from hitting. He then says, "Could you please hold up, I lost something out here, I'll be just a minute."

He walks out to the designated 50-yard practice green and places the golf ball he is holding on the green. He has just won his bet. By the time he returns to the tee line and picks up his winnings, the man he has just beat out of twenty dollars is leaving and shaking his head. Dave just shrugs his shoulders and starts hitting practice balls.

I decide to walk up the tee line and start a conversation with him. I tell Jimmy to watch my back although he is busy hitting the free bucket of balls. I guess he wants to appear inconspicuous.

I move up the tee line and stop to watch Dave hit some shots. I will be looking for a reaction when he first sees me because I am still sure the person who blew up the plane was in the crowd watching while I was taking pictures Sunday morning. I sit on a bench directly behind him and he finally turns around and looks right at me. I hope this ends better than my encounter with Stan (the man).

"That was quite a scam you pulled on that guy, he did not seem like a very happy camper when he left."

He replies without any hint of recognizing me, "No, he wasn't, but I'll bet if I really had taken the shot and missed, he would have taken my twenty."

He then drops a ball down on the grass, looks back at me and says very confidently, "Twenty says I can do it for real, you want some?"

I have been watching him hit a few shots and it looks as if he is leaving everything out to the right of the green, so I say, "Sure, but let's make it fifty."

After all, he is betting with the other guys twenty.

I want to put a little pressure on him and besides that, I am gambling with SIL money. I figure he realizes he is leaving it out to the right and therefore he will compensate to the left and since the wind is coming from right to left, I feel the odds are in my favor.

He agrees and makes the swing. He misses the green about five feet to the left. *I wonder if I am supposed to split my winnings with SIL. No way.*

He looks back at me as I hold out my hand. He gets into his pocket, pulls out a wad of bills and hands me a fifty.

"I sure wish I had more time to get that back but I have a 9:00 tee time and it's already 8:50," he says with an unhappy camper sound to his voice although he is smiling. "Maybe I'll see you around later and you'll give me a chance to get even. Do you play poker?"

"No, poker is not my game, but let me give you a business card. If you need any help with your game before the World Am, give me a call and I'll give you a discounted rate."

"How do you know I'm playing in the World Am?" He quickly asks.

"Oh, just a guess, but if I don't see you, good luck next week."

"Teaching pro huh, maybe I will give you a call. Do you take checks?"

I laugh, "I don't think so, cash only, in advance."

He smiles, shakes my hand and heads over to see the starter. I think I kind of like this guy. As I am walking back down the tee line toward Jimmy I hear Dave say, "Hey Farmer, what are you doing here?"

He then points back at me and says, "Watch that guy, he just took fifty from me, he's good."

I have a gut feeling Dave is not the assassin but now I have lost the element of surprise with my next suspect.

☜☞

Andy, the farmer, walks over to me and says, "So you took fifty from the Police, that's quite an accomplishment. He doesn't lose very often."

I look him directly in the eyes. "Oh, I guess I just got lucky."

The Farmer is about 5'10", two hundred pounds with sandy red hair peeking out from under his John Deere ball cap. He actually looks like a farmer.

I shake his hand and say, "I'm Mickke D, are you playing in the World Am next week also?"

Andy stares back at me with cold, dark eyes but his face never changes expression. He does not recognize me from anywhere, or so I thought.

"Say Mickke D, did you ever spend any time in Korea? You sort of look like a guy I met over there."

"Sorry, Mr. Bottier, I never made it to that part of the world."

"Look here Mickke D, how do you know my name? Did the Police tell you?"

"I guess he did or I was just lucky again."

"Well, I hope you don't plan on taking money from me. I'm just a poor farm boy from Michigan who came down here to play in this here World Am thing they have going on next week."

I reply with a partial grin. "Michigan huh, do you guys ever play Ohio State?"

"Well, not very well recently I'll have to admit, but listen here, I'll tell you what I will do right now. I'll just bet you that Michigan beats Ohio State next year and I'll only take ten points."

I too quickly reply, "I'll take that bet with one small change. No points."

His eyes are darting with excitement as he quickly replies, "Well, how much Mickke D? Make it easy on yourself."

I shoot right back at him, "How about a hundred and I'll give you an address right now where you can send the check."

He extends his hand and we shake. He then smiles at me like a Cheshire cat and I just know I am in trouble.

When it comes to Ohio State/Michigan football, I sometimes allow my loyalty to get me in trouble. One might say, I open mouth, insert foot. He explains to me what he has just said and that is that Michigan will beat Ohio State. He did not say in which sport. I took for granted he meant football. Therefore, if Michigan beats Ohio State in any sport next year, I lose. He gives me a card and says I can mail the check to this address. I see no reason to give him one of my cards.

Well let me see, I won fifty from Dave and I probably just lost a hundred to Andy. I suppose I will have to add fifty to my expense account with SIL. I am going to guess that Andy is going to look up Dave right away, give him the good news, and probably rub it in a little bit. Andy is not the assassin, I am sure of that.

Jimmy gets a big chuckle out of my first two encounters. I get to hit about ten balls from the large bucket. Machine Gun Kelly hit the rest of them. We spend a little bit of time chipping and putting; then we opt to go back to the clubhouse and wait for our last suspect to arrive.

‽

We are watching the check-in area at Possum Trot and about 11:30 a man checks in and Karen points over toward us. Paul Hills walks over to introduce himself. I turn my back and look out the window as he approaches. As I turn to say hello there is just the slightest look of surprise and anger on his face.

He hesitates for a split second and then says, "Hi, I'm Paul Hills and I guess I will be playing with you fellows today." He is smiling but I notice tension in his face.

We all shake hands and we introduce ourselves. Jimmy says he is looking forward to playing with him today. I keep quiet and just observe but I know I am looking into the eyes of the assassin. Something about him signals danger, as if the soul behind the eyes has faced this scenario before and is not afraid.

Paul is good. He gets his composure back in a split second. Still smiling, he says he is going over to the range to hit some balls and practice his putting for a while. He will see us on the tee.

He does not look like an assassin. He is about fifty, a little bit heavy, dark hair and has the look of a Boy Scout leader, not a killer.

After he leaves, I look at Jimmy and say, "He's the guy. I see it in his face. He recognized me from the airport on Sunday. I just knew the killer was in the crowd watching."

"Are you sure? He seems like a nice guy."

"I am sure, he's the one."

Jimmy's usually happy face turns serious. "Now I wish I had brought my gun. How do we want to do this?"

I am not sure. How do you handle spending four or five hours with an assassin on a crowded golf course?

డ్‌సా

As Paul leaves the Possum Trot clubhouse, he is ticked-off and livid. Mickke D was the person taking pictures at the airport after the explosion. What are the odds of playing with him on a golf course in Myrtle Beach, home to more than a hundred golf courses?

Paul does not think he recognized him because he was wearing a disguise at the time, but to spend four or five hours with him on the course may jog his memory. There is only one thing left to do. Paul picks up his golf bag and tells the starter he is going over to the range to practice for a while and hit some balls. After he reaches the practice area, he continues around the driving range office and walks across the road to the parking lot. He throws his clubs in the back of his Highlander and leaves the course.

డ్‌సా

Jimmy and I sit in the clubhouse for about ten minutes contemplating how we are going to handle the afternoon with an assassin in the next golf cart. If Paul did recognize me and if he thinks I recognized him, will he try to retaliate on the course or will he run?

Jimmy says, "Well, if he takes off we don't have to worry about spending the day with him in the next cart."

I reply, "No, then all we have to worry about is being assassinated by him later."

Neither one of us comes up with any realistic ideas. Jimmy suggests we always hit short of him so he will never be behind us. We discuss just leaving but I need to be positive Paul is the assassin. I hope by talking with him and asking some pertinent questions, I can be sure.

When we get to the bag drop, I show Jimmy which pocket on my bag has my gun in it just in case we get in a real bind and I am away from the cart.

I give our ticket to the starter. He points to a young flat-belly with a ponytail. "This is Lee Donaldson; he is part of your group but we can't seem to find your fourth. He went over to the range to hit some balls but I can't find him there or anywhere else."

Jimmy and I look at each other without saying a word. He ran. We have the right person. Paul is the assassin.

I walk over to Lee and ask, "Did you know Mr. Hills?"

He replies, "Well, not really, I met him on the casino boat last night and he talked me into playing with him today for a few bucks. You guys want a side bet?"

He sounds sincere about not knowing Paul so I tell him no thanks but I do ask him if he knows what type of a vehicle Paul is driving. Lee says he is driving a white Highlander with Nevada plates. The fact that he knows this does not surprise me because most gamblers are very observant people and Lee is definitely a player. From the look of his tan, he probably plays golf five or six days a week.

Jimmy and I gather up our golf bags. I tell the starter to save out ticket and give it to the next twosome that comes by. We leave Lee wondering what is going on; he is now a single with no one to play with. We approach the lot cautiously just in case Paul is waiting to ambush us. We look around and see no white Highlander. The assassin is gone.

As we drive back to River Hills, Jimmy wants to know what I am going to do now. I tell him I have done my job by figuring out who the assassin is although I did it a lot faster than I had anticipated. *Good thing there is that $5,000.00 bonus because I did not make a whole lot on two days of per diem work.*

I will report my findings to SIL and go back to my average every day way of life. At least I didn't get shot, I didn't have to shoot anybody and I now know that I've still got that investigative sense about me. This could be the start of a new career as long as the demons continue to stay away. So far, so good.

Chapter 20: Paul's Revenge

The closer Paul gets to the North Towers, the more upset he becomes. Not only has his two weeks of golf in Myrtle Beach been ruined, his cover may have been blown.

He needs to make sure he cannot be traced. He paid for his condo at the North Towers in cash and the address he used is a post office box in Vegas. He is good up to that point. He has another set of tags for his vehicle and he has two other condos he owns outright if things get warm in Vegas. Only the condo in Vegas is in his real name, the other two are not. Bogus bank accounts have been set up to make automatic monthly withdrawals for POA fees and utility bills. He makes all deposits in cash and in disguise. He has done his handicap through an online handicap service company so they can't trace him back to an actual golf course. This could become a problem if he were to win. He hopes he has covered all of his bases, but only time will tell.

He decides he should not go back to Vegas right now; he will be better off at one of his other condos. He owns one in Charleston and one in Panama City Beach, Florida. Charleston is too close to Myrtle Beach so he opts for Panama City Beach, which is home to one of his favorite courses, The Hombre.

He goes out to his SUV and changes his Nevada tags to Florida tags. He loads up his clubs and luggage. However, before he leaves town, he wants to leave Mickke D a little taste of what happens when you mess with the assassin.

He remembers seeing the name Mickke D somewhere so he looks in the phone book and discovers Mickke D Real Estate and Landscaping on Sea Mountain Highway in North Myrtle Beach. He finds no other Mickke D listed so it has to be him. He rips out the phone book page and stuffs it in his pocket.

He puts on his disguise, buys a one-gallon plastic gas container at the local Ace Hardware Store along with tape, rubber gloves, wire, a bag of rags, and a kitty litter box. He stops at a gas station, fills up his SUV and the container.

His next stop is the nearest mall and Radio Shack where he purchases a new disposable cell phone and an extra battery. The manager at Radio Shack asks him for a lot of personal information and Paul finally says as his gaze sharpens, "Look, Frank," gazing at the man's nametag, "do you want me to buy this or not? I can go to Circuit City and get the same thing for less."

The manager looks into Paul's eyes as chilly fingers dance along his spine. The manager blinks first and rings up the sale. Paul pays in cash and leaves.

He next drives out behind the mall and parks in the middle of nowhere. He needs to assemble his present for Mickke D. He puts on the gloves, places the rags in the kitty litter box, and soaks them with gas from the one-gallon container. He places the soaked rags and some gas in a large sealable lined plastic bag, which he had in his vehicle. He wires the new battery to the cell phone, twice the power, tapes the phone to the plastic bag, and then runs a wire to the battery and phone and another wire inside the bag. He seals the bag but is sure to leave plenty of air inside the bag.

He has just constructed a firebomb, which he can set off at any time just by dialing the disposable cell phone number. The spark from the battery will ignite the fumes and the rags. The air inside the bag will allow it to burn and melt the plastic bag. The rest is history. Even if by chance it doesn't work, Mickke D will get the message when he finds the bomb. Sometimes just the thought of what may have happened can be very scary but if it doesn't work there can always be another time and place for Mr. Mickke D.

Next, he puts on some coveralls, gets his 9mm Luger from the glove compartment, screws on the silencer and puts the gun in his pocket. He puts on a different ball cap and drives over to Sea Mountain Highway. He drives past the address on the phone book page several times and notices just one car in the parking lot. He figures Mickke D is still on the golf course. He elects to take a chance. He places the firebomb in a large canvas tote bag and marches in the front door.

Once inside a very attractive, tall, thin woman with medium brown hair, feverishly working on her nails, meets him. She introduces herself as Jean. Paul, in a very charming way and with a big smile, explains that he is here to service the copy machine for Mickke D Real Estate. Jean tells him to follow her and she takes him down a poorly lit hallway to the last office on the right. The reception area was bright and airy but the hallway leading back to the other offices is just the opposite. He says he won't be long and thanks her for her help.

Suddenly she wrinkles up her nose and blurts out, "You smell like gasoline. What have you been doing?"

Paul has to think fast, "Oh, the smell. I was filling up a container for my mower and I spilled some gas on me. Sorry, I guess I didn't get it all cleaned off."

Either Jean is very lucky or Paul is very lucky. Maybe both of them are very lucky, because Jean is about to ask him for his business card and ID. He anticipates her question and reaches into his pocket for his gun. Both turn when they hear a noise outside. They look out the window as the UPS truck pulls up in front of the office.

Jean turns and excuses herself but says she will be right back. Paul takes this opportunity to place the firebomb under a desk and out of sight. If she does come back into the office, she will not be able to see the device and if she smells gas, he hopes she will think it is just a lingering smell from him being in the office.

Once she leaves and he has planted the bomb he finds the copy machine, opens and closes the top a few times just to make some noise. He leaves the office, shuts the door and walks toward the reception area with the empty tote bag.

He tells Jean, who is talking to the UPS driver, while working on her nails again, that he needs a part and will come back tomorrow to finish the job. He smiles again and asks her what time she opens in the morning. She tells him she will be there at 9:00am. He says he will see her around 10:00 tomorrow.

Jean has no idea how close she has just come to buying the farm. Paul does not like to kill someone without a contract and payment, but if push comes to shove, he will. He will justify it in his mind simply as survival of the fittest. He hopes she gives the UPS driver a big Christmas bonus this year because he may have just saved her life.

He stops a few blocks away from Mickke D's office next to an out of the way dumpster and removes his coveralls, puts on gloves and gets rid of everything he has left over from building his fire bomb. He empties the remainder of the gas into the dumpster and throws in a lighted match, props open the lid with a small stick, and slowly drives away. The police will just think some kids started the fire.

He elects to go through Charleston on his way to Panama City Beach. He will spend the night at his condo and maybe play some golf before going on to Florida. He is still angry. He will get back at SIL somehow, someway.

Chapter 21: Mickke D & Barry

After dropping Jimmy off next door, I go home and place a call to Barry. "Barry, it's Mickke D. How are things in Culpepper?"

He answers in a very subdued voice, "Not much going on here, do you have any good news for me?"

"Yes. I know who the assassin is."

There is silence on the other end of the phone. Finally Barry says; his voice slightly perky, "Who is it?"

"It's Paul Hills."

"Are you sure?"

"I'm 99.9 percent sure. He recognized me at the golf course and left before I had a chance to talk with him. He must have remembered me from the airport when I was taking pictures of the crowd."

There was silence again on Barry's end, "Okay, great, nice job. Fax me your statement and a written report on exactly what took place with names, dates, and times. I'll have your check in the mail this week along with the bonus."

I thought I would feel elated after talking to Barry but I have just the opposite feeling. He is keeping something from me. He knows more than he wants me to know. This whole thing is beginning to smell and it isn't the kind of smell you lick your lips over.

I had no more than ended that thought when my phone rings. "Mickke D, its Barry. I have one more small favor to ask you. A possible witness in an ongoing investigation of ours died in Murrells Inlet a few weeks ago. It was a hit and run accident. He had no family. I contacted the police down there about our case and asked them to send me his personal effects. They told me they could not mail them to me, that someone would have to pick them up and sign for them. Could you stop by, pick them up, and mail them to me? You can bill me for another day plus expenses."

"Sure, do I need any paper work?"

"No I already faxed them the paper work. Tell them who you are and that you're from SIL. Tell them you want the personal property of Rusty McRichards."

"No problem, I'll go down tomorrow and pick them up."

"Thanks Mickke D, I really appreciate this."

Now I'm really confused. What is Barry up to and who is Rusty McRichards? Why didn't he pick up Rusty's personal property while he was in town and why is he asking me to pick them up now? I'm beginning to think this investigation is not quite over so I guess I'll see what I can find out on SIL's quarter.

ॐॐ

Actually, Barry had just found out that Rusty McRichards had no family and that he may have had something on him, which could lead SIL to the mapmaker. Barry doesn't trust his informant to pick up Rusty's belongings because he has a long record. Mickke D is the next best thing, clean, local, and completely controlled by Barry. Or so he thinks.

Chapter 22: The Fire

Paul is sitting in his condo in Charleston, around 1:00am in the morning and he has just finished watching one of his favorite movies, "Caddy Shack". He arrived in Charleston about 7:00pm, had a nice dinner and has just been chilling out in his very comfortable condo. He smiles, picks up his cell phone and dials the number of the firebomb cell phone.

☙❧

My phone rings. I gaze at the clock and 1:45am is flashing into my blurry, sleep-filled eyes. Who in the world could be calling me at this un-godly hour? Nothing good has ever come from a call in the middle of the night. My first thought is that it is one of my ex-wives. Maybe she got into the sauce and decided to call and harass me.

Again, I blame my ex-wives unfairly. Actually, it is Jean from the office, "Mickke D, sorry to wake you up but the office caught on fire and you need to get down here right away."

"What happened?" I ask her in a rather confused and sleepy tone of voice.

"We don't know. Thank goodness the fire department got here quickly and put the fire out before the whole building went up in flames."

"I'll be there in a few minutes."

As I'm getting dressed, I have a spine tingling thought. Maybe the assassin is trying to send me a message. If I'm right, I guess I should be thankful he didn't blow up or burn down my house, at least not yet.

I get my .45 from the dresser drawer below the clock. I place the gun in the small of my back and put on a tee shirt and light short-sleeve windbreaker. This could be an ambush but I doubt he would try anything in front of a crowd of people. I am very observant as I leave my house to go to my vehicle. I notice nothing out of the ordinary.

I pull into the parking lot at the office about twenty minutes later. I notice fire trucks, police cars and a small crowd milling around. There is a strong smell of smoke in the air and I can still see burning embers inside the building and on the roof. I spot Jean with her husband Bob and walk over to them.

"Hey guys, is anyone hurt?"

Jean replies, "Not that we know of."

"Does anyone have any idea how the fire got started?"

"We don't know but the police said they want to talk to you when you get here," Bob says.

Before I start looking around for the person in charge, I go back to the Trailblazer and hide my 45 under the seat. It is probably not a good idea to talk to the police with a loaded gun on me. I find a police officer and tell him who I am and that I need to talk to the guy in charge. The officer laughs and says I need to talk to Sam. He directs me over toward a group of firefighters and police. I walk over and ask for Sam. No wonder he laughed, Sam is not a he but a she.

I introduce myself to Sam. She pulls me aside and asks point blank, "Mr. MacCandlish, do you have any enemies?"

"Please call me Mickke D and why do you ask officer," I look at the badge hanging from her neck, "Concile?"

"Please address me as Detective Concile. And I'm asking because the fire department found evidence of a fire bomb in your office."

I smile and say, "The only enemies I may have are several ex-wives but I don't think any of them are smart enough to do this," as I point to the smoldering building.

Detective Concile does not smile back. This is just what I need, a police detective without a sense of humor. "No detective Concile, I can't think of anyone right off hand." This time I do not smile.

She stares at me for a few seconds and then says, "Aren't you one of the guys who had their plane blown up Sunday at the Grand Strand Airport?"

When I first met her tonight, I thought she looked familiar. Now I remember, she was with the police investigating the plane explosion, but she was not one of the detectives who interviewed me.

"Not really, I drove my friends to the airport but the plane belonged to them, not me. They were old Army buddies of mine who came down for the weekend to play golf. I lost a very good friend in that explosion."

She looks at me and says she is sorry for my loss. She actually sounds sincere.

She asks me a few more questions and then tells me in a very authoritative tone of voice that she will expect me at the North Myrtle Beach Police Station tomorrow morning between 10 and 11 to give a written statement. Again, she is not smiling.

I smile and say, "Yes, Detective Concile, I will be there."

I go back to where Bob and Jean are standing.

I ask both of them if they saw anyone strange around the office yesterday and Jean says, "Oh, my goodness, a man came to work on your copy machine."

"What did he look like?" I ask.

"He was white, about six feet tall, had on coveralls, goatee, moustache, ball cap and dark sunglasses," she blurts out. "He sounded like a really nice man. He didn't stay long, said he needed a part and that he would come back tomorrow. However, do you know what? He smelled like gasoline, said he had spilled gas on himself while filling up his mower."

"Did you tell the police about him?"

"No, I didn't think about it 'till right now."

I point in Sam's direction. "You should probably tell Detective Concile over there about the man."

Jean and Bob go over to see Sam and I go home to try and get some sleep before my grilling at the police station tomorrow. I probably was correct. The assassin was in the crowd watching at the airport. He did recognize me at the golf course from being at the scene of the explosion. He knew I had something to do with SIL.

Chapter 23: Sam

I am on my way to the police station and after giving my statement today, I am going to go on down to Murrells Inlet and pick up the belongings of Rusty McRichards and ship them off to Barry. I have a funny feeling Rusty is also a part of the puzzle.

I am not concerned about giving my statement to Sam. After all, I took hundreds of statements myself while working for Army Jag at Fort Bragg.

Sam takes me into her office, which is rather small, poorly lit, and very cold. It's then that I get my first up-close and personal look at Detective Sam Concile. She is a very attractive woman probably about my age, mid forties. She has bleached blond hair. Even in the dimly lit room, I can see the dark roots and she is dressed more like a real estate broker than a police detective might be. However, as we all know, looks can be deceiving.

"Please be seated Mr. MacCandlish."

She doesn't beat around the bush. She pulls out a folder, lays it on the desk and launches her attack, "Mickke MacCandlish, aka Mickke D, former Army Special Forces and Investigative Officer for Army Jag at Fort Bragg. I haven't found any record, not even a speeding ticket since you've been in the Myrtle Beach area. Real estate broker, landscape architect, golf teaching pro. Seems like the all-American boy. Anything else I should know about you, Mr. MacCandlish?"

I cannot believe she has all of that information and nothing about the helicopter landing in the fairway behind my house or the altercation at Crab Catchers.

I answer, "Not that I can think of, that about covers it, except you didn't mention my three ex-wives, maybe they are still not happy with me."

"I have that information, but I don't think it has anything to do with the case, does it? Were any of your divorces messy enough for them to want to get back at you for any reason?"

"No, not really, they told the judge I had issues and paid no attention to them which, of course I denied. However, they ended up with a big settlement, they seemed happy. I just thought I may get a smile from you."

She has a ring on her finger. I wonder if her husband has ever seen her smile. When I was growing up, I was taught to smile a lot, talk nice, and dress appropriately.

She quickly comes back at me, "I never smile when I'm working; now tell me about the man who came to service your copy machine yesterday."

"I don't know anything about that, detective. The first time I knew anything about it was last night when I heard it from Jean. That was when I told her to tell you about him. My copy machine works fine, or at least it used to."

"Okay, tell me about your friends from the airport?"

"What do they have to do with last night's fire?" I ask rather curtly.

She crosses her arms over her chest and stares at me with bemused eyes. Nary a sound falls from her pursed lips. It's as if she is daring me not to answer the question.

"I can't tell you much, they own a company called SIL and they came down for a weekend of golf. I had not seen them in over fifteen years and one of them did not make the trip back."

"We checked with the Grand Strand Airport and they show your friends scheduled to leave but there is no record of them arriving at the airport. Since you took them to the airport when they left, did you also pick them up when they came in and if so, where was that?"

"Don't really know detective, they just sort of appeared at my backdoor."

Sam looks at me with a smirk on her face, not a smile, and says, "And I have a funny feeling you are not going to elaborate on that, are you?"

I give her the cold shoulder look this time and don't answer her question. I just shrug my shoulders, arch my eyebrows and stare at her. The interview is quickly becoming a game of interrogation chess.

Sam has a disgusted look on her face. She throws a yellow legal pad and a ballpoint pen on the table. She then proceeds to tell me to write everything down I have just told her and not to leave town without checking with her. *Sounds like she got that line from an old movie,* I think.

"Is there anything else you want to tell me, Mr. MacCandlish?"

I opt not to tell her about my business deal with SIL until I find out the real reason for my friends visit to the beach.

"No detective, that's about it."

እ⁓

Detective Sam Concile doesn't believe a thing Mickke D has told her except the part about his three ex-wives. The problem is that she has no proof or evidence to prove otherwise. Her gut tells her that Mickke D is probably a decent person but he is hiding the truth. And she wonders what "issues" he had with his ex-wives.

She is the lead detective in the fire at his office and she is working on the plane explosion at the Grand Strand Airport. As far as she is concerned, they are both connected. However, unless someone starts telling her the truth, she has no way of figuring out who the bad guys are. She is sure it is not Mickke D or his golfing friends, although she is still having trouble collecting detailed information on SIL.

Sam orders officers Stratten and Woolever to tail Mickke D for the rest of the day to find out if he is up to anything fishy. She informs them to just find out where he goes, who he talks to and report to her in the morning.

"But be careful or this guy will spot you, he's ex-Green Beret and he's probably investigated more crimes than both of you combined."

"We'll be fine, Chief," they both say in unison.

"I told you not to call me Chief, my name is Sam."

She goes back into her office, shaking her head.

እ⁓

I have followed a few people during my career at Fort Bragg, so I figure out very quickly Sam has put a tail on me. I am beginning to think that she doesn't trust me or maybe she is a good detective and just doing her job.

I need to find a way to lose the tail. I am on my way to the police station in Murrells Inlet and I don't want Sam to find out about Rusty McRichards, at least not yet.

The majority of the stoplights along the Grand Strand are very long lights so if I time one correctly I will be able to lose my pursuers at one of these lights. As I approach the intersection of 17 and 22 near the Tanger Outlet Mall and the Myrtle Beach Mall, I notice the cross street traffic is backed up which means the light is getting ready to change. As I approach the intersection, the light turns yellow and then red, but I continue on. This will not be the first time someone has run a red light in Myrtle Beach and surely not the last. The car following me has to stop.

Now if I can just get to the split at Business 17 and Bypass 17 before they catch up, I may be able to lose them. As I near the split, I notice another white Trailblazer in front of me taking Business 17. I follow the Trailblazer but I turn off into the parking lot of the Carolina Opry and Pirates Voyage. I pull beside two vehicles, which will block my pursuer's view of my SUV. I watch as the unmarked police car continues down Business 17 following the other white Trailblazer.

I wait for about five minutes to be sure they do not turn around and back track. I see no sign of them. I go back out to Business 17 and take an around about way down to Murrells Inlet via 31.

৵৽

Stratten and Woolever reluctantly call Sam and give her the bad news. "Sorry Chief, I mean sorry Sam, we lost him."

Sam almost curses but instead she says, "You lost him; you've only been gone twenty minutes, how could you lose him already?"

She hangs up and shakes her head again. She thinks to herself, *Mickke D, you're good.* Then after looking around to make sure no one is watching, she actually smiles.

Chapter 24: SIL

(Fifteen years earlier)

Back at Fort Bragg, Barry, Bill, and Ted are planning their last vacation before they muster out of the army to start their new company. They are taking a thirty-day leave and are genuinely looking forward to the time away from army life.

They are hitching a ride on a cargo plane from Fort Bragg to Charleston, South Carolina, where they will board a salvage ship on its way to the Bahamas. They will work their way over to the islands. They are not paid but they get free room and board and all the while they are gaining experience in the art of treasure hunting and deep sea exploring.

They have been doing this for the last three years and have loved every minute. Each year they have delved into a different aspect of the salvage business and are keeping daily journals of all they have learned.

This year they plan to work with the divers on an actual wreck on the sea floor. Their ultimate goal is to own their own salvage ship and search for treasure all over the world.

The problem with this lofty goal is the type of ship they would like to own is very expensive and they probably will not make the kind of money they require by just being spooks. Therefore, their vacation will end in Miami, completing plans for the real money-making business end of SIL.

After three weeks at sea and one day on land, they catch a commercial flight out of the Bahamas to Miami. They make several business calls once they arrive.

They also plan to make some time for the ladies while they are in town. None of them has had any type of a relationship while at Fort Bragg because they are afraid someone will slip up and say too much about their future plans. However, in Miami the gloves are off.

They are planning to start two side businesses at SIL. The first is the sale of illegal arms, including but not limited to everything from small arms to Stinger missiles. They will not actually handle any of the physical weapons. They will be the intermediary on the deals, although they will provide transportation, if needed, for a fee.

They will find buyers for the sellers and sellers for the buyers, and of course, both parties in the transaction will pay them well for their part in the deal. There are times when neither party in an arms deal wants to know who the other party is or for the other party to know who they are. That is where SIL comes into the deal. If asked, one or both parties' identity will stay a secret.

The second business they are establishing is the farming and transportation of human organs. This will work the same way, buyers for sellers and sellers for buyers. SIL will get a call from a donor and then it will be their job to find a person or organization looking for that organ. This business is very hush, hush so SIL fits perfectly into the equation.

Chapter 25: Gary and Dean

(Earlier)

Gary Sherman puts in a call to Dean Rutland, "Dean, I read about the death of Trever Byers. Had he written his report for Brazile before his untimely demise?"

"As a matter of fact, he had started on it. His widow gave me the draft and all of his notes at the funeral. I'm just happy the senator was not available to attend the funeral or he may have received it."

Gary hesitates and then asks, "What was the verdict?"

"It wasn't good so I edited all of the bad stuff out and did the report over myself before handing it to the senator."

"Thank you, Dean, I'll make sure there is a bonus in your envelope next time. Keep me advised."

Gary is becoming apprehensive and a little bit nervous about Dean. He is the only link between him and the killing of Trever Byers. He is not sure if Dean would ever use any of their phone conversations to blackmail him later. Those phone calls could implicate him in the killing. He has always made his payments to Dean in cash so there is no paper trail but the phone calls are a different matter.

He has no idea who Dean hired to kill Trever Byers and he does not want to know. He also does not want any kind of a trail back to him. He has two choices: One, he can continue to keep Dean on retainer and hope nothing goes wrong. Two, he can have Dean eliminated and hope that Dean has not anticipated this and made plans. He decides to hold off for now and see how things transpire.

రావిరి

The murder of Trever Byers is weighing heavy on the mind of Dean Rutland. He is becoming very concerned about Gary and Barry. Gary doesn't know Barry and Barry doesn't know Gary but Barry and Gary both know him. He is the only common link to the killing of Trever Byers. If he should die, they would both be safe from implication in the murder. He is angry, but only with himself. How could he have allowed himself to become a part of cold-blooded murder?

Dean is more afraid of Barry than Gary. He knows Barry's background. Barry will not hesitate to get rid of him if he thinks there is any chance of him spilling the beans.

Gary is more of a businessperson and not a killer, but he could hire someone to do it for him. Dean needs to purchase an insurance policy and then let Barry and Gary both know that he has one. If they do not know, the policy is no good. He needs to make it very clear to them that he should live to a ripe old age.

Dean elects to write down everything that has transpired between the three of them. He starts with the illegal campaign fund payments to Senator Brazile. He includes the retainer fees to himself and the payments to Barry to have Trever Byers killed. He includes as many dates and times as he can remember.

He rents a box at the local Mailboxes in town, pays in advance with cash for ten years. He then mails the letter with the information to himself. He figures ten years will be a good length of time for his insurance policy. Now the only problem is how he gets the authorities to open the box upon his premature death. He would hope that if he dies, the police would look into all of his safe deposit boxes. In one of them, next to some old jewelry, they will find a key to the mailbox taped to an index card inside an envelope. On the card he writes, *I am truly sorry.* If he dies accidentally, who cares, the truth will rear its ugly head.

Chapter 26: SIL

Barry and Bill finally have a solid lead. They know the name of the assassin, that he lives in Las Vegas and drives a white Highlander SUV. It's time for another trip to Sin City. However, this time they hope the outcome will be better.

They are still waiting for the insurance company to settle the claim for the Gulf Stream, which they say they can't until the police department in North Myrtle Beach files a final report on the accident, which of course has not happened as yet.

Barry has leased a twin-engine turbo prop and is billing the insurance company. So far, they are paying the lease but that won't last forever. He has his pilot's license so he lays off Rob Logan, his regular pilot until he gets the new company plane. He will fly them to Vegas to see if they can find Paul Hills.

Before they leave, they check on the Internet for Paul Hills in Las Vegas and low and behold, there are three of them in town. This sounds much too easy and of course, that is what got them into trouble the last time. They underestimated the assassin, which will not happen this time. They pack up weapons, explosives, and whatever else they think may be useful to take with them. However, one thing is for sure, this time they will be more attentive to business.

They land at a small field just outside Vegas, different from the one they used the last time. They rent a car, not a spooky black SUV, use fake names, and cash, and proceed into the city. They check into a medium-priced hotel along The Strip and go out for dinner. They choose to have a nice meal and a full eight hours of sleep before going on the hunt for the assassin.

The following morning, after a huge breakfast, they proceed to check the addresses they found on the Internet. Two of them are single-family homes and neither one of them think Paul would live in a house. He probably is a condo guy. The third address is a condo complex located next to a nice resort. It is an attractive, well-secured building. All of the tenants are using pass cards to get in the front door. This looks and feels like Paul's type of domain.

They drive around the area several times looking for a white Highlander but come up empty; of course, it could be parked in a garage somewhere. They park in the resort's over-flow parking lot across the street from the condo complex and begin the tedious job of a stakeout. They see little to no activity. Barry would like to just follow someone into the building, break down Paul's door and shoot him. Cooler heads prevail and they elect to be patient for at least an hour or so. Bill brought along a Steve Berry novel so he begins reading.

After two hours of forced patience, the mail carrier shows up and Barry opts to take a chance. Bill continues to read.

Barry goes up to the mail carrier and says in a very soft, can you please help me, tone of voice, "I'm trying to locate an old Army buddy of mine, Paul Hills. Does he live in that building?" Pointing toward the address, they had found.

"Yes he does, but he must be out of town because his mail is being held at the Post Office. But you didn't hear that from me, if you know what I mean."

"You know, I sort of thought that. I have been trying to call him for days now and no one answers. Thank you very much and I did not hear anything from you."

As the mail carrier leaves, Barry is thinking. *They should fire your sorry ass. You don't tell a stranger that someone is out of town.*

The guys need to go to Plan B, but they are not sure what Plan B is, so they improvise.

Plan B actually turns out to be quite simple.

"Let's talk to the neighbors and use the Army buddy approach," Barry suggests.

They put on dark glasses, ball caps and wait for someone to come out of or go into the building.

They elect to take turns questioning the complex dwellers. Bill gets the first shift and as an older man approaches the building, he gets out of the rental car and does his thing.

"Excuse me sir, do you live in this building?"

"Why, yes I do young man. How can I help you?"

"I have an old Army buddy who I think lives in this building, but I have been unable to get him to answer his phone. Do you happen to know Paul Hills?"

"Why, yes I do, seems like a nice man. I've talked to him several times. He isn't around all the time, travels quite a bit, some kind of a sales job I think he said."

Bill continues, "Do you have any idea where he could be off to this time?"

"Not really, he doesn't talk much but when he does, it's usually about golf. He loves to play golf."

Bill continues, "Any particular course he prefers to play?"

"Oh, he likes all of the courses around here but I think he once said his favorite course of all times is The Hombre in the Panhandle of Florida along with some courses in Charleston, South Carolina."

They now have another lead, although still a long shot. Barry opens his laptop and gets on the Internet. The Hombre Golf Course is located in Panama City Beach, Florida. They did bring their clubs along so if this turns out to be a wild goose chase, they can play a little golf while deciding on their next move.

While online, Barry checks on small airports in the Panama City Beach area and finds one which will work for them. They call ahead, make arrangements and proceed to the plane. Barry figures it will take six to seven hours with a good tail wind to get there.

☙❧

Paul is finally enjoying himself. He is in Panama City Beach. He has played golf every day, laid on the beach, met a few women, played a little poker, and is just enjoying the good life. However, he has not dropped his guard. He is always aware of his surroundings. He is always on the lookout for the unexpected in his line of work, *something to do with sales, I think.*

He never takes the same route twice and he is always looking in his rear view mirror, whether it's to the golf course or the grocery store. When he arrives at the golf course, he drives around the parking lot at least three times and is looking for anyone sitting in his or her car for any extended period. He always tries to park his vehicle away from other cars if possible and he has a weapon in his golf bag, just in case. He is almost paranoid when it comes to being careful, that is why he left Myrtle Beach; he felt he was no longer in control.

Chapter 27: The Judge

Judge Cadium is scanning the obits in The Sun News and he whispers to himself as if there may be someone else in the room with him, which of course there isn't, "Oh, my god, that's Rusty from the restaurant. Yes, the same Rusty who gave him the old coins. The same Rusty who said he trusted attorneys. He really doesn't know what to think or if he should contact anyone about the coins he still has in his possession. Someone else has died who was involved in some way with the map and the coins. His mind is going in several different directions at the same time.

He does not have to worry about making that decision very long. He receives a call from the local police that same morning.

Officer Dick Smoltz calls to inform him, "We found your business card in Mr. McRichards' coat and we thought you may be his attorney."

The judge hesitates for a second and then replies, "I was doing a small job for Rusty. How can I help you?"

Officer Smoltz continues, "Judge Cadium, we have been unable to locate any next of kin for Mr. McRichards. All we have is his driver's license. Can you come down to the station and ID the body?"

"No problem, officer, I will be down right after lunch."

"Thank you judge, I'll see you then."

TC did not realize retirement was going to be this stressful. After his wife of thirty years passed away two years ago, he moved from Maryland down to South Carolina and the Pawleys Island area of the Grand Strand. His plan was to relax in the sun, walk on the beach, spend time on his boat, search for sunken treasure, have a few drinks, maybe meet a new soul mate, eat in some great restaurants, and live the good life. He can kiss those grandiose plans good-bye.

His new best friend Trever Byers is dead and he withheld information from a police officer. He meets Rusty McRichards in a coffee shop one day and now he is dead, reportedly killed by a hit and run, drunk driver while crossing the street. He is beginning to get a complex.

❧❦

As TC enters the police station in Murrells Inlet, he is not sure what he will tell Officer Smoltz. The officer on duty at the front desk calls Officer Smoltz and then tells him to go down the hall and it's the last door on the right.

He enters the office, shakes hands with Officer Smoltz and sits down.

"Judge Cadium, it is very nice to meet you. We don't get many federal judges in our little town. Thank you for taking the time to come down this afternoon."

"Retired federal judge and I'm afraid I didn't know Mr. McRichards very well but if there's any way I can be of help, please let me know. By the way, I really enjoy your little town."

This produces a huge smile from Officer Smoltz. "Well, before we get down to questions and answers, let's get the ID of the body taken care of."

The officer leads him down a hallway to a make-shift morgue and shows him the body.

"Yes, officer that is Rusty McRichards."

"Thank you judge, that was easy, now let's go back to my office."

Back in his office, Officer Smoltz continues, "We went to Mr. McRichards' condo but no one there seemed to know him. His closest neighbors are out of town and no one seems to know when they may return. Since we found your business card in his coat pocket, I called you. How long have you known Mr. McRichards?"

"Not long, I met him at a coffee shop along the beach, but he did not say much about his personal life, let alone his family."

The next thing out of Officers Smoltz's mouth blows his mind. "Well, since you seem to be the only person who knows him and you seem to be his attorney, I would like to give you his personal effects to hold until we locate any family. I'll have the body moved to the morgue in Conway. Will that be a problem with you?"

"Not at all."

Officer Smoltz hands him a plastic trash bag, which contains all of Rusty's personal effects. He can't wait to see if the coins are in the bag. He says good-bye and leaves.

As soon as he gets to his car, he starts going through Rusty's things. The suspense is killing him. He checks the side pockets and the inside pocket of Rusty's sport coat and finds nothing. It is the same old sport coat he had on the day he met him at the coffee shop. He then sticks his finger in the lapel pocket and low and behold, he finds his business card with the other coins scotch taped to the back of the card. No wonder the coins were not mentioned. The police never found them.

He cannot believe his eyes, how did the police miss this. He doesn't know and doesn't care. He now has all the coins that Rusty discovered and the police don't know about any of them. They only found the first card that he gave to Rusty and not the one that he wrote the receipt on and gave him.

He throws Rusty's belongings in the back seat and drives home to plan his next move. Life is becoming very complicated for him right now. So far, besides himself, anyone who has any connection with the coins or the map is dead. He is certainly glad he never told Freddy what they were doing that day or that he had drawn a crude map and mailed it to Trever.

Chapter 28: Trever

(Earlier)

About two weeks after he is hired by Dean Rutland to do consulting work for Senator Brazil, Trever Byers is contacted by Fred Park of The Justice Department. They want him to be, clearly, a double agent snitch.

It seems the Justice Department is looking into possible illegal campaign financing allegations against Senator Brazile. They need someone close to the organization to help with the investigation. Trever is probably as close to the senator's inner circle as they are going to get. Since he is a die-hard Republican Conservative and Senator Brazile is a die-hard liberal Democrat, Trever has no problem taking the job. Of course, Dean did not ask Trever's political affiliation when he hired him for the consulting job. Trever can now double-dip. He receives a paycheck from both parties.

Senator Brazile wants him to look into what consequences might occur along the Carolina coast if offshore drilling was to take place. In addition, the Justice Department wants him to see if someone may be trying to influence Senator Brazile with illegal campaign funds.

He is in seventh heaven: He is receiving a nice pension from ATF, Brazile's office is paying him a consulting fee, and the Justice Department is paying him to spy on Brazile. Life is good!

He loves the Carolinas, and he loves being near the ocean. He spends a lot of time along the coast meeting with environmentalists, marine biologists, and tourism representatives from the Outer Banks in North Carolina and the Grand Strand area of South Carolina.

They take him deep-sea fishing and show him areas of concern. Someone is always taking him out to dinner for fresh seafood and drinks every evening. He also finds time to play some golf, which is his real passion, and the courses along the North Carolina coast and the Grand Strand area around Myrtle Beach are some of the most beautiful courses in the world. Life could not be better!

He is planning to play Bald Head Island again tomorrow and meet his friend Judge Cadium for lunch to discuss a treasure map which the judge mailed to him. He and the judge are self-proclaimed salvage consultants, even though they have never found much in the way of treasure. They do have a great time searching.

Trever sends out two communiqués. One to Dean Rutland, which says, like several of the others, that offshore drilling itself will probably not be a problem, but any type of a spill will be devastating to the Carolina coast. Damage to marine life, coastal wildlife and tourism, especially in the Myrtle Beach area of South Carolina and the Outer Banks region of North Carolina, could run into the billions of dollars. He tells Dean he is preparing a detailed report, which should be ready in about two weeks.

His second message goes to Fred Park, his contact at the Justice Department. He tells Fred he is looking into the illegal funds issue as much as he can without making Dean or the senator suspicious. So far, he has found nothing.

What bothers him most is that he has not been contacted by someone from the oil industry to give their side of the story.

There have been several press releases in the local papers about the oil industry's take on offshore drilling and the huge savings it will bring to the American people, but no personal contact from anyone directly to him.

It is common knowledge that he is in the area and that he is working for Senator Brazile. He is to give the senator his opinion on the pluses and minuses if offshore drilling was to take place.

No one from the oil industry is giving him their take on the pluses and minuses and he is not about to ask them for their opinion. If they are not concerned then he is not concerned. He will give the environmental, marine, and tourism side of the equation only.

His only thought is that big oil knows the only shot they have to get to Senator Brazile is through illegal campaign funds. So far, he has been unable to prove that theory.

He is going to suggest the Justice Department look into Dean Rutland's bank account and see if it leads them anywhere; follow the money.

He never gets to make that phone call.

Chapter 29: The Senator

Senator Brazile pushes the phone button for his secretary Connie Smith. "Yes senator, how may I help you?"

"Connie, see if you can find Dean and tell him I need to see him right away."

She has been with the senator for a long time now and she can tell by the sound of his voice that R. Gene is upset. She calls Dean's cell phone and gets his voicemail. She leaves a message. She adds 911 at the end.

Dean Rutland has been thinking about how he will let Gary and Barry know that he has a life insurance policy but has been unable to come up with a plan. He notices his cell is vibrating so he checks and gets Connie's 911 call that the senator needs to see him post haste.

He is in the next building so he proceeds to Senator Brazile's office to see what fire he has to put out this time. If it weren't for the extra money he gets from Gary Sherman, he probably would have left the senator a long time ago.

When he arrives at Senator Brazile's office, Connie smiles and motions him to go right in. When he gets inside, the senator calls Connie and asks her to hold his calls and he is not available to anyone, except the president.

Dean had been with the senator for more than ten years and he cannot ever remember a call from the president when he was in the room, so the odds of that are not very good. Maybe it's just wishful thinking.

The senator motions for Dean to sit down and then he gets right to the point. "Dean, I think we may have a problem." The senator's hands seem to be playing with everything on his desk.

Dean is always amused when he uses the word *we* when he really means *he* has a problem.

"What's the problem, senator? Has the press found out about your earmarks for the next budget?"

Senator Brazile informs Dean he received an anonymous, unlisted call on his private answering machine saying an investigation into illegal campaign contributions is very probable.

"Have you heard anything?" Brazile asks.

The question catches Dean off guard, but he does not waver, "No, senator, I haven't. This is news to me."

"Well Dean, you're in charge of that. Look into it right away and get back to me ASAP," he snaps.

"Why the concern, senator, we've had audits before and nothing has ever come of them." He studies the senator's nervous hands and wonders why he is so concerned.

"I was told that the person who was looking into this was Trever Byers. However, in case you have forgotten, someone murdered him not too long ago. He was supposedly working for Justice as well as for us. If that is true, I am really going to be upset with you and the Justice Department. You for hiring the guy and Justice for hiring him to spy on me and for thinking I am doing something illegal. I want answers."

He slaps his hand hard on the desk and stands abruptly.

"I'm on it, senator," Dean says as he marches out of the office.

❧

Connie is not happy with Dean Rutland as he leaves the senator's office. He is in such a huff; he does not even give her a second glance. The main reason for her displeasure with him is that Connie and Dean have a semi-relationship going on. *Semi* to her means only when she wants it to be.

❧

As Dean leaves the senator's office, he is confused. Why did the Justice Department recruit Trever Byers to work for them? Worse yet, do they know something about Trever Byers' death, not reported in the papers?

Of course, the fact that Trever is working for the senator as a consultant is not a secret. Who tipped off Justice that there might be a possible problem? Gary Sherman? Maybe he wasn't sure he was getting enough bang for his buck.

Therein lies the problem. He's not getting any bang for his buck. Dean is channeling all the money from Gary Sherman into his own bank account and not to the senator's campaign account. Therefore, you might say he is double dipping. He keeps the senator's money and the money Gary pays him under the table.

He figures that if the senator never gets the money, there is no way he can be involved with illegal campaign financing. Therefore, eccentrically Gary Sherman has hired Dean as a front row lobbyist. He does not know if that is illegal or not and he figures Gary Sherman will never know the difference.

He needs to try to figure out what Justice knows. He remembers a woman he dated a few times named Liz Woodkark. She works for Justice and maybe he can get some answers from her. They parted on somewhat friendly terms. Actually, Liz dumped him when she caught him with another girl on a night he told her he was too tired to go out. Maybe she has forgotten about that.

He finds Liz's number and calls her, "Liz, Dean Rutland, how are you?"

"Dean Rutland, I'm surprised you're not too tired to call me." (She has not forgotten).

"Liz, I'm just calling to see if you can help me with a problem Senator Brazile is having."

"So, Mr. Rutland, what is the senator's problem?

"Liz, the senator is hearing rumors that the Justice Department is going to investigate him for campaign finance abuse. Now I know you are not allowed to relate any inside information but if you did happen to hear anything about it and you replied *no comment*, I will consider that an affirmative answer to my question."

"Dean, if I do give you an answer to your question, does that mean you may take me out for that dinner you were unable to make the last time?"

"Liz, no matter how you answer the question, I would love to take you out to dinner."

Liz hesitates for a few seconds and then says, "Dean, I have no comment about your question."

He has his answer. "Liz, I'll call you next week, keep the weekend open."

He now knows that Justice is looking at the senator and possibly looking at Dean himself. He hopes after dinner and drinks at his place, Liz will provide him with more information about the inquiry. Politics is a dirty business but hey, someone has to sacrifice. Moreover, for an older woman, Liz is a real fox.

$\approx \ll$

After Dean leaves his office, Senator Brazile locks his office door. He goes back to his desk and calls Connie.

"Make sure I'm not disturbed, Connie, I'll call you back when I'm ready for calls and visitors."

Connie thinks this is a little strange. He did not add, unless the president calls. She wants to call Dean to find out what went on in the meeting but she does not think that would be a good idea while she is at work. Dean did not even look her way when he left, which also is strange.

The senator sits down at his desk, gets a key from his top middle desk drawer and unlocks the bottom enclosure on the left side of his desk.

He stares at the .38 Special hooked to the inside of the door, which makes it easy to get to in case an unwanted intruder breaks into his office and forces him to unlock the desk door. He pulls out a large gym bag which he told Connie held of all things, his gym clothes. He accidentally had it out on the desk one day when she walked in unannounced. Connie looked at him funny, but she did not pursue a line of questioning. She is a good employee and knows when to keep her mouth shut. From that point on, he never gets his gym bag out without first locking his door.

The senator opens the bag and nervously touches around $800,000 in cash, mainly $100 dollar bills neatly packaged in $5,000 packets. He turns the bundles over in his hands, then shoves them back in his gym bag, locks it in the desk and goes to his private washroom to wash his hands. This was what the Ssenator was concerned about when he called Dean to his office. He has been collecting cash for his retirement and walking around funds for several years. He is concerned this is what the Justice Department is looking into. He does not want to get caught with his fingers in the cookie jar.

The senator devised a plan to receive payment for the earmarks he gets into Senate bills. When someone comes to him with a request for money, he will first read the entire request and decide if it makes any sense and if he thinks he can get it through the system without a lot of trouble and backlash. He does not accept every request and he does not ask every person or organization to give to his retirement and walking around fund.

Once the request is accepted and he decides he needs a donation, he will call the person into his office and let the other party know what he is looking for but in a roundabout way, so as not to be too forward with his request for a donation.

Let's say someone wants $500,000 for a new library, the senator will ask for a $5,000 cash donation for his campaign fund once the earmark is approved and the money is received. Therefore, he receives the donation after the benefactor receives their money. If he received the payment before, that, by law, is a bribe. The senator doesn't want to know and doesn't care where the $5,000 comes from as long as he gets his donation.

In the end, the requesting parties get their earmark and the senator gets his donation. It would not be easy to prove otherwise. All transactions are in cash and there is no paper trail. All of his requests come from constituents who do not want the wrath of Senator Brazile to come down on them. Besides, they just received a nice big earmark and if they ever want another one, the cost of doing business to them is very small.

Chapter 30: Barry & Bill

Barry and Bill leave Vegas early and arrive in Panama City Beach late morning. Barry has called ahead to the small airport just outside of town and had the manager of the airport reserve a full-size van so they will be able to transport all of their guns, explosives, and the other materials. They have enough stuff with them to start a small war in a third world country.

They pick up the van and pull it sideways beside the plane so no one can see what they are loading into the van. The side entrance also makes getting in and out in a hurry a lot easier. Bill has with him some dark vinyl covering to put on the inside of all the windows except the driver and passenger windows and the windshield. They don't want anyone to be able to see inside and spot the weapons.

They go to the beach to look for Paul Hills. They have decided not to stay in a condo or hotel this time; they want to be able to get in and get out in a big hurry if necessary. If they need to stay overnight, they will sleep in the van or on the plane.

To them this is war; they are not playing games. Their foe is good and they know it, and they are prepared this time. The one thing on their side is that they hope Paul does not realize they are on his trail and coming in for the kill.

They drive up and down the beach looking for Paul's white SUV and they drive through parking lots and parking garages. Each time they spot a white Highlander, they stake it out and wait until someone comes to the vehicle. So far, the people who show up do not fit the description given to them by Mickke D.

After four hours of looking around the beach, they elect to go to The Hombre and take a chance that he may be there. They arrive at the golf course about twenty minutes later.

They meander cautiously through the parking lot and notice two white Highlanders. They now have to make a major decision.

Do they wait in the parking lot to see if Paul shows up or do they leave the somewhat safe confines of the van and try to find him?

Barry says, "You stay with the van where you can see both vehicles and I will go take a look around the clubhouse and see if I can spot him."

Bill replies, "Sounds like a plan, we should put our cell phones on vibrate and that way if either one of us spot him, call the other one and give his location."

Barry then adds, "Whatever you do, do not confront him here except as a last resort, we need to follow him and find out where he is staying and then we'll make final plans."

The biggest problem for Bill is the fact that there are two white Highlanders to watch. The biggest problem for Barry is that Paul may remember him from the airport the morning of the plane explosion. Barry puts on dark glasses and a ball cap before leaving the van. Since they brought their clubs with them, Barry grabs his putter and a couple of golf balls, changes into a beach shirt and proceeds toward the putting green.

Bill elects to park the van at the end of the lot where he can see everyone leaving the course and traveling toward the parking area. He will also be able to see if they get into either one of the white SUVs.

కొ౼

Paul Hills has just reached the 18th green at The Hombre. He is playing pretty well today. If he two putts from thirty feet, he will shoot 80. As he reaches down to mark his ball, the hairs on the back of his neck begin to tingle, a warning, as if someone is watching him. He has been in the killing business for quite a few years now and he has always been able to sense when something is not right. He automatically switches to self-preservation mode. His nerves are alert, his mind thinking like the hired assassin he has been for many years. He does not have a weapon on him but he knows there is one in his golf bag.

Barry recognizes Paul from the description Mickke D had given him. He calls Bill and says the man they are looking for is here.

Paul misses his first putt but the second is a tap in, so he does end up with an 80. He surveys the area as he shakes hands with his playing partners, Jim and Anita Stippler, from Ohio, who have a second home in Panama City Beach, and Doug McMullan, a doctor from Atlanta who is attending a convention in Panama City. Doug decided to skip the afternoon seminar and play golf instead. It was a good group and they had a lot of fun, but fun time is over for Paul.

He needs to assess the situation and make some quick decisions. Is something wrong? Is someone watching him? In addition, if he is being watched, how does he handle it? He looks around and sees nothing out of the ordinary. He stays on full-alert mode.

Jim asks, "Do you guys want to go into the clubhouse and have a drink while I add up these scores?"

"Sure, but I'll pass on my score," Doug replies.

Paul plays along, deciding the group will provide excellent cover. "Sure, sounds good to me and I think Doug owes me a couple of free physicals anyway." He had made some bets with Doug during the round and of course, he won.

The Hombre does not allow you to take your golf cart out to the parking lot to drop off your clubs. You leave them at the bag drop, bring your car around and pick them up. Of course, they clean your clubs and someone will put your clubs into your car, which equals another tip. This works out well for Paul because he does not want to go out into the parking lot right now. He sneaks the small revolver from his bag into his pocket.

He scans the bar area as they proceed into the grillroom. The only person who doesn't fit is a guy seated at the bar with a ball cap, dark glasses, long pants and a silk Tommy Bahama sports shirt. He remembers seeing him practicing on the putting green as they were finishing up on 18. He must have just arrived minutes before they did.

Paul thinks he has unusual attire, since the temperature is almost ninety degrees outside, way too hot for long pants and he is wearing dark glasses in the grillroom. If they were the type that changes tints, they would have lightened up by now. In addition, he is dressed excessively nice for a ball cap, maybe a straw hat but not a ball cap. He does not fit. Paul's second sense is correct. Someone is watching him. Now the big question; is there more than one and if there is, how many and where are they?

His first priority is not to get into a gun battle here at the golf course. He needs to flee and then he will pick the battlefield. He likes to play offense, not defense. His motto is live to fight another day.

About ten minutes after Barry leaves the van and walks over to the putting green, Bill watches as a middle-aged couple leaves the clubhouse and walk toward the parking lot. The couple go to one of the white SUVs and get in, back out and drive up to the bag drop to pick up their clubs. The man does not look at all like the description Mickke D gave them. Bill then receives a call from Barry telling him he has spotted Paul. Bill figures the other SUV has to belong to Paul Hills.

He makes a decision. He gets out of the van, opens the side door and gets a tracking device from among the vast array of materials he and Barry have brought with them. He jogs over to the remaining white Highlander, sticks the tracking device up under the left rear wheel well, and runs back to the van.

In the van, he uploads the tracking device code into his hand held personal GPS system. The tracking device on Paul's SUV begins to beep on Bill's screen. He then calls Barry and tells him what he has done. They now have a fix on Paul. He can come back to the van.

Paul sits with his golf group, pretending to listen as they chat away. The man at the bar with the dark glasses and ball cap hasn't looked once in their direction but Paul still suspects SIL.

Paul's prime suspect at the bar reaches into his pocket, pulls out his cell phone and speaks into it. He then stands up, leaves a few bills on the bar, and walks out. He still does not look their way.

At the table, Doug says to the group, "I think I should get back to the convention center and catch the end of the afternoon session. Again nice playing with you this afternoon and Paul, if you're ever in Atlanta, stop by and I'll pay you what I owe you." He hands Paul his business card.

Paul replies, "Doug, I just may take you up on that someday."

Jim and Anita stand up and say that they should go also. Everyone shakes hands all around. After a short, friendly argument, Doug picks up the bar tab and they all move outside.

Paul stays with the group out to the parking lot. As he gets closer to his SUV, he notices a gray van parked at the end of the lot. It is too far away to see if there is anyone inside. He presses his automatic door opener quite a ways away from the vehicle just in case they have planted a bomb. That would be a great way for SIL to get back at him. He holds his breath and closes his eyes but all is quiet, nothing happens. Just as he turns to go to open his vehicle door, the car next to his lowers the passenger side window. Paul fingers the gun in his pocket, stays slightly behind his vehicle and waits.

The man inside leans across the front seat and says to him, "Just wanted to let you know some guy stuck something under your wheel well while you were inside, I guess he didn't see me sitting here. I think somebody may be trying to keep track of you."

Paul relaxes the grip on his weapon, smiles and says, "Hey thanks man, probably my wife's PI."

At least now, he does not feel quite as nervous about turning the ignition key. If they want to track him, then he is probably safe for now. He backs out and drives up to the bag drop to pick up his golf clubs. He pushes the button, which unlocks the back compartment door. The attendant puts his clubs in and as Paul walks past the rear wheel well, he slides his hand under the edge and just like a magician, palms the tracking device. He places it in his pocket as he pulls out a tip for the attendant.

As he pulls away from the bag drop, he checks his rear view mirror and side mirror to see what, if anything, the gray van is going to do. The van doesn't move. Paul has the tracking device in his pocket and now he must figure out how he can get it placed somewhere else so that the guys in the van can't track him, but he must do it in a way so that they do not see him dispose of it.

❧❧

Barry and Bill watch as Paul pulls away from the bag drop and they monitor him on their GPS system. As he leaves, the small light begins to blink and a soft beep is heard, showing that there is movement on the part of the tracking device. It is working perfectly.

Barry starts the engine but Bill puts a hand on his shoulder and says, "Take it easy, we don't want him to get spooked, where ever he goes we have him. Let's stay back so he doesn't run."

"Yeah, you're right. I just want to eliminate him so bad I can taste it. We'll give him a ten-minute head start."

❧❧

As Paul leaves the golf course, he keeps an eye out for the van but it is nowhere in sight. Paul figures that whoever is in the van does not know that he found the tracking device, so they are in no hurry to follow him. This will give him a chance to switch the tracking device and send his pursuers on a wild goose chase. He spots a gas station coming up with several cars parked at the pumps. He pulls in behind a black SUV where a woman is pumping gas.

He gets out of his vehicle and with a big smile on his face, he walks up to her.

"Excuse me ma'am, I think I'm lost, do you know where The Hombre golf course is located?"

She smiles and says, "Oh yes, let me finish filling this and I'll point you in the right direction."

As she turns to replace the pump, Paul replies, "I'll close this gas cap for you," and as he does, he attaches the tracking device to the inside of her wheel well.

కం—ళ

Barry and Bill notice that the SUV has stopped and they both look at each other.

"Maybe he stopped to get gas," Bill says.

Barry answers, "I don't know but I think we should get on the road, I don't trust him one little bit."

He starts the van and they pull out of the parking lot onto the highway. The GPS system lights up and starts beeping again; Paul is on the move. Barry slows the van so as not to get too close and they continue on their way.

కం—ళ

Paul thanks the woman for the directions and follows her out of the gas station. The black SUV turns left, goes to the stop sign, and turns right, which puts her back on the same road that Paul was just on. Paul turns right and pulls behind a dumpster where he can see the highway in his rear view mirror. He watches as the gray van passes his location and continues down the highway. He smiles, but there is a deep anger in the pit of his stomach. He is livid. Why can't they just leave him alone? If they want a war, they will have one.

After watching the van go by following the woman in the black SUV, Paul elects to go back to his condominium, pack up and leave town. He figures that since they came to the golf course, they do not know where he is staying or they would have just waited for him there. His condo is only five minutes away and he gets there in less than three. He hurries inside where everything is ready to go. He has learned to live out of his suitcase just because of a possible situation like this. He is packed and back in the Highlander in less than fifteen minutes.

As he leaves the condo, he thinks back to the gray van parked in the golf course parking lot. Now that he thinks about it, he remembers that the vehicle was a rental because it had a rental tag. This means they must have flown into Panama City Beach so therefore they had to leave their plane somewhere. They had to bring weapons and there is no way for them to get weapons onto a commercial flight.

He has a choice: He can leave town now or he can find the plane and do some more damage to SIL. He checked out the entire area before he bought the condo in Panama City Beach and he knows of one small, isolated airport just outside of town. He opts to go over there and look around before leaving town. If their plane is there, great, if not he will go to Charleston. He figures they have found his place in Las Vegas. As he nears the airport, he is thinking about what he has in his vehicle that he can use to destroy a plane.

Paul can build anything and he has redone his Highlander so that he can carry weapons and explosives with him at all times. He just hopes that if the police ever stop him, the officer does not have an explosives search dog with him.

He has taken the back seats out of the SUV and cut away the backs of both seats. He took out the springs and padding and replaced the back of each seat with a wooden tray. He attached the tray in the same way as a tray back on an airplane. He can just unlatch the lock and the whole tray opens to the side on each seat. He designed and built small shelves and access cubbyholes to house all his weapons of small destruction.

On the inside, one seat houses small handguns and a broken down assault rifle. The other seat has C-4, blasting caps, throw away cell phones, extra batteries and room for his disguises. A large blanket drapes over the back seat to disguise the two storage areas.

He stops about a half mile away from the airport. He changes into coveralls and a ball cap. If the plane is there, he will be ready. He parks behind a line of crape myrtle trees, making it difficult for office personnel or SIL, if they are near, to see him.

He strolls into the office, smiles and says to the person behind the desk, "Hey, I'm here to clean a plane, is that it parked over there?"

The man sitting behind the desk gets up, smiles right back at him and says, "Well, who the hell are you and what the hell are you talking about?"

"I told you, I'm here to clean a plane. I met two guys at a bar last night and they said they were looking for someone to clean up the inside of their plane so here I am. Is that it over there? They said it was a twin engine something or the other. I just know how to clean and don't know much about airplanes."

The man looks at Paul as if he is crazy. "I can't just let you go onto their plane without someone giving me an okay."

Paul quickly asks, "So that is their plane?"

"Sure that's their plane, but I don't know you from the man in the moon."

Paul has wasted enough time; he pulls a .357 short barrel revolver from his pocket and puts it against the old man's forehead.

"It's a good thing I like you mister or you would be on your way to heaven or hell by now. Is the plane locked up?" he asks as he pulls the hammer back on the .357.

"Yes sir, it is, but I will be happy to get you the key."

He looks at the nametag on the man's shirt and says, "I thought you might, Nick. This is your lucky day. Get me the key and I am going to tie you up, shut you up and when the guys return, tell them their old friend says hello."

Paul came prepared; he has duct tape and rope in his coveralls. He gets the key from Nick, ties his hands behind him and puts duct tape across his mouth.

"Nice meeting you, Nick and have a great day, oops sorry, you already had a great day, you're still alive."

He sits Nick down behind the counter.

He just has to hope that no one comes in and finds Nick before he is finished with the plane. However, if Barry and Bill show up then all hell is going to break loose.

He gets what he needs from the Highlander and goes over to the plane. He takes four sticks of C-4, blasting caps, a cell phone and new battery onto the plane. Within ten minutes, he is back in the SUV and driving out of the airport. He stops and changes back into his regular clothes. He then dials the number of the cell phone he planted on the plane. A huge explosion ensues another fireball leaping high into the air above the airport and SIL just lost another plane.

He smiles and says to himself, "Hey this is fun; maybe I should just go into business blowing up planes."

≈◦*≈*

Barry and Bill cannot figure out why Paul is going over the bridge to Panama City and away from the beach. They have been following his vehicle for almost twenty minutes now and Barry is getting concerned.

Bill finally offers a reason, "Maybe he's going into Panama City for dinner."

The *ping* on their GPS finally settles down in a rather upscale single-family housing development. Barry slows the van trying to locate the white Highlander. They notice a woman getting out of a black SUV about three houses up and the closer they get to her the louder Bill's GPS starts beeping. As the van reaches the black SUV the beeping becomes a solid sound and the screen displays a message that they are at their destination.

"What the hell is going on," Barry says to no one in particular, "Where is the white Highlander?"

They just look at each other and then Bill finally says, "He switched the tracking device, that no good son-of-a-bitch!"

"Oh, my god, the plane," Barry yells out as he turns the van around, squeals the tires and heads back toward the beach.

"Slow down, we can't afford to get stopped with all of these weapons in our vehicle," Bill yells from the passenger seat.

"Yeah, you're right, plot me the fastest path to the airport."

≈◦*≈*

Paul had no sooner uttered the words, "It's fun to blow up airplanes," when he blurts out, "You dumb bastard, why didn't you just wait until the guys got onto the plane and then made the phone call. Your troubles would then be over and SIL would no longer be chasing you."

He decides it is time to change tactics, instead of being on the defense; it is time to go on the offense. He tried to give them a warning in Myrtle Beach by just blowing up the plane; he had not planned for one of them to die. They can't pay him the money they owe him if they are dead. He set the fire at Mickke D's office when no one was around and he is guessing no one got hurt. Why can't they figure out that if they will just pay him what they owe him, he will go away?

He is going to Charleston and once he gets there, he will plan his attack. He will have several hours of drive time to come up with some ideas. He will consider this as just another assignment and plan everything out to the last detail, except this time he is going to enjoy the kill and not look at it as just another job with a paycheck. The paycheck this time will be freedom, he may even retire. He has more than enough money in bank accounts all over the world to last him for the rest of his life. He can travel and play golf wherever and whenever he wishes.

Chapter 31: Mickke D

I sit in the parking lot of the Murrells Inlet Police Station for about ten minutes to make sure I have lost my tail before I go inside. Officer C.A. Bernett meets me at the front desk and asks if she can help me.

"My name is Mickke MacCandlish and I am supposed to pick up the personal effects of a Rusty McRichards for a company called SIL," I tell Officer Bernett.

"Oh sure, I remember getting that call and we checked out SIL, everything seems to be okay. They seem to know people in high places. Wait here and I'll get them for you."

In about five minutes, Officer Bernett returns empty handed and she is with another officer, Dick Smoltz.

"Mr. MacCandlish, I'm afraid there has been a mix-up here," Officer Smoltz says. "I was not told about SIL wanting the personal effects, so I gave them to Mr. McRichards' attorney about a week ago. Do you want me to call the attorney and see if I can get this straightened out?"

I think about it for a second and then reply to the two officers, "Sounds like a plan to me, I'll just take a seat and wait."

Officer Smoltz leaves but returns in a couple of minutes with the bad news, "Sorry Mr. MacCandlish, he is not answering his phone. Why don't I make you a copy of his business card and you can call him and if he has any questions, have him call me. Here is my card."

I take the copy of the attorney's card and the officer's card and leave. I am not sure what to do next.

As I approach my SUV, I still don't know what I am going to do. I guess it won't hurt to call the attorney and see if he will give me the effects. He either will or he won't and he may be able to give me some information about Rusty.

I look at the copy of the business card and notice it reads Retired Federal Judge. I'll bet he knows people in high places also.

Since there is an address and it's not far away, I opt to just go over and see if I can find him. It's harder to say no in person than it is on the phone. I drive to the address on the card.

It doesn't take long to figure out the address on the card is not an office address. Retired Judge Thomas Allen Cadium lives in Heritage Plantation, a very upscale part of Pawleys Island. As I pull into the half circle driveway, I'm thinking, *nice place, judge.*

As I walk up to Judge Cadium's front door, I notice two cars parked in the brick paved, circular driveway. One is his because it says THEJUDGE on the license plate but the other one has a Virginia plate. I figure he has company but I proceed to ring the doorbell anyway.

After a few minutes, I hear someone inside and then a man's voice asks, "Who is it?"

I think this is a bit strange unless he is concerned about something or he is hiding something. I answer, "My name is Mickke MacCandlish and I was given your business card by Officer Smoltz at the Murrells Inlet Police Department."

The judge unlocks and opens the door. "What can I help you with Mr. MacCandlish?"

"Please call me Mickke."

"And you can call me TC, now what can I help you with Mickke?"

He seems a little irritated so I get right to my reason for being at his doorstep.

I answer in what I consider a very investigative voice, "I am doing some leg work for a company investigating a federal case which may involve Rusty McRichards. I was told to go to the Murrells Inlet Police and pick up Mr. McRichard's belongings and when I got there they told me that they had already given everything to you by mistake."

I hand him the business card I received from Officer Smoltz.

He motions me to follow. "Come in Mickke, I have Rusty's things out back, follow me."

The house is huge; we go through the greatroom, which has eighteen-inch Italian marble tile on the floor. The kitchen has the same tile, just a different shade, and it is almost as large as the greatroom. Very impressive. We go down three steps to a large Carolina room, which opens out into the pool area. The pool is at least thirty by fifty feet long. A screened enclosure covers the entire area of the pool.

Sitting by the pool on their lounge chairs are two beautiful girls sipping on who knows what and who cares what. They have on itsy, bitsy, teeny, weenie, yellow poke-a-dot bikinis.

I stop dead in my tracks and TC chuckles, "Mickke, these are the North twins, Lorrie and Maggie."

"Hi, Mickke," they both respond in unison.

"Hi, girls, please call me Mickke D."

"Oh, what a cute name," one of them says.

TC touches my shoulder and leads me out to a storage building in the back yard. The entire yard is huge and has a beautiful eight-foot high hedge encompassing the entire back yard. We walk up to the metal out-building, probably purchased at Lowe's and he relates to me this is where he keeps his lawn equipment. He enjoys taking care of the grass himself. He opens the door, which has no lock, and picks up a large plastic storage container. I think it odd he would put the effects with his lawn paraphernalia, but hey, to each his own.

"This is all there is Mickke and you are more than welcome to take it all with you, including the container."

I gather up the container and say goodbye to the twins. I wonder if they would like my red boxers and refer to me as pops?

"Nice home, TC."

As if he was reading my mind, TC smiles, thanks me and says, "The twins aren't bad either, are they?"

"No, sir, they are not."

As we approach the front door, he stops and looks me in the eyes, "Mickke D," and he emphasized the D, "Those twins are not for my pleasure; they are the daughters of my current girlfriend. I let them come over and use the pool whenever they wish and they take care of cleaning the pool and twice a month, they clean the house. They keep the pool much cleaner than they do the house. Also, they make beautiful decorations when I have unexpected company like you pop in."

"Actually, I was just getting ready to applaud you for your choice of decorations and ask you what you are taking to keep up with those two fine creatures."

"I have a difficult time keeping up with their mother, let alone the two of them."

I opt to change the subject before I get myself into trouble and besides he is starting to open up a bit. It is time to ask some more case questions.

"TC, how long had you known Mr. McRichards and where did you meet him?"

It is always nice to ask two questions at a time, I learned that from watching presidential news briefings on TV.

"Not long, I only met Rusty one time, in a coffee shop on Pawleys Island. I shared a booth with him and I gave him my card when he told me he was having trouble with the VA. He kept getting the run around from the local VA office in Myrtle Beach. I said the next time they give you a problem, show them this card and tell them I am your personal attorney."

This was the story he had dreamed up after getting the call from Officer Smoltz. It is nice to practice saying it aloud.

"I guess the police found my card on Rusty's body and called me."

"How did Rusty die?" I ask, trying to keep the flow of information moving along.

"I read in the paper that he was struck by a hit- and-run driver in Murrells Inlet and they have yet to find the person responsible. Why are you asking so many questions? Should I hire an attorney?" He laughs. "And, by the way, what is the federal case Rusty was involved in?"

"I really don't know the answer to that question, I'm just the messenger."

I think for a minute and then ask, "Why do I get the impression that even though you did not know Rusty that well, his death really bothers you?"

"Mickke D, it's just that within the last four to six weeks, two people that I know were both killed and one of them was murdered."

"If you don't mind me asking, who was the other person?"

"Oh, it was a good friend of mine. We spent a lot of time together on my boat looking for sunken treasure. Of course, we never found anything worth very much. He was murdered on Bald Head Island while playing golf."

Bingo. TC is the link between Trever Byers, SIL, and Rusty McRichards.

After a slight hesitation, I say to him, "Sorry for your loss, what happened?"

"Well, no one is sure except that he was found near one of the tee boxes back in the trees with a hole in his heart. I had driven up there to have lunch with him and I end up finding out he had been killed."

"And they don't have any suspects?" I ask the question even though I am sure I know who the killer is.

He answers, "No, it's just like Rusty McRichards death, they know what happened, but they have no idea who did it. I am seriously considering hiring a private investigator to look into my friend's death. Do you know anyone in the area you might recommend?"

"Maybe, let me think about that and I will get back to you."

I shake hands with him, we exchange business cards, and he says I can call him anytime. I get into the Trailblazer and head north. I like the man, but I sense he didn't tell me everything.

Chapter 32: Bambi and Thumper

(Earlier)

Two weeks before Barry and Bill make their second trip to Vegas; Barry has Bill gather all of the available newspaper articles about the murder on Bald Head Island. After reading the articles, Barry comes up with one name which he cannot explain. Why had Thomas Allen Cadium gone to Bald Head Island to have lunch with Trever Byers? The articles were very vague about the relationship between Trever Byers and Judge Cadium.

According to the articles, Judge Cadium is a retired federal judge who lives on Pawleys Island, and the two of them have been friends for about two years. Not much more information is available about him except that he is a widower.

Barry wants to know more about him and to find out if he knows anything about the missing treasure map. He calls a part-time investigator who has worked for him before. The investigator lives in Virginia Beach and her name is Cindy North.

Cindy has done a couple of jobs for SIL over the past several years and she will be perfect for this job. She also has two twin daughters who have also been on SIL's payroll a few times. Barry remembers the twins being as mean as a cornered snake if you ever got them ticked off at you. He had always referred to them as Bambi and Thumper, from an old James Bond movie. The twins didn't like the nicknames Bambi and Thumper.

He calls Cindy and tells her he has a job for her and the twins. They are going to Pawleys Island, South Carolina, rent a nice condo for a month or two, and then get up close and personal with Thomas Allen Cadium. He tells her he needs to know what the relationship is between Judge Cadium and a man named Trever Byers. He also warns her that Mr. Cadium is a retired federal judge and that he is no dummy.

Cindy and the twins agree and take off for Pawleys Island three days later. The family is able to pick up and leave because they all work for a medical billing service and as long as they have a computer, they can work from anywhere. The twins have never been to the Myrtle Beach area and they are looking forward to spending time at the beach and hitting the local clubs.

Barry is not sure Myrtle Beach is ready for the twins! They can cause a lot of havoc in a very short period of time. They are both black belts and can fire an M-16 with the best man around. When they tell a man *no*, they mean it. The last time SIL hired them, he had to bail Bambi and Thumper out of jail twice. Thank God they had not killed anyone.

He tells Cindy to have the twins on their best behavior; he does not want anyone killed or put in the hospital. Cindy says she will keep a close eye on them, but they have slowed down quite a bit in their old age. They were twenty-eight years old on their last birthday.

Cindy will have no problem doing her job but keeping the twins in check could be another problem. She has a long talk with them before they head south. They promise to avoid any trouble unless someone else starts the trouble first. The only problem with that is that most times trouble follows them around and then usually someone gets hurt. Look out Myrtle Beach; Bambi and Thumper are on their way to your fair city.

Chapter 33: Barry & Bill

The airport is just far enough away from the beach that the only people who hear the explosion are Paul and Nick. The black smoke is about the only thing that looks out of place in the area.

Barry and Bill notice it right away. As they drive into the airport, no one is around, just the smoldering shell of their airplane. They pull up to the office and go inside.

"Is there anybody here?" Barry calls out.

They hear a noise behind the counter and notice Nick. Barry goes behind the counter and pulls the duct tape off his mouth but leaves his hands tied behind him.

"What the hell happened to our plane, Nick? I thought you were supposed to look after it?"

Nick coughs a few times and then finally answers, "Sorry, guys, a man came in, put a gun to my head and told me if I did not give him the key to your plane, he would kill me."

"Did he say anything else?" Barry slowly asks.

"He said to tell you that your friend said hello. I'm really sorry fellows, I had no choice."

Barry turns to Bill and tells him to call 911 on the office phone and tell them someone destroyed their plane and that we found a person dead in the office. Before anyone can blink, Barry pulls out his gun and shoots Nick right between the eyes.

"What the hell are you doing Barry, have you gone mad?" Bill screams at Barry.

"Just shut up and get everything out of the van except our golf clubs and hide everything out back in the bushes," Barry calmly replies. "The police will think Paul killed him. Our story is that we came down here to play golf and somehow he found out and followed us. He had blown up our other plane in Myrtle Beach and killed our partner. We then call the rental company, tell them we need to drive the van back to Virginia, get a room, come back and get the weapons in a few days and head north. We will blame everything on Paul. We'll stay around and play golf for a few days, how about The Hombre; it looked like a nice course."

Bill just shakes his head and goes out to the van to hide the weapons.

The police and fire trucks arrive in about twenty minutes. A police detective takes Barry and Bill's statement. They inform the police about SIL and mention a few high level names. The detective advises them they can leave but to stay in touch in case they are needed later. Barry tells the detective they will be around for a couple more days to finish their golf vacation before heading north.

☙❧

Bill is getting very upset with the way Barry has been acting lately. It is almost as if Barry has gone off the deep end and now he has killed Nick for no reason whatsoever. Then all he can think about is playing golf. The man has a problem. He is so obsessed with killing Paul that everything else has taken a back seat. SIL has some very influential clients in Washington. Bill thinks that Barry is afraid that if they find out SIL ordered an assassination, SIL will lose all credibility and the business will fail.

In addition, the arms deals and the human organ sales have almost completely stopped and the cash flow for SIL is close to zero. Bill wants to get out but he is just not sure how to go about it. Bill realizes Barry can be a very nasty person. He wants to be very careful about what he says and when he says it. In addition, Bill is now a part of two murders, Trever Byers and now Nick at the airport. Although he did not personally pull the trigger, he is still an involved participant. It is time for Bill to make some hard decisions. Does he turn himself in and cut a deal or does he just leave the country and disappear?

Chapter 34: Mickke D

As I drive up Route 17 to Little River, my mind is going in several different directions. One direction is the lovely North twins. I wonder if they would refer to me as pops like Paula Ann did but that is just a fleeting thought of days gone by and it does not last very long. After all, I am old enough to be their father or uncle. In addition, I have a funny feeling that the twins are not as innocent as they try to portray. I will surely look into their background the first chance I get. Maybe I can talk Detective Concile into doing a background check on them, but then again maybe Ms. Smiley will tell me to take a hike or worse, yet she may want to know why I want the information. It may depend on how pissed off she is that I lost the tail she put on me.

I'm also thinking about what TC said about needing a private investigator. After today, I will no longer be on SIL's payroll and besides that, I think Barry and Bill have been messing with me. My only problem would be if Barry finds I am looking into the murder of Trever Byers on Bald Head Island. Barry can be about as mean as a rattlesnake when backed into a corner. I have a funny feeling SIL is more involved in the murder than they want me to know, but right now I am beginning to feel like I really need to find out what happened on Bald Head Island and who is behind the murder. Of course, I'm really not sure I can take on another business. I'm already spread thin.

Not far up the road, I decide to find a place to eat since I skipped lunch today. One of my favorite restaurants on the south end of the beach is Angelo's. They have great steaks and a wonderful Italian buffet. I am ready for a medium rib-eye with pasta on the side. I am not disappointed.

As I leave Angelo's, the sky turns dark and it begins to rain. I can see lightning in the direction I am going and I know that traffic will soon begin to slow down.

When the sun is out and the temperatures are high, you can drive up and down Highway 17 and not realize there are 300,000 tourists in town because the majority of them are on the beach; however, when it rains, they are all out on 17 looking for something to do, somewhere to go or somewhere to eat. I opt to get off on Highway 544 and go up to 31 and take it into Little River which will eliminate a whole lot of curious tourists who are about to leave the beach.

As I get on 31 and proceed north, the sky becomes darker, the rain heavier and the lightning more spectacular. My mind and my demons start to wander back to a time many years ago when I was in Colombia chasing the drug cartel and training the Colombian Army.

આ∽ઌ

I had received information from air surveillance that they had spotted what looked like a cocaine refining plant out in the middle of nowhere near our training camp. At the plant, they process the cocaine before distribution. My contact stated they spotted tents, three deuce and a half trucks and about ten cartel soldiers with weapons. The information came from a drone plane operation. My people did not believe the cartel spotted the plane and that the cartel soldiers and the cocaine should still be there.

If we had an agreement with Colombia, we could have gone in and dropped a few bombs on the site and that would have been the end of the refining plant, but we don't have an agreement and since no U.S. troops were allowed in the country, except as training personnel, we had to do it another way. We had to go into the field, find them, and then eliminate the refining plant.

I checked the local weather forecast and found that we were supposed to have thunderstorms with heavy rain and lightning from about 2100 hours until 0200 hours. This did not sound like a very nice night to go hiking in the jungle. However, I also figured the cartel would think the same way and they would not be as ready as they normally would. Any type of an edge is always a plus and maybe the difference between life and death in an operation like this. I had been teaching the Colombian troops this and now it was time to see if the teacher could not only talk the talk but also walk the walk.

I had put together a plan of attack by about 1500 hours. We would leave the base training camp around 2000 hours and we should be at the location between 2300 hours and 2400 hours. Besides myself, I was taking along Sgt. Mark Yale, a good old boy from the Jackson, Ohio, area. We would be the only U.S. troops on the mission.

I also recruited 15 Colombian soldiers I thought could follow orders and they also understood and spoke a little bit of English. We had English classes each day before training began and all of the soldiers had to pass a speaking and written exam before they graduated. By graduating, they qualified to receive more pay from the government so all of them trained and studied very hard.

We armed each of the Colombian soldiers with a fully loaded M-16 and ten extra magazines. Mark, who was acting as my radioman, had an M-16 and a grenade launcher. I had an M-16, my .45 pistol and four hand grenades on my ammo belt. We also had two mules with four 5-gallon gas cans per mule. Once we found the plant, we planned to burn it to the ground.

We were a motley-looking crew as we left base camp around 1950 hours and moved out into the jungle for a five-mile hike to meet an enemy who knows that if they lose the cocaine and live, death will be the penalty for living. They would fight to the end to keep us from getting their cocaine.

We were not very far away from our base camp when it began to drizzle. Everyone knew it was going to rain so ponchos were the dress code. We also knew to try to keep our weapons and ammo as dry as possible. I asked Mark to do a como check with headquarters in Panama. If things really got hairy and we needed help, they would provide air cover and rescue. The only problem was that it would take them a while to get there so actually the brass just wanted us to keep them advised of the mission. We were pretty much on our own.

I had been on missions before with an occasional jackass or two, but never with two mules. The mules brought up the rear and we planned to leave them with one soldier about one half-mile from the objective. Once we secured the objective, the soldier would bring the mules for the final job of burning the area. The burning part sent a message to the drug cartel. We *would not only find you, we would destroy you and the cocaine. We hoped to end up with several captives so we could maybe get some good information on the drug cartel. This usually did not happen. The cartel had strict rules about capture. You would die for the cocaine or they would kill your family.*

The closer we got to our objective, the darker the sky became, the harder it rained, and the lightning seemed to be striking all around us. The mules did not mind the rain, but they did not like the thunder and lightning. We decided to drop them off about a mile away instead of a half-mile. It would be too dangerous in case they started acting up and making noise. We left two soldiers with the mules instead of one. I guess if I were one of those mules with four 5-gallon cans of gasoline strapped to my back with lightning bouncing all around, I would be a little upset also.

Mark and I continued with the thirteen remaining Colombian soldiers toward our objective. When we get within the one half-mile area, I call up Lucky, one of the soldiers who is familiar with the area, and tell him to go on ahead and give us a detailed account of what the camp looks like and what kind of security is in place.

The Colombians were very good in the jungle at night because they grew up in the jungle. Lucky returned (we called him Lucky because he had been shot twice on our hikes and he kept coming back for more) in about twenty minutes and told us that the camp was going full bore. There were two guards on duty and the camp had claymores around the perimeter.

The fact that the camp was working at night is good news and bad news. The good news is that we would be able to see the glow of lights long before we got there and the bad news was that they were in a hurry and did not plan to be there very long. We saddled up and headed out with Lucky leading the way. Before long we started to see a soft glow ahead of us and the closer we got, the brighter the glow became. We could hear the sound of a generator.

We stopped about two hundred and fifty yards away from the camp and Mark and I went on alone. I wanted to see how they had their claymores set up and to check out the actual lay of the land. It did not take long for me to find out.

Mark and I received training in jungle warfare and we both taught jungle warfare to the Colombian Army so we were not new to the idea of sneaking through the jungle at night and engaging the enemy. However, the ante goes up when you knew that you just may come face to face with a Claymore mine.

The Army described the M18A1 Claymore as a directional anti-personnel mine. The Claymore was shape charged and fired shrapnel in the form of 700 steel balls about the size of "birdshot" out to about one hundred meters across a 60-degree arc in front of the device. It would definitely get your attention. The M57 firing device, or clacker as we called it, fires the Claymore. More than one Claymore could be "daisy chained" together so that one firing device could activate all Claymores in the chain. Another method of firing was by using trip wires but not as successfully. The cartel wasn't quite good enough to get the trip wires set up properly and they usually failed.

We had two items in our favor and one against us. The two in our favor were the sound of the rain and thunder, along with the sound of the generator, which of course was much louder close to the camp. The thing against us was the lightning. An electrical charge detonates the Claymore. A lightning strike could set off every Claymore around the camp. This would not be good. Mark and I will not be happy campers. We will probably be dead campers.

I decided that the best plan for the entire patrol but the worst plan for Mark and I would be to find all of the Claymores and turn each one of them around, facing into the camp. If it worked, the cartel will end up killing or wounding themselves with no danger to us or our patrol. If it didn't work, well, then we would go to plan B, and since there was no plan B, we would worry about that later.

I instructed Lucky that if we did not contact him within fifteen minutes after he heard the Claymores go off, to pack up and proceed back to base camp.

Lucky just smiled and said, "No problem, but you like bad cat, you always find way back home."

I just smiled and left with Mark.

As the lightning danced around us, Mark and I found the first Claymore. We detected no trip wires and there was a "daisy chain" attached. I turned the Claymore around by just flipping the mine and then Mark followed the chain left and I headed right. We would meet at the end of the chain, hopefully, and then get the hell out of Dodge!

The water running off my brow was not all raindrops; it was good old-fashioned nervous sweat. We were both about as nervous as a long tailed cat in a room full of rocking chairs. However, this is our job and we trained hard to do the task and then get nervous. I told Mark there should be sixteen Claymores around the camp. That was the normal amount deployed by the Cartel, four in each direction. I figured it would take a good forty-five minutes for us to do our thing and we were right on schedule. As I finished my eighth Claymore, I heard a soft bird whistle, which was Mark's signal that he was close. We met up in about five minutes on the far side of the camp and compared notes. Mark says he had turned eight and I confirmed that I had turned eight. So far, so good.

We had been very fortunate up to this point and now it was time to leave. We moved quietly and quickly away from the camp. When I estimated we were about one hundred yards away we found two good-sized trees to get behind. I motioned for Mark to fire a round from his grenade launcher into the camp and I fired a whole magazine from my M-16. There was no response for about a minute and then AK-47 rounds began to whistle above our heads, as we became intimate tree huggers. Next, there was a huge explosion that sounded like a small bomb exploded. It was the sound of sixteen claymores all firing at the same time.

Then there was stillness and the light from the camp began to fade. The only sounds came from the lingering rain pelting down on the jungle canopy, an occasional lightning strike along with the sound of distant thunder. The silence was deafening. We waited for a few more minutes but the silence remained, no yells, no commands, no moaning from wounded soldiers.

I told Mark to get on the radio, call Lucky, and have him bring up the patrol and the mules. We now had to clean up and get out of there before someone starts checking on the camp. A large cartel force could show up at any time to find out why they had lost radio contact with the camp. Time was of the essence.

Lucky shows up in about fifteen minutes with the patrol and mules. Mark and I led the patrol into the camp very cautiously. The lights had vanished so we needed to use our flashlights to see what had happened. I warned everyone to be careful; you never knew if a wounded cartel soldier was waiting to ambush you.

No one in the camp was alive. The first thing we did was count bodies. The drone plane had spotted fifteen warm bodies and we found fifteen dead bodies. Five were cocaine workers and ten were guards. Along with the gasoline cans, we brought cameras and finger printing kits. We numbered each body, took pictures, and fingerprinted each one. That information would help headquarters determine to which cartel clan this group belonged. We removed all the bodies from the camp area. I would send a special patrol later to bring back the remains. The odds were good that when they returned the bodies would be gone.

We poured the gasoline around and set the camp on fire. If the cartel did not know something was wrong before, they would surely figure it out very soon. The fire would not do as much damage as normal because of the rain, but the cartel leaders would get the message. The cartel lost fifteen workers and soldiers. They can replace them, but more than that, they had lost millions in cocaine, which went directly to the bottom line. That would get their attention.

We arrived back at base camp just before sunrise. It was still raining and we were wet, tired, and ready for bed. I did not get much sleep and Mark had the same problem. It took a long time for both of us to get the memory of that night out of our systems. For one of us, it took a lot longer.

My escapades were written up in the Special Forces Monthly Review, giving of course an unknown location, but not as a heroic mission completed without any injuries or fatalities to our troops, but as one they did not recommend for anyone else to copy.

In private, Mark and I were congratulated on the success of our mission by headquarters but told never ever do anything so stupid again. Trust me, I never did. I returned to the States soon after that mission, one reason being there had been several death threats on my life. There was a reward worth hundreds of thousands of dollars to bring my head, dead or alive, back to the cartel.

Chapter 35: Mickke D & TC

A flash of lightning, the crash of thunder, and all of a sudden I am back in the real world. I awake from my daydream in a clammy sweat, just in time to make the turn from 31 onto 9 heading into Little River. It is still raining and I do not remember driving from Surfside to the turn off onto 9. It was as if my eyes were watching the road but my mind was back in Colombia and it was a scary feeling. I was not in control.

I have not thought about that night in Colombia for many, many years. I hope the dreams do not return along with the sleepless nights and the feelings of depression and remorse. I was trained to put death and killing behind me and move on. However, we all handle death, especially when caused by our own hands, in our own separate ways. There were times when I did not handle it well.

I try changing the subject in my mind, to forget about that night in the jungle. I change the agenda to thinking about several questions which I need answered. First, why has Barry not told me about the connection between Trever Byers and TC? Second, I do not think TC is telling me the entire truth about his visit to Bald Head Island. Third, what is the deal with Lorrie and Maggie? They are just too good to be true. First thing in the morning, I will ask Jimmy to have the FBI check out the twins and their mother.

❧❦

As TC comes back through the house and into the pool area, he notices the twins are packing up.

"Do you girls have a hot date tonight?" he asks.

Maggie answers, "Not really, we are going to meet Freddy for dinner and clubbing. Your new friend is cute, is he married?"

"I have no idea Maggie but I'll find out for you."

The way he knows it is Maggie is because the twins always wear necklaces, Maggie's has an "M" at the bottom and Lorrie's has an "L." He wonders how many times the girls exchange necklaces and then mess with some person's mind.

He is well aware that Cindy and the twins are too good to be just a chance meeting in a grocery store. He has not just fallen off the turnip truck. He did an Internet check on Cindy and the twins. It showed they moved here from Virginia Beach not Columbus, Georgia, as they told him. Cindy's record was clean but the twins have gotten into quite a bit of trouble along the way but nothing serious. So what, Cindy is good in bed and the twins are nice window dressing around the neighborhood. Besides that, he has introduced the twins to Freddy and now he is a very happy camper. Oh, to be young again.

He has been very careful about what he says around Cindy and the girls. He is not so sure about Freddy. He would just bet that the twins have some very persuasive powers. The good thing is that Freddy really does not know that much and he knows nothing about the map he sent to Trever Byers.

Little does TC know that this will be the last time he will see the twins and Cindy. The next morning when he calls Cindy, he gets no answer and when he tries her cell phone, it is no longer in service. He drives over to their apartment but it is empty. Cindy and the twins have packed up and left town in a big hurry.

More bad news: He hears on TV that a man died on the beach last night. The police say it was a murder. The man was Freddy. The police have the suspects in jail after a phone tip from an unidentified female. The suspects were in bad shape. Freddy must have put up a hell of a fight. He wonders if the twins could be involved in any way.

Now he has another dilemma. Does he tell the police about the relationship between Freddy and the twins or will they figure it out on their own?

☞∽◈

The twins met Freddy the previous night at Senor Frogs for dinner at Broadway at the Beach. There are some great clubs there so you can have dinner and walk to the clubs. Things started going downhill at the second club the twins and Freddy visited.

Freddy is a great looking guy with a great accent and therefore some guys get very jealous of him. In addition, what makes it worse is that he has two beautiful girls with him. He is a very easygoing person but he knows that some guys, particularly after they have had a few too many, think they are much bigger and badder than they really are. Just because of that fact, he has learned not to drink more than one beer per hour, always have a good full meal ahead of time and do a lot of dancing to wear off the alcohol.

He and the twins are having a good time until three lowlifes think that he has one too many girlfriends. They start making passes at the twins and of course, he and the twins just ignore them. This goes on for about thirty minutes and finally Maggie has had enough. She goes up to the leader of the three losers and gets right in his face.

In a very subdued but stern voice she says, "If you don't leave us alone, I am going to cut your dick off, stick it down your throat and you are going to choke to death on your own penis."

As she finishes her little speech, she grabs his balls and squeezes very hard, tears begin to flow from his eyes and he cannot speak.

"Now do you understand me, numb nuts?"

Her foe can only move his head up and down in an affirmative manner.

It is so noisy and crowded in the club that no one hears or sees what Maggie does or says to the number one stooge. Of course, Lorrie knows what is happening but Freddy has no idea, he has never seen the girls in action except in bed.

Maggie loosens her grip on Mr. Loser and he gasps for air.

She smiles and says, "Nice talking with you friend. Don't forget what I just said."

She walks over to where Freddy and Lorrie are and tells them, "I don't think they'll be bothering us anymore tonight."

Lorrie smiles and says, "I can't believe he's still standing."

"Remember, Mom told us to be good," Maggie replies.

Freddy has no idea what either one of them is talking about so he just shakes his head and agrees.

Freddy has one bad habit. He smokes! Cigarettes are bad for your health is a phrase we have all heard. Well, if Freddy did not smoke, he may still be alive today.

He tells the twins he is going to step outside for a smoke and the twins do not notice that the three stooges follow him. Freddy has no chance at all. He no sooner lights up his smoke then there is a knife in his back, and he is being herded out to the parking lot. One stooge sticks a paper towel in his mouth and the other ties his hands with a plastic tie. The stooges have done this before.

Lorrie looks around the bar for the lowlifes, she is keeping an eye on them to make sure Maggie's message got through to them.

"They're gone Maggie, the bad guys are gone!"

The twins search the bar and cannot find them. "Come on, they must have followed Freddy," Maggie says as she grabs Lorrie and charges out the front door.

As they get outside, they can see in the distance four figures going out to the parking lot. One of them looks like Freddy. Lorrie and Maggie have just turned into Bambi and Thumper and they are not happy campers.

As they arrive at the parking area, they notice a car leaving in a big hurry. The twins locate their car and follow after the vehicle they think has Freddy. They follow the car down to the beach, jump out, and run after the people who have him. They catch up with them very quickly on the beach. It is late night and the beach is deserted.

"We thought you may come after your boyfriend, nice of you to make it so easy for us," Maggie's lowlife friend says.

Maggie very quietly replies, "Where is he?"

"Oh, he is right over there in the surf, but he won't do either one of you any good anymore. But now don't worry, we are going to see that both of you get everything you have coming to you, several times each."

Lorrie looks at Maggie and whispers, "Now remember, mom told us not to get into any trouble."

Maggie smiles at Lorrie and replies, "You're right but she also said we can defend ourselves if someone else starts the trouble."

"You're right Maggie, let's kick some ass."

The twins are not afraid. They jump on the three assailants like a Tasmanian Devil on fresh road kill. By the time they are finished the bad lowlifes are bleeding, bruised and out cold. The only plus on their side is they are not dead, at least not yet.

The twins rush over to Freddy, who is not so lucky. They find him lying in the surf beneath a velvet sky bleached by a nearly full moon. He stares up at them with eyes that are gazing somewhere other than here. He suffered several stab wounds and it looks as if his neck is broken. Maggie searches for a pulse but comes up empty. She is beside herself. She wants to kill all three of the assailants right now but Lorrie pulls her away.

"We need to call 911 and get the hell out of here. We can't bring Freddy back and the cops will have the guys who killed him."

Lorrie calls 911 and reports a murder. She then throws her phone in the ocean. Even if they recover the phone, the saltwater will have destroyed all the information on it.

Just to make sure the bad guys stay, the twins give them a few good kicks before they leave. Maggie finds her friend on the ground and gives him a swift kick to the side of the head.

"I told you to leave us alone!" she yells as she kicks him again.

They can hear the sirens so they look back at Freddy one last time and go back to their car.

When the police arrive, two of the bad guys are moving around but Maggie's lowlife friend is still out cold and may be that way for a long time. They are too embarrassed to tell the police they had their butts kicked by a couple of girls, so they say Freddy started the fight and they were just defending themselves. Later, after a full investigation, the police charge them with murder, but they never implicate the twins.

Mom is going to be very upset, the twins are both thinking on their way home; they are right, mom is livid. They decide to pack up and head back to Virginia right away. While the twins are packing,

Cindy thinks she had better call Barry and give him the bad news. She makes the call.

ॐॐ

Barry's cell phone rings at one o'clock in the morning. He and Bill have rooms at the Holiday Inn on the ocean in Panama City Beach. He answers and it's Cindy.

"I hope I'm not calling too late but we have a problem," Cindy says with a choked voice.

"What's the problem Cindy, have the twins ended up in jail again?"

"Not yet Barry, but they were out clubbing with one of Judge Cadium's friends tonight and the judge's friend was killed."

She closes her eyes waiting for him to go off on her but there is silence on the other end of the phone.

After a few seemingly endless seconds of silence, he replies in a rather calm voice, "Okay, Cindy, tell me what happened. Did the twins kill this guy?"

"Of course not. The girls were out with Freddy hitting some of the clubs and he went outside to smoke. The next thing the girls knew, someone kidnaps him and the twins are following the car down to the beach where they find him dead."

"First of all, who is Freddy?" He asks.

"He is a friend of Judge Cadium's and he helps him on his boat. The girls were getting info from him because the judge was very evasive about anything that happens on the boat."

Cindy is speaking almost too fast for Barry to understand her.

"Now Cindy just slow down a little bit, what did they learn from Freddy?"

"Well, the girls told me that Freddy told them that he and the judge were out off of Pawleys Island looking for something but that the judge never said what they were looking for."

"Ok, now Cindy, are the girls okay and did they do anything wrong that could reflect back on SIL?"

"I don't think so, but you know the girls, sometimes they get carried away."

"All right Cindy, here's what I want you to do. Grab the girls, pack up your things right now, tonight, and go back to Virginia Beach. Don't stop until you get there. Do you understand? When you get home, send me a statement and I will see that you get paid."

"Thanks Barry, we'll be on our way within an hour." Cindy is relieved that he has not raked her over the coals.

He smiles. He has his answer. The judge was looking for treasure and he was the one who sent the map to Trever Byers.

He hopes the twins did not do anything too drastic and the police do not find out about them and track the girls down. He figures if worse comes to worse, he can get by with telling the police the girls are working on a case for SIL. It has worked before to get Bambi and Thumper out of trouble.

Chapter 36: Mickke D & Blue

I sleep in until almost 7:30 the next morning after my meeting with Judge Cadium and my daydream about Colombia. I did sleep okay last night; my demons did not rear their ugly heads again. After my orange juice and oatmeal, I go next door to Jimmy's house and ask him to check out Cindy North and the twins.

"I thought the job was over Mickke D, what happened?" He asks.

"I learned some things yesterday that makes me think there is more to this than what I had originally thought."

"So does this mean you may have some more work for me? That was fun the last couple of days. By the way, do I get paid for any of this?"

"As a matter of fact, yes you do. You can have all of the golf lessons you will ever need free of charge."

"But Mickke D, you already give me free golf lessons."

"I know, but now it's forever, so you had better live for a long time and make sure I stay alive to give you free lessons."

He smiles and we high five.

కలల

I leave Jimmy's house and opt to work in the yard. This will give me some time to relax and contemplate my next move.

As I begin working in the yard, which I really do enjoy, I notice my neighbors' dog staring at me from across the street. He is part German shepard and part husky. He has pale blue/white eyes and is just about the friendliest dog I have ever known. His name is Blue and he is my best buddy. It's great to be able to get your dog fix with your neighbor's dog and not one that you have to take care of yourself.

Blue very seldom barks but when he does, there is usually something serious going on and I have never heard him growl at anyone or anything. I have seen some very scared people walking or riding bikes down our street when Blue comes charging at them from around the corner of the house. There is an electric fence around my neighbor's yard and Blue does respect the fence but not all the people know the fence is there.

He wants them to play with him or feed him. I think half the people on our street give him dog treats. When I feed him, I make him sit and give me a high five before he gets his treat. He is very spoiled. In addition, I hate to say this, but he is one strange dog.

Blue loves to dig. They are not small little holes but huge holes. Sometimes when he's digging, I can only see the backend of his body and the rest of him is in the hole. About once a month, my neighbor comes out and fills in the holes that he has dug. He just lays there and watches her do her thing. Then after she finishes, he waits until she goes back inside, then he looks all around the yard and across the street to see if anyone is watching. If he doesn't see anyone, he starts digging again and within thirty minutes, he has this humongous hole back again. He digs right next to the driveway and several of my neighbors friends have had their car wheels stuck in the holes and have been unable to get out without help.

He loves the rain; he will lay out by his holes in the rain and sleep in a mud puddle. He also enjoys jumping up on cars. He will jump up and just sit there and admire his yard and his big holes. Personally, I think Blue's elevator does not go to the top floor.

He likes to chase me, in his yard, when I get on my Trikke for a little exercise. The Trikke is a three-wheeled self-propelled means of transportation with no pedals and is an excellent way to work out. It's sort of like cross-country skiing on pavement. I watched a commercial on TV and it really looked like fun. It does take a little time to get used to making it go and it does not like inclines. It took me a long time to figure out how to go uphill. Since I was not out doing physical labor at the time, I thought it would be good for me. They filmed the commercial at the beach in California on flat smooth ground. River Hills is smooth but not flat, I guess that is why it's called River Hills. Overall, I do enjoy the Trikke, I get my exercise and Blue gets his by chasing me up and down his yard.

I get started on my yard and about one hour into my project, I hear a vehicle coming down the street. The speed limit on all streets in River Hills is 25 mph and this guy has to be doing 40 plus. As he nears my yard I give him the slow down sign and he comes to a screeching halt at the end of the cul-de-sac and jumps out of his pickup truck. I can tell by his behavior that he probably drank his lunch and he took more than a normal lunch hour.

I am standing in my driveway with my shovel and rake preparing to put leaves and debris in my trash bag. Now the rake I am using is not a normal rake. It is about four feet long with a pink wooden handle and a little pink head. One of my ex-wives left it in the garage and it works great for the task I am doing.

As the man gets closer, he is yelling something about me giving him the finger, which of course I did not. I gave him the palms down sign to slow down. I doubt very much if he would have been able to tell the difference. He is smashed.

I notice that he has a carpenter's belt on and the only weapon that is visible is a claw hammer and a screwdriver. The closer he gets to me the louder he gets and the more pissed off I am becoming.

I am a very easygoing type of person until someone pushes the wrong button. Nevertheless, what I have to remember is that the army trained me to kill quickly and quietly. I have had to learn self-control as a civilian, which sometimes has not been easy. My ex-wives can attest to that.

As the carpenter comes up to me, I can smell the alcohol on his breath. He reams me a new asshole and then I politely say, "Are you finished?"

I try to explain to him that I had not given him the finger but that I just wanted him to slow down because there are kids who ride bikes and retired people in the neighborhood who walk in the street or back out into the street with their cars. I could tell he was not listening and did not care.

Always remember one thing: If you are going to get into a fight, think you are going to get into a fight, or just think there is a good chance of a fight, there is one thing you should do. Always land the first punch! Do not be a hero and let your opponent hit you first.

The split second the carpenter reaches for his hammer and utters the words, "nice rake, Alice," I move the handle of the rake around and pound it into his solar plexus.

Now some folks have called me Alice on the golf course when I leave a putt three feet short but never in my own driveway and he should never have made fun of my pink rake.

As he starts to fall forward, I put my right leg behind his left leg and push him back with the rake. He falls on his butt holding his chest. I place my left foot on his chest and push him to the pavement, the handle of my cute little pink rake in the middle of his throat. He raises his hands in surrender. The fight is over.

I am about to let him up when I hear another vehicle coming down the street, also going too fast. Here comes another pickup, it stops by the other pickup, and two new carpenters get out and head my way. I also hear noise from behind me and I am beginning to think things are not going well; the odds are not in my favor. I'm thinking, three to one, not bad; four to one, not good.

"Mickke D, do we have a problem here?" a familiar voice asks.

My neighbor Jimmy walks up and stands beside me. As I mentioned before, he is a big man and not the type of person you really want to piss off. I guess we made a physical impression on them, because the two smaller carpenters stated their friend had made the wrong turn and they would get him out of here.

I let the guy up and as he leaves with his two friends, here come two more cars, except these have blue lights flashing, but no sirens.

Now wait a minute, I have a helicopter land in my backyard and no one shows up; I watch a fight in a public restaurant and no one shows up, but I have a small disagreement in my front yard and two police cars show up. What's wrong with this picture?

So now I have three carpenters, two pickup trucks, two police cars with lights flashing and Blue is barking his head off. I can just see the neighbors peeking out of their windows saying, "We need to get rid of this guy, he's bringing down the neighborhood."

The police officers get out of their cars and walk up to us. Officer Doan and Officer Dunn look around and Doan says to no one in particular, "Is there a problem here?"

I answer, "No officers, just a little misunderstanding, it's all straightened out now."

Doan looks at Dunn and says, "Let's look at some drivers licenses and get some names."

Dunn walks over to the three carpenters and Doan looks at Jimmy and me. We reach into our pockets, get out our wallets and hand our licenses to him. He looks at my license and laughs. Now I know my picture is not that great but I didn't think it was funny.

Doan looks over at Dunn and says, "Hey Dunn, guess who I've got over here?"

"I give up, who, Al Capone?"

"No, it's Mickke D, the guy who gave Woolever and Stratten the slip after a ten-minute tail, remember everyone was laughing about it in the squad room?"

"Oh yeah, well guess who I've got over here?"

"Okay, I give up, who, the Three Stooges?"

"No, three guys who have had too much to drink."

"Okay, call it in and I'll get a statement."

I tell Officer Doan what happened and he seems to believe me. He asks if there is anything, he can do for us. I ask him if he could speak to the three carpenters to make sure they do not decide to come back when they sober up and try to get even one way or another.

Doan walks over to the three carpenters and says, "Gentlemen, and I use that term only because I have to, if anything happens to Mr. MacCandlish or any of his property, whether it is your fault or not, I will see to it that all three of you go to jail. Is that clear?"

All three nod their heads in agreement.

Doan and Dunn load the three workers into their cars and then Doan says, "There are two tow trucks on the way to collect the pickup trucks. I will be sure and tell Woolever and Stratten you said hello. I will also make sure Detective Concile knows you are back in trouble again. She put out a memo saying to keep an eye out for you."

"Thanks for your help officer and please give Sam my love," I reply with a smile.

"Yeah, right," Doan quirps.

Both officers' get back into their cars, with the three carpenters, and leave.

Jimmy looks at me and says, "What was that all about, this is supposed to be a nice, quiet neighborhood. When do I get to deck someone?"

"I don't know what happened, I was just raking the yard and then all of a sudden everything goes downhill. And I didn't deck him, I just gently shoved him down."

"Yeah, with your little pink rake, Alice," Jimmy says as he walks away laughing.

ॐॐ

I finish with the yard and elect to go ahead and mail Rusty's belongings to SIL. I figure that once I do that and send them a bill along with the package, my employment with SIL will end. I will then call Judge Cadium and tell him that I know of someone who can help him with the investigation into Trever Byers murder and Rusty McRichards' death. Me. Of course, I think I already know who killed Trever Byers but I don't know who hired him or why he was killed.

I take a shower, change clothes, box up Rusty's things and I am just about to go out the door to the Post Office when my phone rings. It's the judge.

"Mickke D its TC, remember me, the guy with the two beautiful mermaids around the pool?"

"Sure, I remember. This is spooky, I was just thinking about giving you a call. What can I do for you?"

"Have you read The Sun News this morning or listened to the local news?" he replies.

"No, I haven't, what did I miss?"

I used to enjoy reading the paper every morning until I got into this investigative thing with SIL and since then I have seen very little TV and I have read few newspapers.

"Remember I told you I have had two people who I know die recently. It is now three. Another close friend of mine was killed at the beach last night. In addition, my girlfriend Cindy and the twins are gone. They packed up and moved out overnight."

"I'm sorry, who was killed last night?"

"His name was Freddy Rioz. He was a friend who helped me on the boat."

Things are getting more complicated by the minute. Another of TC's friends dies and the twins are gone. Furthermore, what's this about a boat? I wonder if it's as big and beautiful as his home at The Heritage?

I tell him I would like to help him with the investigation and that we probably should not discuss this on the phone. I will meet him in the food court at Coastal Grand Mall in an hour.

I pick Coastal Grand Mall because there are too many people dying around him. There's less chance of a problem in a very public place with a lot of people and possible witnesses everywhere. But mainly, I don't want to drive all the way down to Pawleys Island again. I just came from there not too long ago.

He agrees to meet me at the food court. I hope he is open and forthcoming with me because I think he has not been completely truthful up to this point. Maybe this third death will help him decide he had better be upfront with someone, and if not me, maybe the police. It will be his decision.

I have just sat down in the food court at Coastal Grand Mall when I see TC coming in the back entrance from the parking lot. I hold up my hand and he comes over and sits down.

"Do you want anything to eat or drink before we get started?" I ask.

"Black coffee would be great, thank you."

I bring back his coffee and a Diet Pepsi for me along with a large order of fries and ten or so packets of ketchup, just in case he needs something to eat. If not, the fries are all mine.

I figure the direct approach will be the best way to get him to tell me the truth.

"TC, if I'm going to be working for you to find out what happened to your three friends and if there is any connection between the three of them, I need you to be completely honest with me.

He tells me almost everything without hesitation. I think he is starting to get a little bit nervous and concerned about his own mortality. He goes into detail about meeting Rusty, the coins, making the trip to Bald Head Island and finally finding the other coins in Rusty's jacket. He keeps an ace in the hole, the boat sweep and the map.

We agree on financial terms and shake hands.

I'm beginning to feel like Jim Rockford all of a sudden, a real PI. I wonder if I need some type of a license.

Chapter 37: The Assassin

It is 2:00 in the morning as Paul Hills turns off I-95 onto South Carolina 64, a two-lane highway, on his way to his condominium in Charleston. He is going to try to relax for a couple of days before making plans to get back at SIL.

He notices a set of headlights coming his way on this desolated, dark, stretch of road. Abruptly and without warning, those same headlights begin to swerve from one side of the road to the other. As he takes his foot off the accelerator, he notices the lights seem to go off the side of the road and start going up and down as if bouncing. He starts to put on his brakes but it is too late, the vehicle comes back onto the road, crosses the yellow line and slams head on into Paul's Highlander.

The headlights belonged to an eighteen-wheel, fully loaded tractor-trailer. The driver had fallen asleep and by the time he is jolted awake, he is just along for the ride. He tries hitting the brakes but he is traveling too fast to be able to stop before he collides with Paul's SUV.

It is very still, Paul is going in and out of blackness. He knows something is wrong but he is not sure what. His body is numb but he hurts all over. His mind is still somewhat working and he is ticked-off as he thinks to himself, *I don't believe this, dying on a lonely highway, no final gunfight, no going out in a blaze of glory, what a silly way to die and besides that, I still have never had a hole in one.*

He blacks out again. When he comes to, he sees ghosts dangling from hangman nooses held by a huge supreme puppeteer. The faces of the ghosts are of the sixty plus people he has killed during his life. They were just faces to him, not really living human beings. Their suffering and deaths meant nothing to him, a man purged of emotion and empathy many decades ago. Now he wonders if they felt the same way he is feeling now and if they are all waiting for him somewhere in the great beyond to take their revenge.

They were right, he thinks, *your life does pass before your eyes as you die,* but so what, he will not live to tell anyone. He blacks out again and when he comes to this time, his mind wanders back to all the women he has known in his life. He has never been married, never been a father, and never attended his child's baseball or soccer games. Another dangling ghost appears with the face of a lovely girl from Wisconsin named Ola. He will never know it, but he did have children, twins, a boy and a girl. He had an affair with the lovely Ola from Wisconsin. He hated the name Ola so he nicknamed her Bunny. He stayed with Bunny for about a month, but decided he was becoming too involved with the affair. It was time to leave. He left without ever saying goodbye.

Of course, he left no forwarding address so Ola had no way to get in touch with him to tell him about his kids. She tried but no one seemed to know anything about the father of her children. He had dreams about her occasionally and every once in a while, he would wonder if maybe she could have been the one he let get away. This is one of those times.

His thought about not going out in a blaze of glory is mistaken. This time when he comes to, he smells the smoke and senses the fire. He tries to scream but there is no air in his lungs to form the words. The fire erupts and before long, flames engulf the Highlander. Next, the ammo stored in the fake back seats begin to go off and Paul has what he wants, a final gunfight in a blaze of glory. He smiles, then drifts off hand in hand with all of his past ghosts into a bright yet foggy tunnel, thinking about his never-to-be hole in one. The assassin is dead.

∽∽

Barry and Bill come through Charleston three days behind Paul. They remembered the neighbor in Vegas mentioning courses in Charleston. They drive around town looking for any white Highlander they can spot. They drive through condominium developments and several golf courses but to no avail. They go to the courthouse and check tax records but nothing exists for Paul Hills. Barry wants to stop at police headquarters and ask questions but Bill tells him that is probably not a good idea since their van is full of weapons, surveillance materials, and explosives. They spend the night in Charleston and the next morning travel up I-95 to Culpepper.

As they see road signs for Myrtle Beach, Bill turns to Barry and asks, "Should we call Mickke D and see how he's doing?"

"No, I don't want Mickke D involved in this any way, shape, or form."

"Why do you say that? I thought he did a great job finding the assassin for us. Maybe he can find him again?"

"That's the problem, he did too good of a job. I do not want him nosing around in this anymore. If he starts looking, he may find out a whole lot more than we want him to find out. And if that happens, do you want to be the one to eliminate him?"

Bill is silent for a few minutes and then he says, "No, I would not relish that assignment."

Barry turns to Bill and says, "Yeah, me neither, but could you do it? Could you pull the trigger?"

"I don't know, could you?"

"Sure, if I thought there was no other way and my life depended on it, sure, I could pull the trigger and so could you."

There was very little conversation between them for the rest of the trip. The thought of killing a friend like Mickke D did not sit very well with Bill. If Barry is willing to kill Mickke D then Bill is right in thinking he will be willing to kill him, as well. Maybe that was what Barry was trying to get through to him. He will do whatever it takes to finish the job, friend or no friend.

అ~⋚

Four days later at SIL headquarters, Bill is doing his usual checking of reports of unexplained and unusual deaths across the nation. SIL keeps a file on such things just in case they ever need the information later, for an ongoing case.

A report comes in from the State Police in Charleston, South Carolin. It states that there has been an accident involving an SUV and a tractor-trailer. The SUV was a Highlander and the driver was dead. The part that makes it unusual is that they have been unable to identify the driver and ammo was going off at the scene of the accident. The police found burned C-4, weapons, and ammo at the location.

Bill makes a copy of the report and takes it directly to Barry's office.

"Oh, my god, he's dead," Barry slowly stammers as a smile frays the edges of his mouth.

"We don't know that for sure, but it sure sounds like him," Bill responds as a strange ill at ease feeling passes through him.

"Well, Mr. Cutter, why don't you see if you can confirm my beliefs one way or the other? If he is dead, we can move on to things that are more productive. We can stop hunting him and see about finding the treasure map that Trever Byers had on him."

"Okay, let me see what I can find out."

Bill leaves Barry's office wondering if he should have kept the report to himself. If the assassin is dead, he could be next.

When Bill gets back to his office, he looks up the number for State Police Headquarters in Charleston. He calls the number and gets Detective Susan B. Wallace. She was the person on duty the night of the accident and therefore the lead detective.

"Detective Wallace, this is Bill Cutter in Culpepper, Virginia and I work with Special Investigations Limited. I had an accident report come across my desk from your locale and I think I may have some information about your John Doe."

"Slow down a minute Mr. Cutter, who the hell are you and who the hell is Special Investigations limited?"

"Sorry detective, check your Homeland Security Code File and look up 14BOF-17," Bill replies.

"Hold on," Susan says as she pulls a codebook from her locked desk drawer.

After a few minutes of silence, she comes back on the phone and says, "Okay, so now I know who you are and that you know people in high places, what do you have for me?"

"We have been searching for a man named Paul Hills in relation to a murder on Bald Head Island, North Carolina, several months ago and your John Doe was driving the same type of SUV as Mr. Hills."

"Mr. Cutter, so do thousands of other people. What makes you think our John Doe is Mr. Hills?"

"We had spotted Mr. Hills in Panama City Beach, Florida, but he got away from us and we thought he was headed to Charleston, where he possibly owns a condo. We could not find him in Charleston and I think the reason is that he was killed in the accident."

"Did you check in with anybody here while you were searching for Mr. Hills?" She asks.

"No, Detective Wallace, we usually try to stay out of the lime light, if you know what I mean."

"What you mean, Mr. Cutter, is that you're one of those spook companies and you pretty much do as you damn well please."

"I'm sorry detective, did you get up on the wrong side of the bed this morning or are you always this pissed off? I can have someone call your supervisor if you wish, but I would rather not do that."

There was silence on the phone and then she replies, "You're right, Mr. Cutter, I apologize, it's just that the accident scene was a scary situation. There was ammo going off everywhere and then we were unable to find anything on the victim to identify him."

"Detective, if you don't mind, I am going to fax you everything we have on Paul Hills and then you let me know if you think he could be your John Doe."

"That will be great, Mr. Cutter, and again I apologize for my rudeness. I will get back to you as soon as possible."

Bill hangs up, shakes his head, faxes the information to Charleston, and reports to Barry.

Chapter 38: Mickke D

I get up the next morning after my encounter with the carpenters and my meeting with TC, answer some e-mails, return some phone calls and plan my day. One of my e-mails was from Patti Michelle Court, one of my golf students. She is having some problems and wants a nine-hole playing lesson. I e-mail her back that I am tied up right now but I will get back to her next week. Patti has taken a series of lessons and does very well but always seems to choke on the course.

I figure I should make a trip up to Bald Head Island and see what I can find out from the authorities at the scene of Trever Byers' murder. Again, you always learn more in person than over the phone.

It is another beautiful Chamber of Commerce day so I am looking forward to the trip.

I arrive around 1:30pm on the island. The ride up is great and the ferry boat trip over to the island is exuberant. For some reason I just feel pleasant today, as if something good is going to happen.

I rent a golf cart and get directions to the police station. On the way, I pass North Carolina's oldest lighthouse, Old Baldy, commissioned by Thomas Jefferson. I remember when Jimmy and I were up here to play golf, he wanted to climb to the top and look around. I told him to go ahead without me. Just be sure and take pictures.

Police Chief Marty Vette answers my knock on the door and for some reason as I introduce myself and quickly flash him my old Army Investigative License, I think I have met him somewhere before. He looks familiar to me.

I say to him, "Chief Vette, have we met before?"

"Mr. MacCandlish, if we have, I'm sorry but I don't remember it."

At age forty-five and three wives later, my memory is not what it used to be. In addition, it has become very selective. However, I know I have met this man. Maybe it will come to me later.

"Chief Vette, I was hired by Judge Cadium to look into the death of Trever Byers."

"Oh, yeah, the guy who was shot at the golf course. I wish you a lot of luck. I have been unable to find anything on the person who did that," Marty replies.

"Could you tell me what you did find, evidence wise?" I pleadingly ask.

"Sure. I found golf cart tracks leading from the golf course over to the tidal creek where I suppose he had a boat waiting. I found the condo he had rented, paid for in cash with a name that belongs to no one. The condo was cleaner than church on Sunday morning and there was not a print anywhere."

He finally takes a breath and stares at me.

"That didn't give you much to go on, did it? Did the feds come over and take a look?" I ask.

"Oh hell yes, they were all over the place, but they don't like to share information. We'll get back to you when we know something was all I was told."

"I know what you mean Chief; it's like pulling teeth to get information from them. Do you think anyone would mind if I go over to the golf course and look around?"

"Let me call Justin, the golf pro, and have him get someone to take you out to the scene of the crime. However, do me a favor, if by chance you find something please let me know. Don't pull a fed on me."

I promise him I will share any new evidence that I may discover.

He smiles as if to say, *yeah right, sure you will.*

He calls the golf course and sets up the trip to the murder scene. I thank him for his help and proceed over to the golf course to meet Justin.

సౌళ

As soon as his guest leaves, Police Chief Marty Vette makes a second call, "Hey, one of your old buddies is up here nosing around. He said his name is Mickke MacCandlish. I remember him as Mickke D."

"Thanks Marty, I'll take care of it," the voice on the other end of the phone replies.

æ✑

It takes me about ten minutes to get from Chief Vette's office to the golf course. Justin is waiting for me in the pro shop.

"You must be Mr. MacCandlish; Marty said he was sending you over and for me to take you out to the crime scene. Are you ready to go?"

"Yes, sir, let's do it."

We leave the pro shop, get into his golf cart and wind our way out to the tee box on number 6. He is very talkative about what happened that day. He is also apologetic about bringing the golf cart back to the pro shop before anyone in charge had a chance to look it over.

"Were you the first person to see the cart after the shooting?" I ask.

"Yes, one of my rangers spotted Mr. Byers' body back in the tree line along with his pull-cart and clubs. He rushed up thinking he might have had a heart attack or something but when he got there, he noticed the blood on his chest. He found no pulse and then he called me on his radio."

"So then, what did you do?"

"I got on the phone and called 911 plus Chief Vette. I went into the clubhouse and told Mr. Cadium that we had found Trever and that he was dead. I then took my assistant pro and went out to see what was going on."

"What did you find when you got there?"

"A sight that I never want to see again," Justin slowly replies.

"How did you find the golf cart?"

"After the body was brought in I decided to go searching for the missing golf cart. My assistant and I noticed cart tracks in the soft ground and decided to follow them."

"So where did you find the cart?"

"We found the cart at the edge of the tidal creek where an old boat dock was located."

We finally arrive at the 6th tee box and he drives the cart over in the trees where Trever Byers body had been found. It would have been hidden pretty well unless you were actually looking for something, which is what the ranger was doing. Justin then followed the path he had taken the day of the shooting and drove me out to the old boat dock. There was not much to see.

"I've played here before but refresh my memory. Where is the 6th tee in relationship to the clubhouse and the rest of the course?" I ask him.

"That's interesting; it has to be the farthest point on the course away from the clubhouse," he answers.

We exchange small talk on the trip back to the clubhouse and when we arrive, Justin wants to know if I would like a beer. I say sure and as we sit down at the bar, I happen to glance around the room and there are four men playing cards at one of the tables.

It hits me like a ton of bricks. I remember where I met Marty Vette. I played poker with Barry, Ted, Bill, and him maybe sixteen to seventeen years ago one night at Fort Bragg. I remember Barry had invited him but that's about all I remember from that night. I probably lost money so I put that evening into my negative selective memory box.

Isn't that interesting. A guy who Barry invited to play poker years ago just happens to be the police chief on the island where a murder takes place and SIL is investigating the murder. It could be a complete coincidence. Yeah, right. I wonder if Chief Vette recognized me from that poker game and if he did, why didn't he mention it?

I say to Justin, "How long have you been the head pro here?"

"I've been on Bald Head about five years now. I love it here, beautiful course, beautiful location and lots of nice people. It doesn't get any better than this."

"Was Chief Vette here when you came or did he come after you?"

"He was here when I got here. I think he has been on the island for almost ten years. Why do you ask?"

"Oh, no real reason, I thought maybe I knew him from somewhere, but if he's been here that long, it is definitely not him."

I thank him for the beer and drive my golf cart back to the dock area. I catch the next ferry back to the mainland. This has been a very informative day. I learn that the assassin is very good and that he cleans up the scene of his crime like a true professional. He cleaned up so well that it will be very difficult to learn much about the shooting or the killer. But I learn a lot more about Trever Byers' death and that is that Barry knows a whole lot more than what he has told me.

I debate with myself on the way back if I should call Barry and ask him about Marty Vette, but one of us loses the debate and decides not to call just yet. I make a mental note to call TC when I get home and ask him his thoughts on Chief Vette. I could call him on my cell phone but I am one of those crazy people who does not like to talk on a cell phone and drive.

I get back to the house, immediately call the judge and ask him if Chief Vette said anything at the interview that sounded out of place or just not right. TC says not that he can think of, but then again the thing that now stands out is that the interview was very short and sweet and there has been no follow-up at all.

Furthermore, the chief was not the least upset about the fact that Justin had compromised the crime scene when he drove the killer's golf cart back to the clubhouse. It was as if the chief didn't really care that much about the investigation or finding the killer.

I thank TC and tell him I will keep him in the loop. I no more than hang up when the phone rings and it is TC.

"Hey TC, did you think of something else the chief said or did?"

"No, I didn't, but I wanted to know if you would like to take a ride on the boat someday?"

"Sure, sounds like fun, just let me know when."

"How about tomorrow, say eight o'clock my house. We'll grab some breakfast and take her out for a spin."

I hesitate for a few seconds. Eight means I need to leave by seven, which means I need to get up by six. "Sure, I'll see you around eight."

I added *around* just in case I am late.

It sounds to me like the judge has something else on his mind besides just a boat ride. I guess I will find out tomorrow.

మ్రా

I arrive at TC's house about 8:15am. I almost made it on time. At the last minute, I elected to take my .45 along so I had to change into a shirt that will cover my gun stuffed in the middle of my back.

He has bagels, scrambled eggs, bacon, orange juice, and coffee waiting for me. Since it's the middle of the week, I think about asking for oatmeal but the bacon smells so good I decide to cheat and indulge myself. Around 9:00, we take off in his Mercedes and go over to the marina.

We get to his boat, or I would call it a yacht, and proceed out of the marina. TC tells me about his *boat* on the way out to sea.

It is a Carver 450 Voyager w/480 Volvos. Forty-five feet in length, fiberglass hull, diesel powered 560-gallon fuel tank, 150-gallon water tank and 80-gallon holding tank. 480 horse power with a 20-knot cruising speed. It has a beautiful interior and more instruments than I can comprehend. I was right in my thinking, beautiful home, beautiful boat.

He shuts it down about two miles out and we drift. It is another Chamber of Commerce day along the South Carolina coast.

"Mickke D, I hope you don't mind but I did a background check on you."

"Not at all, what did you find?"

"Well, you have quite a resume; you're probably just what I'm looking for."

Puzzled, I reply, "I thought you already agreed to hire me to find out what happened to Trever Byers. Could I have been on another planet when that took place?"

"Oh, no, we're good on that, but I may have another offer to make you."

"Fire away, I'm willing to listen to any proposal."

"Remember when I told you about the coins that Rusty had, well, I forgot to mention that he told me where he found them. Freddy and I took the boat out and we may have found where the coins started out before they ended up on the beach."

"So what you're trying to say is that you may have found the location of a ship wreck with a whole bunch of coins on board."

"That's about it. Are you a qualified diver?"

"You bet, I became diver certified while in Special Forces, I didn't want the Navy Seals to have all the fun."

"Mickke D, I need a partner to help me go after that possible ship wreck, are you interested?"

"Sure, sounds like fun. Tell me more."

He proceeds to go into detail about what he and Freddy had found and how he had made a rough map of the location and mailed a copy to Trever Byers. He also tells me that the police found no map on Trever. He concluded that whoever killed Trever had also taken the map.

Now my investigative wheels are starting to grind. Could that map be the reason SIL wants to find Paul Hills? Barry, Bill, and Ted were always talking about shipwrecks and sunken treasure beneath the sea.

He tells me that he is willing to provide the boat, all the equipment and the capital for the operation. We will split everything fifty-five percent for him and forty-five for me. The extra 10 for him is to cover the expenses.

"Sounds fine to me, let me know when you want to start?" We shake hands to make it official.

Chapter 39: Mickke D & Mrs. Byers

Before leaving TC's house, I ask him for the phone number of Trever Byers' wife. She lives just outside of Washington, D.C. and even though I always like to talk to witnesses in person, D.C. is too far to go for an interview. I ask TC to call Mrs. Byers and let her know I will be calling her. He says he will call her tonight.

I call Mrs. Byers the following morning. "Mrs. Byers, this is Mickke MacCandlish in Myrtle Beach, South Carolina. I was given your number by Judge Cadium."

"Yes Mr. MacCandlish, TC called me last night and said you would be calling me."

"First of all, Mrs. Byers, I am very sorry for your loss. I hope you don't mind if I ask you a few questions pertaining to your husband's death?"

"You mean murder. Not at all, Mr. MacCandlish and please call me Mandi Lee. I am just glad someone is looking into Trever's death. The police and the government aren't doing anything."

"Well, Mandi Lee, you can call me Mickke D. TC feels the same way about the investigation or lack thereof and hired me to see what I can find."

I hear a slight laugh from her. "Rhymes doesn't it? Mandi Lee and Mickke D."

I say, "How did your husband meet TC?"

I asked this same question of TC and I just want to verify that the two stories match.

"They met at a Salvage Convention in Myrtle Beach about two years ago. They have been looking for sunken treasure ever since. I actually saw less of Trever after he retired than when he was working full time."

"Who hired your husband to do consulting work for Senator Brazile?"

"His name is Dean Rutland and he's an aid to the senator."

"Do you happen to have a number where I can reach him?"

"Yes I do, please hold for a minute and I'll get it."

She returns to the phone and gives me the number for Dean Rutland. I ask her, "Was that the only job your husband had?"

She hesitates for a minute and then replies, "No, he was also doing consulting work and getting a check each month from someone at the Justice Department but I don't know who it was."

"Did he ever tell you anything about the work he was doing for Justice?"

"No, he was very open about the job for Senator Brazile but never said much about the other consulting job."

"Do you work anywhere, Mandi Lee?"

"Oh yes, I'm an assistant attorney with the Defense Department."

"And what does an assistant attorney do for the Defense Department?"

"It's classified and if I told you, I would have to hunt you down and kill you."

I burst out laughing. "I'm sorry, but that's one of my favorite sayings. I have just never had it said to me before. I will not ask you any more questions about your job."

"Thank you," she replies and there is no laughter in her voice.

I hesitate for a moment to gather myself and then continue, "Did your husband leave any papers or notes about either one of his consulting jobs?"

"I found the unfinished report he was preparing for Senator Brazile and I gave it to Dean Rutland at Trever's funeral. Then the other day I was cleaning out Trever's computer and I found the same report on his hard drive. Could that be important?"

"Could you e-mail the report to me? I don't know if it's important, but it could be."

"I will e-mail it to you today."

I tell Mandi Lee I will let her know the minute I find out something about her husband's murder. She sounds as if she is good with that. I almost tell her I know who killed Trever but since I can't prove it, I don't.

I'm beginning to wonder what she does for the Defense Department and if maybe, that has anything to do with Trever's death and SIL. I'm also wondering if Trever found out what she was doing and he died because of that. Maybe Mandi Lee has something on SIL. Furthermore, what about Trever's consulting job with the Justice Department? There are whole bunches of scenarios out there. I need to figure out which one is the actual reason for Trever's death.

I receive the e-mail about thirty minutes later. It is a five-page single spaced report, which pretty much says that there will probably be no problem with offshore drilling unless there happens to be a spill.

Trever is very clear that if a spill occurs, the results for the environment, fishing, and tourism industries will be catastrophic. It will cost in the billions of dollars to clean up such a spill and to compensate business for their losses. At the end of the report, Trever says that if offshore drilling were to go forward, there should be many safety controls in effect and someone should be overseeing the day-to-day business of drilling and production. He states that he was not one for more government controls but in this case, the ramifications of a spill would be over whelming.

After reading the report several times, it sounds like a very negative report for the oil companies. Maybe Barry was right. Big oil had ordered the hit on Trever Byers. However, how would they know about the report? It would have had to come from Trever Byers, from inside Senator Brazile's office or maybe even Mandi Lee.

I think it is time to call Dean Rutland.

ॐन्क

I call the number Mandi Lee gave me and get Dean Rutland's voicemail, "Hi, this is Dean, leave a message and I'll get back to you."

"Mr. Rutland, I was given your number by Mandi Lee Byers. I have some questions concerning Trever Byers' death. Please give me a call back at your convenience."

I did not leave my name for a reason. Most people will not return a call if the caller does not leave a name. However, if they are curious or concerned about the call, they will get back to you.

Ten minutes later my phone rings, "This is Dean Rutland returning your call, who am I speaking to?"

I want to see if I can rattle his cage. "Thank you for returning my call, Mr. Rutland. I am looking into the murder of Trever Byers and his lovely wife gave me your number. She said you may have some insight into Trever's death."

Dean's voice gets much bolder and more irritated, "If you do not tell me who you are, I am going to hang up and give the FBI your number. Maybe you can explain to them what you're looking for."

"Oh, I'm sorry, Mr. Rutland, how unprofessional of me. My name is Mickke MacCandlish and I was hired by Judge Thomas Allen Cadium to investigate the murder of Trever Byers."

After a slight hesitation, he replies, "What firm are you with Mr. MacCandlish?"

"Oh, I'm with MacCandlish and Associates, Mr. Rutland, have you heard of us?"

"No I haven't, where is your office located?"

"Myrtle Beach, South Carolina," I answer.

We are playing a game of chess. He is trying to get information from me so that he can get someone to check into me and I am giving him false information so that he will come to a dead end. I can tell by his tone of voice that he is getting uptight with the conversation. It is time to rattle his cage a little bit more.

"Mr. Rutland, I know that Trever Byers was working for you but he was also working for the Justice Department. Do you know who he was working for over there?"

"I'm sorry Mr. MacCandlish, I know nothing about that and this conversation is over. I would highly suggest that you let the police and the feds do the investigating in this case."

I definitely have ruffled Mr. Rutland's feathers. Now the question is who is going to call me, or show up at my door to advise me that I should keep my nose out of this case.

❧❦

Dean Rutland is pissed off to the highest degree of pisstivity! As soon as he hangs up after speaking with Mickke D, he calls SIL and asks for Barry.

Chapter 40: SIL

Bill is in Barry's office when Marty calls. Barry hangs up and looks perplexed as he puts his feet up on his desk.

"Guess who that was, Mr. Cutter?"

"I have no idea." Bill shifts in his chair to see the face Barry has blocked with his feet.

"That was Marty Vette, the police chief on Bald Head Island."

"Oh yeah, you found out Marty was the police chief when you went down there to check and see if they had learned anything about the murder of Trever Byers."

Barry sighs. "Right and I asked him to call me if he learned anything or if there was anything he thought I should know."

"So I guess he had some new information for you?" Bill wonders why Barry is dragging this out.

"Oh, yeah, he said that Mickke D just left his office and he told Marty he was working for Judge Cadium investigating the death of Trever Byers."

Bill's chest tightens. "Wow, that is news."

He watches as Barry's eyes narrow and darken. He knows where his partner's thoughts are going.

Bill breaks the ensuing silence, "You know Mickke D doesn't work for us anymore so I guess he can work for anyone he chooses. Besides that, as far as we know, the assassin is dead, so what can he learn? Did Marty say that Mickke D recognized him?"

Barry lets out a noise like a grunt. "Trust me, Mickke D will figure that out if he hasn't already."

He stares off into space.

"Why don't you call Marty back and check?" Bill says as he notices the set in Barry's jaw, the look of a warrior on his face.

Barry says softly, then louder, as if breaking a trance, "I will. Have you heard back from that detective in Charleston? I would really like to know if it was Paul Hills who died in that accident."

"Not yet, let me go call her while you call Marty."

Bill bolts out of the office, a strong sense of dread weighing him down.

Once Bill leaves, Barry punches in Marty's number. Marty tells him that Mickke D asked if they had met before and he told him not that he could recall. Barry thanks him for the information and tells him to get back to him if he hears from Mickke D again.

Bill puts a call into Detective Susan B. Wallace and she says they are still working on the information but it is certainly looking as if Paul is the John Doe killed in the wreck. Once she is positive, she will get back to him. She is very pleasant this time around.

Bill goes back to Barry's office and they compare phone calls. Barry seems to be much calmer once he learns that the assassin is most likely dead.

As Bill leaves, he turns and asks, "What are you going to tell Mickke D if he calls and asks you about Marty Vette?"

"I'll tell him the truth, I didn't know Marty was there until we started to investigate the death of Trever Byers, and then I'll ask him why he wants to know?"

"Sounds good to me. By the way, if Mickke D is working for the judge, what does this do for our plans to get the map from the judge?" Bill tries to read Barry's face but Barry turns toward the window.

"I really don't know," Barry says slowly. "I would think we need to be very careful if he is involved. Why don't you put together some ideas and I will too. We'll compare notes once we know for sure the assassin is dead."

His voice is monotone, his face, reflected in the window, expressionless. Bill wonders where the friend Barry once was has gone.

శ్రీ

Barry was not disclosing the truth when he tells Bill he didn't know Marty was at Bald Head Island until after the assassination of Trever Byers. He pulls a file from behind the plant in front of the window. He opens it and stares at a recent friend search he'd printed from the Internet. What would Bill think if he knew Barry was lying to him, that he'd picked Bald Head Island because Marty was the police chief there? He seems to be lying to everyone these days. The map had better be worth it.

Marty owed Barry big time. Barry helped Marty get out of a shooting incident while they were at Fort Bragg. A recruit was shot while on maneuvers and Marty was going to be the scapegoat. Barry intervened and got the charges dropped.

Marty was not pushing the investigation because Barry had called him right after the shooting of Trever Byers and convinced him that the shooting was a matter of national security and that SIL would handle the case. It was payback time. Marty kept Barry advised during the entire investigation.

かめ

The following afternoon Bill receives a call from Detective Wallace in Charleston.

"Mr. Cutter, it looks as if you were right, our John Doe is your Paul Hills. We traced him back to a Las Vegas dentist who had filled one cavity. Except for that one filling, we found no trace of the man whatsoever."

"That's great, can you send me that information in an e-mail?"

"I certainly can, and again I apologize for my attitude during our first conversation. If you're ever in the Charleston area, please stop by and say hello. Lunch is on me."

"Thanks detective, I may take you up on that someday."

Bill goes directly to Barry's office with the good news. Good news for Barry, but Bill is wondering if it is good news for him. Barry doesn't need anyone to watch his back now. The assassin is dead.

"That's great news. Let's see if we can put together a plan to get the map from the judge. I have been doing some research on the Internet and if we can find the shipwreck where the coins came from, it could be worth millions."

Bill has never seen Barry this excited about anything except maybe on one of their vacations when they were actually out in the ocean searching for sunken treasure. Maybe he has been wrong about Barry, but then again maybe Barry needs him to help with the treasure hunt. Barry can't do it alone and he doesn't trust anyone else.

Then there is the other unknown factor: How is Mickke D going to play out in this whole thing? He has a funny feeling that Barry is not going to let anyone get in the way of finding the shipwreck and the treasure.

Chapter 41: One Less Witness

Barry and Bill leave the office around 4:00pm and walk down the small incline toward the parking lot. The parking area is tree lined and not easy to see from the office, which is about two hundred yards away. Barry is feeling good since it looks like the assassin is dead and he can move on to treasure hunting.

He asks Bill if he would like to stop and have a beer on the way home and Bill agrees. They decide on The Bluebeery Pub. Barry goes to his SUV. He opens the door and sits down. His Special Forces trained ears hear a *click*. He immediately calls Bill on his cell phone and then he begins to sweat.

Bill calmly answers, "Hey, did you change your mind about a beer?"

"Come over to my vehicle right now and keep your eyes open."

"What's going on?"

"Just get your ass over here right now."

Bill gets out of his car and walks over to Barry's vehicle, which is about thirty yards away. As he gets close, Barry opens the door but does not get out. Bill notices sweat beads on Barry's forehead.

"You don't look good, are you sick?"

"I heard a click when I sat down on the seat. Look under the seat and tell me what you see."

Bill gets down on his knees and looks. What he sees makes him start to sweat. There is a compression detonator charge directly beneath Barry's seat. He armed the charge when he sat down. When he gets up or moves the wrong way, bang he is dead.

"Holy shit, if I were you, I would not get out of that seat for a long, long time. There is a compression charge under the seat and it is armed."

Just as Barry reaches for his cell phone to call 911 and the bomb squad, the first shot blasts into Barry's vehicle. Two more rounds ricochet off the pavement next to Bill, stinging his face and body with a spray of rocky shards. The shooter either just has a handgun or he is a terrible shot.

Bill pulls his weapon and fires a couple of shots in the direction of where he thinks the shots are coming from. "Don't go anywhere, I'll be right back and if I were you I would return fire or he may just walk up here and shoot you."

He turns and sprints up the hill toward the office.

Barry grins and places the call to 911. He un-holsters his weapon and starts firing in the general direction of the assailant. He is afraid to turn his body and fire because he may set off the bomb.

More shots pierce Barry's vehicle as Bill reaches the building and goes directly to his office. He grabs his sniper rifle off the wall rack, opens his desk drawer, puts one round of ammo in the rifle and puts several shells in his pocket. He tells everyone in the office to stay where they are and to get down on the floor. He runs down the steps and out the back entrance.

He has a good idea of where the shooter is located so he circles the area and ends up parallel to where he believes the shooter is firing. He lies down on a small knoll and begins searching through his scope. He spots the shooter about seventy yards away and he is still firing his handgun at Barry's vehicle.

He calibrates his scope and sets his finger on the trigger. He has not fired his rifle in several years but he trained hard for moments just like this. The shooter stands up and points the gun at Barry's vehicle. Bill takes three deep breaths, holds his breath for a count of three and squeezes the trigger. The shooter goes down. The quiet and stillness all of a sudden rings in his ears.

He yells at Barry, "Are you all right?"

Barry does not answer but waves his arm out of the vehicle window. Bill pulls his handgun, slings the rifle over his shoulder and goes toward the shooter's location. He cannot see him but he knows he hit his target. When he gets there, the shooter is not moving. He checks and there is no pulse. He looks at the shooter's face and does not recognize him.

He had reacted to the situation. He did his job. Then another thought crosses his mind. If he had not reacted and just taken cover somewhere, would the shooter have eliminated his problem and killed Barry? Would Barry have tried to get out and been blown into little pieces? He guesses he will never know. He stops by his vehicle, puts his weapon in the back seat and makes a mental note to be sure to clean it.

The police, EMS, and bomb squad all arrive at about the same time. He explains what he found under Barry's seat to the people in charge. The bomb people suit up and look. They confirm what Bill has described to them.

After about fifteen minutes, they devise a plan. First, they carefully remove the driver's side door along with the passenger door and passenger seat. They bring in their medium blow-up air mattress that they use for jumpers and place it beside the door and even with the bottom of the vehicle. Next, they carefully place a harness around Barry so that when the time comes, they will yank him out of the SUV and onto the mattress. There are ropes attached to the mattress so that the minute Barry's body touches the mattress they will pull it and him away from the vehicle. They also erect a steel mesh tent around and over the SUV to help contain an explosion if it occurs. The only open side is where Barry is sitting.

That was the easy part, now for the compression charge. They believe they can push the detonator down a fraction of an inch without setting off the device. Next, they find a 12 x 12 inch piece of 1/8 inch steel plate and drill two holes on each edge of the plate. The holes are to attach bungee cords to the plate and then to the underside of the seat. The idea is to create enough pressure to keep the detonator down when they yank Barry out of the SUV. The attachment of the steel plate and cords would be much easier without large cumbersome bomb gloves working in a confined area.

An hour after they first arrive, the bomb squad has everything in place. Bill and everyone except the people yanking Barry out of the vehicle and the ones who will pull the mattress move away from the area.

At the last minute, they cover Barry with a piece of the steel mesh tent and a bomb suit full-face helmet. They put bomb boots on his feet and wrap his legs from the knees down. Then they start the countdown.

On three, everyone yanks and pulls. All present hold their breath and close their eyes. There is no explosion. The steel plate holds the detonator plunger in place.

It takes Barry about twenty minutes to get everything off and to thank everyone who helped with the undertaking. Barry's SUV is carefully loaded into an enclosed bomb trailer and driven away. The police ask him to look at the dead shooter to see if he knows him. He looks and tells the police he has never seen the man before.

Barry looks over at Bill and says, "Nice shot, Mr. Cutter, I guess I owe you one."

"Just doing my job Barry, do you need a ride home?"

"Yes, I do smart ass and I'll need you to pick me up in the morning, also."

Bill is not sure his saving Barry's life actually matters that much to Barry anymore. Barry's loyalty seems to lie at the bottom of the sea with dreams of treasure and gold.

They both look under their seats before getting into Bill's vehicle. On the ride to his house, Barry is smiling inside. He did know the shooter. It was Glenn Griffin. Why was Griff trying to kill him? The only answer he can come up with is that the assassin actually did call him for a reference and then later told him about the park in Vegas. However, there is a good side to this story. With the demise of Griff, that only leaves Dean Rutland and Bill who know about the arranged killing of Trever Byers.

Chapter 42: Mandi Lee

Mandi Lee Byers is on her way to her monthly meeting. Before she leaves home, she receives an e-mail from Mickke D saying that he thinks Dean Rutland ordered the hit on Trever.

She is a very pretty, petite woman, 5'1" and not much more than one hundred pounds soaking wet. Most of her professors at Duke Law School did not think she would ever make it as an attorney. Most thought her diminutive figure would work against her. They did not know Mandi Lee very well. She finished in the top 10 percent of her graduating class and she became a real bulldog as a prosecuting attorney.

She did not marry Trever Byers until she was forty. He was almost fifteen years older than she and just about ready to retire. I guess you might say it was an arranged marriage of sorts. She needed someone with Trever's background to benefit her later and the best way to control that person would be to be sleeping with him, legally.

Actually, she grew very fond of Trever during their six-year marriage. She was very distraught when she learned he was dead. She almost blames herself for his death.

She found out that Dean Rutland was looking for someone to act as a consultant for Senator Brazile's investigation into offshore drilling. She managed to get her husband's name mentioned in a conversation with Dean and the rest is history.

Mandi Lee works for the Defense Department as an assistant attorney and has little to no status there. Very few people notice her, she makes very little money, but of course, the government has great benefits, including health care.

Her bank account is very sparse, well at least her American bank account. Her main source of income is a monthly check deposited in a bank on Grand Cayman Island. It comes from a shell company set up by the CIA. Mandi Lee Byers is a CIA operative working at the Defense Department.

It was her job to try to convince her husband to approve offshore drilling because the CIA wants to use the production platforms as a foundation to mount their new hush, hush underwater radar/sonar system, which is able to detect the movement of underwater terrorism threats.

They plan to pay the oil companies to allow them to attach a new safety device on their production platforms. Funding for the project will not come from Congress. The CIA does not want the program to go public.

Mandi Lee actually thought that the CIA killed her husband when they found out that he was going to give a negative report to Senator Brazile. Her handler assured her that this was not the case. She is pleased when Mickke D calls her. She wants to know who killed her husband and why.

She walks into a McDonald's, orders a cup of coffee, and sits at a corner table. Ten minutes later another woman comes in, orders coffee and sits down at her table.

Mandi Lee looks up and says, "Hey Liz, how are you?"

Liz Woodkark smiles and replies, "Pretty good Mandi, but I do have some questions for you."

Liz is in her early fifties, strawberry blonde hair, a great body, and striking features. She stays in shape, has a great tan and looks as if she should be living in Key West, not Washington, D.C.

"Sure, what do you want to know?"

"I had an opportunity to speak with Dean Rutland the other night. He was fishing around and quizzing me about who Trever was working for at Justice."

"Let me guess, since this took place at night, did the quizzing take place in bed?"

Liz replies in her best *Gone with the Wind* southern accent, "Why, Mandi Lee, how could you think such a thing?"

"Just in case I'm right, how did he rate on your one to ten scale?"

Liz laughs and says, "I gave him a seven. Not bad, but not toe tingling terrific."

Liz regains her composure and continues, "Have you talked to anyone other than that Mickke D guy about Trever's employment at Justice?"

"No, and when I talked with him, I said I knew nothing about the Justice job. And by the way, I received an e-mail from Mr. Mac-Candlish today saying that he believes Dean Rutland ordered the hit on Trever."

Liz gets a perplexed look on her face. "Why, that no good bastard. I'll take care of that situation myself."

"Any more questions Liz, I have a hair appointment."

"Not for now, I may have an assignment for you in a couple of weeks. I'll let you know."

"If I need to get married again, make sure he's rich and young. I'm ready to try being a cougar."

Liz just smiles, picks up her purse and leaves the restaurant.

Mandi Lee grabs her coffee and follows Liz out the door. Once outside, they both look around for anything or anybody that looks out of place. They then walk away in opposite directions.

Chapter 43: The Attack

It is around 9:00pm and I am home alone relaxing and reading a mystery novel by T. Lynn Ocean, a local author. I'm wearing my red boxer shorts, Ohio State tee shirt, and moccasin slippers. After reading a few chapters, I sometimes slip and in a vain moment, I picture myself as Mike Hammer with a wide brim hat, a moustache, and a cigarette dangling from my mouth. Well, I guess maybe not the mustache and cigarette but definitely the hat.

My cell phone rings and suddenly I return to the real world. My caller ID shows *unidentified*, but I flip open the phone anyway. It could always be a work-related real estate call. The voice on the other end is garbled but I think the voice sounds familiar.

"Hold on a minute, let me get outside. I have poor reception inside the house."

I go outside to the deck. For some reason, on the way out, I gaze at the sky and watch it fade to velvet dusk. There is a smell of storms in the air, a distant flash of lightning and the faint sound of thunder. A chilled gust of wind whisks my face, leaving me in a tranquil and seeming calm. That calmness stays with me as I sit down at the table on the far end of the deck and speak into the phone, "Okay, now who is this?"

"Mickke D, its Barry. Why couldn't you leave well enough alone?"

My calmness all of a sudden vanishes. I feel heat rising to my checks. "Nice to hear from you Barry, but what are you talking about?"

There is a strange echo coming from the other end of the phone as he continues, "I've had several calls about you asking questions concerning Trever Byers' death. I thought we ended that investigation?"

I guess I have my answer as to who is going to show up after I opened the can of worms with Dean Rutland, but why had I failed to see or believe what now seems so clear? Maybe Paula Ann was right. Pops is too old for this stuff.

"You know Barry, you may have ended that investigation but I no longer work for SIL. I'm working for another client now and I'm guessing you don't want me to continue looking into Mr. Byers' death, is that correct?"

The sky is getting darker and the echo in the phone becomes louder.

"I thought you determined that Paul Hills was the assassin?" He replies.

"No, I only determined that Paul was at the scene of the plane explosion and since he ran at the golf course, he is probably the assassin. If he is the killer, my client wants to know who hired him to kill Trever Byers."

I hear a noise below my deck in the back yard. I see nothing but something primal in my brain sets off alarms. I am now sitting in the dark and no one is on the other end of the phone. The night creatures suddenly go quiet, as if a larger, more dangerous predator is on the move. I hear footsteps on the stairs leading up to my deck. My calmness not only is gone, it has turned to fear. I fight a spasm of panic and the demons begin to appear. I push them aside. I have no weapon, I'm half naked, and whoever is on the stairs will get to the top before I can get up and cross the deck to get inside.

I figure I know who it is, so I call out, "Hey, Barry, why not just knock on my door instead of calling to get me outside?"

I remember telling the fellows when they were here to play golf that I had little to no reception inside my house; that I had to go out on the deck to get clear reception. I guess he remembered.

I see a dark figure come quickly up the stairs and move between the door and me. He is dressed all in black. I know that by the way he moves that it is Barry. He has a gun with a silencer pointed at me.

"Get up Mickke D, turn around, and walk backwards towards me with your hands in the air."

I do as he tells me. "Stop and turn around. Keep your hands in the air."

I am about six feet away from him. He pulls off his ski mask. I look him straight in the eyes. His eyes shine with rancor and malice. It is like looking into the eyes of a rabid animal. I am not looking at the same Barry I knew fifteen years ago. A sick feeling clutches my gut. I will myself to show no fear, to get rid of the demons, but the gravity of the situation begins to press down on me.

"Okay Bill," he calls out, "come on up and check him for weapons."

I hear footsteps coming up the steps on the other side of my deck. I start to turn but at my first movement, Barry slams his left fist into my face. It is so quick and in the darkness, I never see it coming. I go down hard.

"Did I tell you to look away?" He bends over and yells in my face.

Bill helps me to my feet and I can feel and taste the acrid tang of blood dripping from my broken nose. Bill does his search, finds no weapons and steps back behind me.

"So I guess this means SIL hired Paul Hills to kill Trever Byers?" I say between drops of blood oozing into my mouth.

"That's right, but that information will not help you now. You've sold your last house, planted your last tree and given your last golf lesson."

Now there is a big difference between thinking you are going to die and knowing you are going to die. If you think there is a chance you may survive, you are not going to take nearly as many chances as when you know this is it.

As former Special Forces, I trained for action, for a more pro-active means of defense. Well, I figure this is it, but right now, I can think of no way out except for a miracle or divine intervention. Since I have never been a staunch religious person, I figure the last option is probably not on the table. Therefore, except for the miracle, I guess I am finally going to find out if there is a heaven or a hell or just plain nothing. At least my ex-wives will not be bugging me anymore and the demons will be gone.

I can sense and hear Bill move to the side but still behind me. I learned my lesson; I do not turn to look this time. I guess he does not want to be in the way if the bullet goes all the way through me. Barry takes a step backward and I cannot see but I hear him cock his weapon. I hear Bill do the same thing.

I notice a slight smirk on Barry's face, which I remember happens just before he makes his move in a martial arts event. My mind quickly comes up with a possible way out.

I am looking directly into Barry's eyes, almost daring him to pull the trigger. I figure that if I fall down and sweep at Barry's legs with my leg, it may cause enough diversion so that one of them may shoot the other one. Then I will only have to deal with the one still standing. My body tenses to make my move. I figure it is my last chance to survive.

All of a sudden, I notice the slightest shift of Barry's eyes and gun to where Bill is standing behind me. The smirk on Barry's face disappears and his eyes deaden from pain and shock. He actually hears the mute sound of Bill's weapon, feels his body recoil backward and then the world as he knows it is gone.

I also hear the sound of Bill's weapon and I feel the heat as the bullet whizzes by my ear. Barry's weapon fires as he is falling; the bullet hits the deck, stinging my leg with a spray of wooden splinters.

I turn and look at Bill, also dressed entirely in black. He has just killed his best friend and saved my life. However, there is still a problem. Bill has his weapon pointed right at me. He pulls off his ski mask, smiles, and then he reaches out with his gloved hand, unscrews the silencer from his weapon, and fires the gun in the air.

"You're lucky, Mickke D, I guess I trust you more than I did him," he says softly.

With his gloved hand, he tosses the gun to me and instinctively I catch it. Now the gun has my fingerprints on it.

"I guess you and Barry had a shootout and Barry lost. Do you want me to get his gun and shoot you in the arm or leg to make it look good?"

"That's okay, Bill, I have a bloody nose and a bloody leg already. If you were planning to shoot him, why didn't you do it before he hit me?"

He laughs, "It was a last-minute decision."

"Who besides Barry wanted me dead?" I ask, still stunned.

"Someone put a contract out on you, and that was all Barry needed to do away with you, he was just looking for an excuse. You were asking too many questions."

"Who sanctioned the contract?"

"If I were you I would check out Dean Rutland in Senator Brazile's office. You owe me one Mickke D, I was never here," Bill says as he puts one hand on the railing, nimbly jumping over and disappearing into the night.

"You're right, I owe you one," I call out as I watch his dark figure glide across the fairway and disappear into the woods. With his training and background, he could survive in those woods for months, if he wanted to, and no one would ever know he was there.

I hear sirens coming my way so I go inside and turn on my deck lights. As I come back outside, I hear footsteps coming up the back stairs, the same stairs that Barry had just come up. It is Jimmy. He has a huge gun in his hand. It has to have a 7-or 8-inch barrel on it.

"What the hell is going on? I heard a gunshot," Jimmy calls out just seconds before he reaches the top of the stairs and notices Barry's lifeless body bleeding all over my deck.

Before I have a chance to answer, he continues, "Is that guy dead? Are you okay? You don't look very good. Nice boxers."

I suppose he notices my bloody face, crooked nose, and bloody leg.

I answer, "I'm fine. I suppose you could say, he won the battle but I won the war. The police are on their way, I would get rid of that small cannon before they get here. What is that thing?"

"I told you mine was bigger than yours. It's a 44 Super Black-hawk with a 7 ½-inch barrel," Jimmy says as he places his weapon in the small of his back and covers it with his shirt.

The sirens stop but I can see the reflections of the blue and red lights on my neighbor's house and I can hear Blue barking his head off. The police have arrived. Car doors slam and I hear footsteps running around the side of my house towards the deck.

I call out, "No need to rush, it's over."

I place the gun on the patio table and I lean against the railing next to Jimmy who is trying to act nonchalant with a cannon stuck down the crack of his ass.

Detective Sam Concile and two officers come onto the deck. The officers look familiar. It is Doan and Dunn from my encounter with the carpenter. It is nice to see familiar faces when you have a dead person on your deck.

Detective Sam speaks first, "Nice boxers, but Christmas is a long time away. Would you mind putting on some clothes?"

I go inside, put on some shorts and return to the deck.

"So Mickke D, what do we have here?"

"That, Detective Concile, is a dead man who tried to kill me."

"And do you know who the dead man is?" She slowly asks.

"Yes ma'am, it is one of my army buddies from the golf trip and the plane explosion."

"And why was he trying to kill you and by the way, you look terrible. Are you okay?"

I'm starting to get a complex. Do I really look that bad?

I am about to answer when the EMTs rush onto the deck. They go over to Barry, feel for a pulse, find none, pronounce him dead, and call the coroner. They look at me and ask if I need some help. *Man, I need a mirror.*

"Well, you can straighten my nose if you want to. I can feel it is not located where it should be."

One of the EMTs puts on new gloves and with a quick yank, puts my nose back in place. I tell him thanks and that I will take care of the cleanup.

"So again, why was this guy trying to kill you? And who the hell are you?" Detective Concile asks, looking directly at Jimmy.

He gets that look on his face like, who me? "I live next door and heard a gunshot. I came over to see what was going on."

"And you who live next door, do you have a name?"

"Oh, sorry detective, I'm Jimmy Bolin."

Officer Dunn chirps in, "We were out here not too long ago on a disturbance call. I have his info on record."

"And what was the disturbance call all about, Officer Dunn?"

"It seems some guys working in the area had too much to drink for lunch, made a wrong turn and ended up down here. These two guys defused the problem before we got here."

"This guy isn't one of those guys?" She points to Barry.

"No ma'am, he isn't."

"Is that the murder weapon?" she asks, looking at Bill's gun on my patio table.

"No, that's the self-defense weapon."

"Is that your gun, Mickke D, and is it registered?" Her voice has a much sterner tone.

This line of questioning is not helping the fact that my head is beginning to throb. I need to answer so that I don't get Bill involved and keep myself out of trouble.

"Yes, it is my gun and no, it is not registered."

"And why is it not registered?"

I think and answer quickly, "It was actually given to me as a gift by the guys when they came down to play golf and I just haven't gotten around to getting it registered yet."

"So it should be registered in the name of one of your Army buddies, is that right?"

"Yes ma'am, if they registered it. But I wouldn't bet a whole lot of money on that."

"So tell me, Mickke D, what happened here this evening? Why is this person dead? And Mr. Bolin, you may leave, but give your phone number to Officer Dunn, we may want to talk to you later."

"Thank you detective."

Jimmy walks over to Officer Dunn, gives him his number and exits slowly down the back stairs; too quickly and that cannon is going to hurt.

I tell Detective Concile that Barry came here and we got into an altercation over a murder investigation I was looking into and he tried to kill me. I explain it was pure self-defense. I tell her to look at the way he is dressed, all in black, a black ski mask and a weapon with a silencer. He wasn't here to play poker or barbecue.

She puts on a pair of gloves, walks over, and picks up the weapon from the patio table. She releases the clip, clears the slide, and states, "There are two bullets missing and our 911 caller said they heard one gunshot and Mr. Bolin just stated that he heard a gunshot."

"I don't know, I guess I did not load the clip completely."

"I find that hard to believe from a person with your background."

"I suppose when I was loading the clip, I wasn't really planning to use it."

She then asks, "I can understand why the dead guy had a gun but why did you have a weapon out here on the deck?"

"I thought I heard some strange noises while I was in the house, so I came out prepared for the worse."

I'm not sure she believes me. She asks several more questions, the coroner arrives, takes the body, and everyone departs. Before she leaves, she tells me not to leave town and that someone will call me to set up an interview.

Chapter 44: The trip to Little River

(Earlier)

There is not a lot of conversation between Barry and Bill on the trip from Culpepper to Little River. The silence is both comfortable and awkward.

Barry has rented a non-descript pick-up truck using a fake ID and cash and changes the license plates once they get out of the city. He received a call from Dean Rutland four days earlier that Mickke D is making waves, big waves. Dean tells Barry there is fifty thousand available if he can make the problem go away. Barry tells Dean to consider the problem taken care of.

He has been looking for a reason to eliminate Mickke D for a long time and now he has one, a cash contract.

Barry is the type of person who has to be in control. He was in control of Bill and Ted until Bill invited Mickke D to join their golf group. From that point forward until they left the army, when Mickke D was around, Barry did not feel in control.

Mickke D just seemed to irritate him at every turn. He just always seemed to have a better idea or a better plan. He always beat Barry on the PT course, at the firing range and on the running track. He always beat Barry on the golf course by pulling off an incredible shot or making a long putt on the last hole.

Moreover, of course, Bill and Ted loved it. They just ate it up. They would ride Barry for days after another Mickke D victory. The only thing Barry excelled in over Mickke D was martial arts and Mickke D was too smart to get in the ring with him, so actually he won that also.

Barry only hired Mickke D to find the assassin because he did not think he would succeed, that he would fail or the assassin would kill him. Within a week, he found the killer. He had won again and now he is zeroing in on SIL and Dean Rutland. If he gets to Dean, he may find someone higher up the ladder and Dean has let him know higher up is not good.

Barry is looking forward to this job and he makes a mental note to take Mickke D out of his will when he gets back to Culpepper.

Bill finally breaks the silence. "How do you want to handle this?"

Barry does not answer for about a minute; Bill can tell he is in planning mode. In special ops, planning the operation is the most important part of the mission.

"Remember when Mickke D told us that he has poor cell phone reception in his house? I am going to lure him out onto his deck around dark and hopefully without a weapon. We go in all black and with silencers. I am going up the back stairs and when I call, you come up the side stairs. I will take the kill shot. You are backup. Do you have any questions?"

Bill shakes his head negatively. Short and to the point, that is how Barry operates. Do not make it complicated.

However, that is not the plan Barry is really planning to execute. This is his chance to get rid of Mickke D and Bill at the same time. His plan is to shoot Bill first because he will be the only other person, hopefully, with a weapon. He will take Bill's weapon and shoot Mickke D. Next, he will take the weapon he used to shoot Bill and put it in Mickke D's hand. It will appear as if they shot each other and by the time they find the bodies, Barry will be back in Culpepper. Problem solved. Then there will be only one person who knows about the assassination of Trever Byers: Dean Rutland.

Bill has listened to Barry's plan and thinks, *yeah right*! He closes his eyes and smiles to himself. However, he is not thinking about Barry's plan; he is formatting a plan of his own. He realizes that Barry has not been himself lately and that he is not thinking rationally. Since the assassination, Barry's demeanor has changed significantly and the attempt on his life in the office parking lot seems to have pushed him over the edge. Bill has this gut feeling that Barry is planning to do away with him as well as Mickke D. He came prepared.

He goes into survival mode. It is now time to fish or cut bait. He cultivates a plan of action with two or more scenarios, depending on the situation.

∂∞∽

As Bill crosses the fairway behind Mickke D's house, he knows exactly where he is going and what he is going to do. He figures Mickke D will not tell the police about him because he has just saved his life. Therefore, no one, including the police, will be searching for him. However, he still does not want possible witnesses to see him.

He crosses the fairway into the woods, cuts across the ninth fairway at Eagles Nest and into the golf course parking lot where they left the pick-up. He gets his backpack out, takes off the black night gear and places it in the backpack. He puts on a reversible sweatshirt and his reversible floppy hat pulled down over his silver-gray hair. He wipes down every area in the truck he may have touched and checks the vehicle for any evidence that he was there. Finding none, he locks the door and takes off at a slow jog toward Highway 17.

He gets about halfway down the road when he sees headlights turn onto the road and come his way. He ducks into the woods and lets the car pass before he continues. He does not want a routine nightly police patrol to spot him or to have anyone see him along the road. He reaches the end of the road and stops at Rickey's Dockside Bar. When he and Barry came up 17 and turned to go to the parking lot at Eagles Nest, there were only two cars at the bar. Now there are two cars and about ten Harleys sitting in the parking area.

He needs to call a cab but he does not want to use his cell phone because the authorities could trace the call back to him. He calmly walks into the bar and asks the bartender if he can use his phone to call a cab.

The rather noisy, probably locals bar, becomes very quiet and everyone seems to be looking directly at him. He keeps his head lowered so no one can get a real good look at his face. The bartender is nice enough to call the number on a business card for him. Anchor Taxi says they will be there in about ten minutes. He quickly walks outside to wait.

Once outside, he starts smiling because this reminds him of another night when he and a good friend were night fishing on a lake back in Greenville.

They were teenagers and about 11:00pm, they were getting hungry. They paddled Bill's Old Town flat bottom canoe over to the dock and walked up the stairs to what looked like a bar for a sandwich. As they walked inside the talking and noise stopped. It seemed as if everyone in the bar was looking at them. They decided to forgo the sandwich, bought two Snickers bars each and left. When they got outside, the talking and noise started again. They ran down the stairs to the canoe and never looked back.

He wonders what ever happened to his friend Steve. They did a lot of fishing together when they were teenagers. He hasn't seen him in years. The last he heard Steve was managing a bowling alley somewhere in Ohio.

He brought along a map of Myrtle Beach so when the cab shows up, he gives the driver a street corner about three blocks away from the bus station. When they arrive, he pays the driver, while again keeping his head lowered so even if the driver wanted to he could not give a good description.

As soon as the cab leaves, he walks to the bus station, goes into the restroom, reverses his sweatshirt and hat and then purchases a ticket to Culpepper.

He arrives in Culpepper about 4:00 in the morning. He was in the back of the bus and slept most of the way. He was surprised that he could sleep at all. He has killed two men within the last month and one of them was a very good friend. He acted on his gut feeling and if he had waited to be sure, he may be dead right now. He did what he had to do and he will not look back. His entire life is now in front of him.

He walks to the office, which is less than a mile from the bus station. He keeps a change of clothes and an electric razor there. He shaves and changes his clothes when he arrives. He takes a box, puts his personal things in and then along with his sniper rifle, transfers everything to the back of his SUV. He is glad he elected to meet Barry at the office.

He goes into Barry's office and finds every bit of information pertaining to the assassination of Trever Byers. He also gets everything he has on the killing and shreds it all.

The first of their three employees begin arriving around 8:00AM. He is in his office waiting for he and Barry's shared secretary, Robyn Pomroy, to get there, hopefully before the call comes about Barry.

Robyn walks into his office looking a little bit surprised, "Aren't we all bright-eyed, bushy-tailed, and early today?"

Bill looks up from his desk and says, "I'm sorry Robyn. I thought I told you, I'm leaving on vacation today."

"Well, if you're going on vacation, what are you doing here?"

"Oh, I just wanted to make sure I got these files to you before I left."

"Where are you going?"

"I think I'll head west. Oh, and by the way, tell Barry he can always reach me on my cell phone if he needs me for anything."

"I'm surprised he's not here, he usually gets in before you."

He says goodbye to Robyn and leaves the office. His duffel bag is packed and he is ready to leave town but he is not going west. He opts to head south. Maybe he will stop in Charleston and take Detective Susan B. Wallace up on her offer to have lunch. She sounds like someone he might like to get to know.

He smashes his cell phone and throws it in the dumpster on the way to his vehicle. He will purchase a new phone later.

Chapter 45: The Second Attack

It's around 10:15 at night and I am sitting in my recliner at home about half asleep and half-watching "CSI Miami." I'm bushed; I have spent the last week meeting with Detective Concile trying to explain to her over and over why I shot and killed one of my army buddies who was planning to shoot me. Of course, Bill shot Barry but I don't want her to know that, at least not yet.

I hear sounds on my roof. Now I have heard sounds on my roof before, but they were always squirrels chasing each other. If this is a squirrel, it is a big-footed squirrel because it is making a whole lot of noise. My .45 is in a drawer in a stand next to my chair. I put it there after the shooting with Barry and Bill. I guess Pops has become paranoid in his old age, or maybe more careful is a better way to put it. Paula Ann would be proud of him.

Now most people would just call 911 and hope the police would come and figure out what the problem is, but being the investigative person that I have become, I pass on 911.

I quietly slip the .45 out of the drawer and put it in my waistband. As a civilian, I have always figured that it is better to have both hands free. There is less chance of shooting the wrong person or thing if you don't have a loaded gun in your hand.

All of the blinds and drapes in the house are closed. I started doing that at night recently where before I never closed anything. I open the drape covering the sliding door, which leads out to my screened-in porch, which then goes out to my deck. The noise has stopped. Maybe it was just a false alarm.

I take out the rod used as a blocking lock, unlock, and open the sliding door. Everything is quiet, almost too quiet. I decide not to turn on the screened-in porch light but I do flip on one of the lights on the deck, which is under an eave. It is not a lot of light, only a forty-watt bulb, but just enough to light up most of my deck.

I slowly move across the screened-in porch and unlatch the screen door leading to the deck.

I have just recently oiled the hinges on the screen door with WD-40 so there is no noise as I cautiously open the door. As I step through the screen door, I hear a yelp from across the street. Blue must have gotten too close to his electric fence. You would think that dog would have learned by now how close he can get before he gets shocked.

As I step out onto the deck, I know something is wrong. Except for the yelp from Blue, absolutely no sounds disturbed the night. It's an old military feeling that you get when you know someone or something is out there with you. The hairs stand up on the back of my neck and a shiver goes through my entire body. I can feel my heart rate increase and the adrenalin begin to flow. It feels almost like a pinball machine but instead of *tilt, tilt, tilt* it is *danger, danger, danger!*

Before I have time to draw the .45 from my waistband, jumping down from the roof is a person dressed entirely in black with a black ski mask covering his or her face. I know it's not Barry. He is dead. If it wasn't for the fact that this person has a 9mm Glock pointed at my head, he or she looks just like a Halloween ninja. I have no time to react. He, I finally notice a flat chest, motions for me to raise my hands.

The next sound I hear is a loud growl and so does my adversary. We both turn our heads and see Blue standing at the top of the stairs leading up to my deck and he is not a happy camper. You could count the number of teeth in his mouth and his white Husky eyes are glowing in the faint light.

As Blue lunges at the man dressed in black, he turns and fires his weapon. Blue goes down. This was all the time I needed. Pulling the trigger is never easy. The act comes with consequences, the fear of which can absolutely paralyze. However, without hesitation and without any demons, I react. I pull my .45 and as the man in black turns back to me, I do a deep knee bend and fire three times. He goes down and I feel a bullet pass very close to my cheek.

I kick the gun away from the body lying on my deck and go over to Blue. He is still breathing. I rush inside to get my cell phone and call 911. I tell them a man and a dog have been shot and that I am more concerned for the dog.

I have just put my cell phone in my pocket when Jimmy comes bounding up the back stairs to my deck with his huge 44 in hand. "Mickke D, what the hell happened, I heard at least five gunshots."

"Jimmy, I'll explain later, right now go across the street and tell Terri that Blue has been shot and we need to get him to the vet."

"You got it. Is that guy dead?"

"Don't know, don't care, just go get Terri."

I had almost forgotten about the man in black. I go over and begin to pet Blue. He whimpers, tries to get up, but is unable to move.

Jimmy and Terri are back in a matter of minutes and they have a large sheet with them. Terri says she has called the vet and he will meet them at the office. We put Blue on the sheet and I help them carry him to Terri's SUV. I tell her that I will explain later and that I will pay the vet bill. Blue just saved my life.

What is spooky about this whole thing is that as far as I know, Blue has never been in my yard, let alone on my deck. Yet he knew that I was in trouble and he came to help me. I'll never refer to Blue as strange again. I owe him big time.

I hear sirens coming down the street, all of my neighbors lights are on and people are standing around outside. After tonight, the neighborhood is probably going to ask me to move. This is far too much excitement for all of these retired folks. I have already heard rumors that my neighbors on the opposite side from Jimmy, Tom and Elaine, have ordered his and hers matching bulletproof vests for Christmas.

The police and my old smiling friend, Detective Concile, with two other plain-clothes detectives are coming up the side entrance of the deck with guns drawn. I have put my weapon on the patio table in plain view and I have my hands in the air. I don't want anyone with an itchy trigger finger thinking I am the bad guy.

Before I have a chance to say anything, Sam says to me, "Mickke D, every time I see you, and thankfully this time you are dressed, something has either been blown up, burned down, or shot. I thought you told me you were a thoughtful, law-abiding citizen with no known enemies?"

She has me there; I am not quite sure how to answer. "Well Detective Sam, I have no idea who that man is but he had a gun pointed at my head, it was self-defense. Oh, and by the way, he also shot my neighbor's dog, which just happened to save my life or you would be out here looking at my body lying on the deck."

"My name is not Detective Sam, it's Detective Concile."

The other two detectives later introduced as Woolever and Stratten look at each other and smile like Cheshire cats as Sam snaps off her reply.

"Now can you get me some more light out here and where is the dog that was supposedly shot by this person?"

"The dog's owner and my neighbor took the dog to the vet," I state as I go inside and turn on all of the deck and porch lights.

"Where is the murder weapon?" one of the detectives asks.

"The self-defense weapon is over there on the patio table and the perpetrator's weapon is there on the deck. He fired twice and I fired three times."

"Looks like all three hit the target, this man is dead," Sam says to no one in particular.

She and the detectives roll the man over and pull off the black ski mask, "Do you know this man, Mickke D?"

I look at the man's face and I am speechless. He almost looks like Lucky, a soldier with the Colombian Army. He was with Mark and me on several raids against the cartel. If it is Lucky, why is he here? Furthermore, why did he want to kill me? I can feel the demons begin to churn in my head again.

I look up at Sam and say, "Can we talk in private?"

She replies, "Don't tell me, it's the husband of one of your ex wives."

"No I'm afraid not, but I need to tell you something off the record."

Sam agrees and we walk over to the patio table and sit down.

"If I'm right, that man is a Colombian Army soldier who I trained probably eighteen years ago in Colombia. I was there doing secret black ops training for the Colombian Army. We raided and burned several large cocaine shipments of the cartel. The army shipped me back to the states because the cartel put a large bounty on my head. I have a funny feeling that bounty is still in effect."

"Wow, Mickke D, you do have a past after all," she replies quietly, "So what do you want me to do?"

"Well, I would sure like to keep this bounty thing a secret if I can. It's bad enough I may have someone from Colombia trying to kill me, let alone half of South Carolina."

"Ok, I'll keep this between us for the time being. I'll see what we can find on this guy and let you know. However, in the meantime, you had better keep your head down; this guy may not be working alone. Do you want me to keep a couple of uniforms in the area for a couple of days just in case?"

"That would be great and it would probably make my neighbors feel a little more secure. I think they're all a bit jumpy right now."

Just as Sam and her people are leaving, Jimmy comes up the back stairs and gives me a thumbs up. Blue is going to be all right. The bullet just grazed his head. The vet said he should be up and about in a couple of days. If the man in black was Lucky, thank goodness, he never was a very good shot.

ॐ॰

I look out of my window several days later and there is Blue sitting by one of his holes with a bandage on his head looking for me. I go over with a treat and he hig fives me just like before.

Terri comes into the garage and thanks me for paying Blue's vet bill and she tells me that she and Blue will be moving to the south end of the beach in about two weeks. She has a new, better job and does not want to spend a lot of money on gas traveling back and forth, so she is moving in with one of her girlfriends. She writes down her new address and tells me I am welcome to visit Blue anytime.

⤖⤗

Blue and I sit in the shade of my live oak tree and watch the movers load furniture all day. Terri brought him over so he would not be in the way. He does not seem to be able to figure out what is going on but I sense that he is confused. When it is time for them to leave, Terri comes over to get Blue. I hand her his leash but he does not want to go. I tell him it will be okay and give him a big hug. Tears flow down my checks as I watch her put Blue in the back of her SUV. As they drive away, I wave and Blue puts his paw up to the back window and gives me a final high five It takes me weeks to get over Blue leaving. I hadn't felt that bad when any of my three ex-wives left me.

⤖⤗

Sam found out the man in black was Lucky, that he had changed sides about six years ago, and that he had probably acted on his own. I asked her what she meant by *probably* and she said that was as good as it was going to get. She could not be sure. I took that to mean I could still be a target, so be careful.

Chapter 46: Mickke D

It has been almost two weeks since the last attempt on my life and since then I have made a few enemies. I called Dean Rutland to let him know that Barry was dead and that I had new information on the killing of Trever Byers. He threatened to have me thrown in jail but that probably won't happen because now he is MIA. No one has seen or heard from him in more than a week. His apartment in D.C. and his house outside Culpepper are both empty. The police are leaning toward foul play. Personally, I think he skipped the country.

Senator Brazile's secretary is also missing and the senator claims to know nothing about either missing person even though they both were working for him.

I figure it is time to give TC a final accounting of what I have discovered and who I think is responsible for Trever Byers' death. I had e-mailed Mandi Lee several weeks ago and told her I thought Dean Rutland had probably ordered the hit on her husband.

I send TC an e-mail with everything I have learned about how SIL hired Paul Hills to kill Trever. Next, SIL went after Paul to cover up their part in the killing. I believe Dean Rutland in Senator Brazile's office hired SIL to make the hit.

I tell him I do not believe Dean acted on his own but so far, I have been unable to find out who hired Dean. I do not think the senator had anything to do with Trever's murder. I would guess it was big oil but I have no hard evidence to back that up. There is no money trail, but I did find out that the report given to Senator Brazile was not the same report that Mandi Lee gave to Dean Rutland. I believe Dean changed the report to show a positive spin on offshore drilling instead of the negative spin from Trever. That alone would implicate big oil.

I report to him that Rusty McRichards' death was as reported in the paper, a hit and run. It had nothing to do with the murder of Trever Byers. The same goes for Freddy. He was just in the wrong place at the wrong time. The twins and Cindy had nothing to do with the murder although they were with Freddy that night. They left town because the girls had been in trouble before and they would be prime suspects. The police found them in Virginia Beach but after signed depositions, they were not implicated.

I also include a statement for my time and expenses. The next day I receive an e-mail from him thanking me for my help and that the check is in the mail. He also says to call him when I am ready to go treasure hunting.

I call him the next day and tell him I am ready whenever he is. We pick a date and I ask what I should bring. He tells me he has everything we need. I ask about a wet suit but he says the water is very warm and we won't need wet suits. I can hardly wait to get out on the ocean and forget about people trying to kill me. Not too long ago I was living a nondescript life and now I am investigating killings and ducking bullets. I'm beginning to think my three ex-wives were not so bad after all.

Before I leave the house and travel to Pawleys Island, I grab my loaded .45 and two extra ammo clips. I am still concerned about the reward on my head from the Colombian Cartel. It's better to be safe than sorry. I am looking forward to this treasure hunt. I haven't spent much time on the water lately and at least it should be quiet, calm, and devoid of bad people.

Chapter 47: The Treasure Hunt

We get to the boat around 10:00am. TC gives me a short history lesson on shipwrecks and what dive equipment he has for us.

He states that more than 2,000 ships have gone down along the coast of the Carolinas, Georgia, and Florida between 1600 and 1900. He also says that salvage hunters have only discovered a very small percentage of those ships. This means there are still quite a few available for us to find.

One of the supposedly treasure-filled ships that went down off the coast of Pawleys Island was *The Queen Beth* around 1680. TC says the coins he has are from that same era. I can tell by TC's attitude that he has fallen in love with shipwreck history and salvage work. He says the ocean, its wide expanses, its endless blue, and its changing moods enthrall him. He also states the ocean has a way of surprising you at times. She can be a real bitch.

As far as equipment is concerned, I am impressed. He has two JW Fisher Pulse 8X hand-held metal detectors. They come with a rating depth of 200 feet and highly mineralized salt water, coral, and rocks with high iron content or magnetic (black) sand, will not affect them. He has eight fully filled Faber High Pressure Steel Dive Tanks and a diesel powered blower that can blow a 15-inch hole in the sand. We'll use the blower when we find something with the hand-held detectors. He also has the CRS to run sweeps if need be. There also is a pulley- mounted Wave Runner in case we decide to try that sport for a while. He has a cooler full of sandwiches, Diet Pepsi, and a few beers for the trip back. This is going to be fun.

We proceed to the location where he and Freddy made their discovery with the CRS. Once we arrive at the location, I opt to show TC the .45 and ammo clips I brought with me. He smiles, goes below, and comes back with a Remington 30-30 lever-action rifle and a full box of shells. He laughs and tells me that his is bigger than mine is and to never take a peashooter to a gunfight.

We both laugh. I seem to remember my neighbor Jimmy telling me the same thing. At this rate, I am going to end up with a severe complex.

TC says he will take the first shift and puts on his gear. After thirty minutes on the ocean floor, which is only about forty-feet deep at this location, he returns to the surface and shakes his head. He finds nothing. He tells me he marked off the grid area he checked with red flags. He says I can go any direction from the marked grid, just be sure to mark the area with flags.

Now it's my turn and I am a little bit apprehensive. I have not dived in more than fifteen years and I probably am not in the best of shape. I suit up and step off the boat and into the water. A brief flash of claustrophobia strikes me flat in the face. I try my best to adjust and ignore it. I know it is just a bare animal reaction, a triggered survival instinct against drowning. I breathe steadily past the momentary twinge of anxiety as I sink deeper into the warm Atlantic Ocean.

Once I get to the soft, sandy ocean floor, I relax and just enjoy the underwater beauty pageant, the multi-colored fish and the trickle-down effect of the sunlight filtering down through the water. I spot TC's flags and proceed to the closest edge of his grid area to begin my search.

Thirty minutes flies by and it is time to go up. I surface next to the boat and just like TC I shake my head in a negative way. I even test the metal detector to make sure it is working. It checks out fine.

We each do four dives and then with no success, we stop for the day. TC says he is going to check some maps he has at home before we try again tomorrow.

I brought extra clothes because he invited me to stay at his house instead of driving back and forth to Little River, which makes a lot of sense to me. Too bad the twins won't be sitting around the pool when we get there.

I realize by the time we return to the house that I have not thought about someone trying to shoot me all day long. My demons stayed in their boxes. Today was great therapy. I hope tomorrow will be just as good.

Our second day is no better, nor is the third. We have done twenty-four dives and have spent twelve hours in the water with nothing to show except withered skin and sunburn.

On the fourth day TC elects to move our location about one-half-mile further out to sea. He tells me he found an anomaly on one of his maps which does not fit in with the contour of the surrounding area and he wants to check it out. We anchor and set up at our new location.

He takes the first shift and while he is in the water, I notice a large cargo ship moving parallel to our location and toward Myrtle Beach. I look for and find TC's binoculars. I take a closer look. Just looks like a big, not fully loaded, cargo ship with the name *The First Strike* painted on her bow. What a strange name for a cargo ship.

I take a second look and think they must have just painted her name because the paint is running down the side of the ships body. I take a third look and I see a man in a boson's chair actually doing the final changes on the name. He is either new or just a sloppy painter.

All of a sudden, TC pops up out of the water and he starts waving franticly. He takes off his dive mask and yells out, "I found it! I found it!"

"You found what?" I yell back.

"A wreck, put on your gear, grab the blower and come on down."

As I am getting into my gear I keep glancing over toward the cargo ship. Something is not right.

I get into the water with the blower and follow the guide rope down to where TC is shoveling sand with his bare hands. The water is clear and I notice the anomaly as soon as I get close to the sandy bottom. It looks like a large nose protruding out from the ocean floor.

TC is waving his arms and motioning me to come over to where he is hovering. I look where he is pointing and I see what looks like the head of a statue attached to a piece of wood. Could it be the bow of a ship?

He wrestles the blower from my hands and fires it up. Sand and silt go everywhere. After a few minutes, he turns it off and we wait for the sandy mist to settle.

Oh, my god, it is a ship!

He continues to blow sand away from the side of our newly found bounty. Quickly letters appear on the side, but only three, *eth*. Could this actually be *The Queen Beth?* What are the odds, first of even finding a shipwreck and second that it could possibly be the one for which you are searching?

My mind goes back to the cargo ship. My gut, military feeling is that something is not right with that ship and I need to get back to the surface, right now. I give TC a hand signal, my hand cutting across my throat and I point up. He looks at me funny but shakes his head that he understands. He grabs the blower and his metal detector and we ascend to the surface.

Once on board, I pull up the guide rope, I tell him to plot our location, and that we are going to take a boat ride. I point toward the cargo ship in the distance and try to explain why I want to get closer to her. He is not happy about pulling up the anchor and argues against leaving our dive site.

After a very stern look from me, he precisely plots our location. As we depart, he is beaming from ear to ear. I can tell he believes he has found his pot of gold at the end of the rainbow.

I ask him to catch up gradually to the ship, which is just limping along at, I estimate, less than five knots. I don't want anyone on board *The First Strike* to think we are spying on them. As we get closer, I get the binoculars and from behind the cabin window, I start to look more intently at *The First Strike*.

Then I see what must have caught my eye before. I spot the muzzle of a .50-caliber machine gun sticking out about one foot from under what looks like a canvas cover. I spent a lot of time in the Army firing that weapon. I would know it anywhere. So why would a cargo ship have a machine gun mounted on the deck? Even around Somalia, where all the pirates are, the ships do not carry such weapons. Moreover, guess what, I don't think pirates infest these waters.

As we get closer, I see men moving around on the deck. They are dressed in some form of military fatigues. I call up to the bridge for TC to take us toward the shoreline away from the ship.

If this were a movie, my next line would be, *Houston I think we have a problem.*

Instead, I say. "I'm going to be very blunt about this. I think that cargo ship is full of terrorists."

"Gee, Mickke D; tell me what you really think. Damn, that's heavy. Can you prove that? Should we call someone?"

I think back to my military training. I was once told in a survival class *when an operation begins to go bad, anything can hurt you, including doing nothing and that action is doing something, reacting is making it happen.*

"No and yes," I answer, "My phone has no bars out here, does yours work?"

"It sure does, I have it hooked up to an exterior antenna. We can also use the ship to shore radio onboard."

"They could be monitoring the ship to shore. I need to call an old friend at Fort Bragg, so let me use your cell phone."

I find the number in my cell phone and then use his phone to make the call. Colonel Townsend answers after about five rings. "Townsend here," he barks out.

"Colonel T, it's Mickke D. How are you?"

"Mickke D, how the hell are you? Say, I was sorry to hear about what happened between you and Barry."

"Thanks Colonel, but I don't have time for small talk. I need a favor."

"You got it. How can I help?"

"I need you to contact some of your Marine, Navy, or Coast Guard friends for me. There is a cargo ship off the coast of South Carolina near Myrtle Beach. I think it's full of terrorists with machine guns and I have no idea what other weapons could be on board."

"Don't you think that should be a call to Homeland Security?"

"I don't know anyone at Homeland Security and I can't prove what I just told you."

"So you want me to get my head chopped off, is that right?"

"Yes, sir, couldn't happen to a nicer guy, Colonel."

It's quiet on the other end for a few seconds and then he says, "Okay, but I hope you're right. What's the name of the ship, any

ID number and exactly where is she located? Also, what makes you think she's a threat?"

I give him the information I have and he says he will get back to me. Just as I hang up TC yells at me, "Mickke D, you had better look at this."

I take the binoculars and don't believe what I am seeing. The men on board are rolling what look like fifty-five-gallon drums off the deck of the ship into the peaceful blue Atlantic.

TC sheepishly says, "Maybe they are going to pollute the beaches with used oil."

"Or maybe the barrels are filled with explosives. Do you have a tide chart with you?"

He goes below and returns with a chart in his hand. "The tide is going in toward the beach."

I am now in full-alert mode. "How long do you think it will take those barrels to reach the beach?"

He thinks for a minute and then replies, "I would guess less than two hours."

"So by the time they get to shore the boat will be long gone. I need to find out what is in those barrels."

"And how do you plan to do that, or do I really want to know?"

"Is that Wave Runner full of gas?"

"Yes it is. What are you planning to do?"

"I'm going to ride over and take a look at one of them."

"And what if they decide to start shooting at you?"

"Well, if they do, I'll have the answer to my question."

Just as I start towards the Wave Runner, TC's phone rings. It is Colonel Townsend. "Mickke D, I just got off the phone with the Coast Guard. They tell me there is an area around Myrtle Beach where two different radar systems don't quite meet. They actually were tracking the ship on radar but it is gone now. They said it must be in that void area. They should have it back in about thirty minutes. They seem to think there is nothing strange about the vessel except that the crew is experiencing radio problems. The Coast Guard cannot communicate with them."

"Well Colonel, that not so strange ship is now dumping fifty-five-gallon barrels into the ocean about one every thirty seconds. We figure those barrels will reach shore in less than two hours."

"So what do you want me to do?"

"I would like you to stay on the line while I take our Wave Runner over and look at one of the barrels. You need to scramble a squadron of fighter jets right away. If I'm correct about the terrorists thing, they are going to have to take out *The First Strike.*"

"Mickke D, I hope you're right. My ass is going to be in a sling if you're wrong."

"Thanks Colonel. I'm on my way."

I look at TC and say in a very authoritative tone of voice, "If something happens to me, tell the Colonel to bring in the planes and take that ship out. Do you understand?"

He shakes his head *yes.* He then lowers the Wave Runner into the ocean. I push the start button and it roars to attention. Thank god, I wore my cut-off jeans and not my regular swimming trunks to dive in today. I always wear a belt with my cut-offs. I stick my 45 under my belt on the left side and my two ammo clips under my belt on the right side.

I start by running circles around TC's boat. If they are watching, I want them to think I am just playing around with the Wave Runner. Then I spot a barrel about a hundred yards away and I gun the Wave Runner. I want to take a quick look and then get out as fast as possible.

I make it to the barrel with no problems. It is indeed a fifty-five-gallon barrel. It is old and rusty but watertight. I can plainly see one big flaw on the barrel. I doubt if it came with a battery operated detonator on the lid. The barrel is sitting too high in the water to have anything heavy inside. Whatever is inside must be light and small. I'm guessing C-4 or one of those new plastic explosives.

I know the only way you can detonate C-4 is with an electrical charge. Therefore, if I'm right they can be several miles away and still detonate the charges. They will probably wait until the barrels get close to the tourist-filled beach.

I see the bullet hit the water next to the barrel just mille-seconds before I hear the shot. I don't think. I just react. I pull my .45 and fire a shot at the detonator on the lid of the barrel. The detonator is shattered into bits and pieces and the barrel does not blow up. It has to be C-4. Bullets are peppering the water around the barrel and the Wave Runner. They are getting my attention.

I wheel the Wave Runner around and move quickly back toward TC and the boat. As I approach, I see TC with his rifle fir-ing back at the cargo ship. I motion for him to stop.

I pull alongside the boat and tell him, "Save the ammo, you can't kill that big boat with that little rifle. But thanks for making them keep their heads down for a couple of minutes."

"Colonel Townsend said he was calling the Marine base in Beaufort to send up some F-18s to help us out. He said they will be here in about fifteen minutes."

"Great, are they still dumping barrels?"

"Yes they are still dumping barrels about as fast as they can unload them."

"TC the barrels have C-4 in them with a detonator on each barrel. We need to fire at the barrels and sink as many as we can the sooner the better. I'll take the Wave Runner and you take the boat."

The next sound I hear is the sound of a .50-caliber machine gun. Whoever is operating that gun is a good shot because he hits TC's boat at least twice. It is time to leave. We are sitting ducks.

"Move in toward the shoreline and then come back head on to the barrels. That way you will be a smaller target. I guess I should ask you, are you up for this?"

"You bet, those guys are pissing me off. They are shooting up my boat."

"Okay, but keep moving from side to side. Don't give them a good target. In addition, don't get real close to the barrels. They can detonate them from the ship. Once you get a good distance, just let her drift and start firing. Since the tide is going in, you will stay farther away from the ship but in front of the barrels. And for God's sake, keep your head down. We need to get back to that wreck."

I look at my watch. I figure we have ten minutes before the fighters arrive. We need to sink as many of the barrels closest to shore as we can before they get here.

As we depart, the .50 caliber is firing as fast as it will fire and the men on board are shooting at us with what sound like AK-47s. I have TC follow me and then after we get a good distance away, we move slowly toward the floating barrels. As we get closer, I figure the people on board the cargo ship realize their mission is no longer secret and start detonating the barrels. I motion for him to back off. The only living creatures they are going to kill out here are fish. I wonder what all those tourists on shore are thinking right now. Maybe they think it is some sort of a training drill.

Then I hear the sound of fighter jets coming up from the south. The Marines have finally arrived. I have never been so happy to see a Marine in my entire life. They make their first pass without firing. The bad guys on the cargo ship aren't very smart, instead of waving and acting friendly, they start firing the .50 caliber at the planes. Not very smart.

On the next pass, the fighter jets fire air to surface missiles at the ship. They also strafe the ship with cannon fire. The battle is over. The cargo ship explodes in a huge ball of fire. We watch as it slowly sinks into the sea and disappears.

On their next pass, the F-18s tip their wings and head back to their base. Mission accomplished. I'm just glad they realized the good guys were in the small boats because they did a real *damn-damn* on the big boat. *The First Strike* just struck out.

The next sound I hear is a Coast Guard cutter. She is coming full speed toward our location. I take the Wave Runner over to TC's boat and we load it back onto the crane and place her onboard.

I look at TC and say, "Are there any beers left in your cooler, I could sure use a drink."

After a few minutes, the cutter pulls alongside TC's boat and asks if we are okay. I tell them we are fine and that they need to either sink or retrieve the remaining barrels in the ocean and that they probably contain C-4. The commander of the ship says to me, "Are you Mickke D?"

"Yes, sir, I am."

"Colonel Townsend says to tell you it is a good thing you were right or he was going to have to whip your ass."

"Well, I am certainly glad I was right, because I do not need an ass whipping from Colonel T. Thanks guys, we appreciate your help and tell those Marine pilots we also thank them."

"Actually guys, we want to thank you. You just stopped a major terrorist attack. A large number of those tourists enjoying this lovely part of the world could have died. By the way, what were you doing out here today?"

TC looks at me and then he answers, "Oh, we were just doing some diving and enjoying the beautiful day."

"Well, I'm sure glad you were here, being alert and paying attention. Thanks again. Oh, and by the way, we would appreciate it if you do not discuss this with anyone until you both can be debriefed. Someone will be in touch with you tomorrow."

We do not go back to the dive site but move back toward Murrells Inlet. We have had enough fun and excitement for one day. TC thinks we should keep the fact that we may have found a shipwreck to ourselves. I agree with him.

Chapter 48: The Cover-up

The following morning, my phone rings at 7:00am. I am sound asleep, dreaming about Blue and I sitting in a large bowl filled with potato chips and popcorn. We are so happy.

"Mickke D, it's Colonel Townsend. I suppose you're up and about by now?"

"Oh, you bet Colonel T, I already did my three-mile run, had my shower, and I'm just now fixing breakfast."

The Colonel was always a stickler for PT. Actually, I haven't run a total of three miles since I left the Army.

"The brass from D.C. wants to meet with you and Judge Cadium around 1000 hours this morning at the Myrtle Beach Convention Center. Come to meeting room B on the second floor. I'll call the judge and let him know."

I suppose I have no choice but to attend, so I tell the Colonel I will be there.

I get to the convention center about 9:45 and TC is already there. He walks over and softly says, "Remember, we found nothing. I don't trust big brother."

I nod my head and we sit down at the table. Several high profile people are present including Under-Secretary of Homeland Security Bob Reiter and the governor of South Carolina, Melissa Craig. Colonel Townsend is also there, along with a lady introduced as Patty Cambridge, the director of South Carolina Travel and Tourism.

Mr. Reiter begins, "Judge Cadium and Mr. MacCandlish, we would like to thank you both for what you did yesterday. You both went far beyond the call of duty by risking your lives to protect Americans against a terrorist attack. We recovered one complete fifty-five gallon barrel and it was filled with ten sticks of C-4 and wrapped with about twenty pounds of nails, screws, nuts, and bolts. We estimate there could have been around five hundred barrels on board the cargo ship. If detonated on or near the beach, it would have killed or wounded hundreds, maybe thousands of tourists. In most cases you would be receiving medals and a parade for what you did yesterday but since what happened yesterday did not really happen, you can forget the medals and the parade."

I look at TC and we are both perplexed and surprised.

Governor Craig breaks the silence, "Gentlemen, the State of South Carolina and everyone along the Grand Strand want to thank you for your bravery yesterday. However, after an all-night session on the phone with Washington, we have determined that if this attack gets out to the public the terrorists will have won. The news will shut down the tourism trade along the coast of South Carolina and probably North Carolina as well. The economy of both states will be devastated."

Ms. Cambridge adds, "We would really appreciate it if neither one of you discuss this attack and whatever you do, no book deals. We would like both of you to sign non-disclosure agreements."

That scenario about the book had not entered my mind, but the thought intrigues me. "So, in other words, we should just keep our mouths shut and move on?"

Mr. Reiter continues, "Yes, Mr. MacCandlish, that is correct and of course we will see to it that Judge Cadium's boat is repaired. As far as everyone is concerned, yesterday was a joint realistic training exercise between the Marines and the Coast Guard. No one was actually ever in any danger. We will profusely apologize for not notifying the local authorities ahead of time."

Governor Craig puts her elbows on the table and rests her chin in the palms of her hands. She looks directly at TC and me, "There is one more thing we would like to add as a token of our appreciation. Homeland Security has supplied satellite photos of your location yesterday afternoon and it almost looks as if you may have been treasure hunting. If that is correct, I am afraid you were within the three-mile limit of the United States and South Carolina. And if by chance you would have discovered something it would have belonged to us."

I can see that TC has the same sick feeling as I do, but I also remember her saying something about a token of appreciation.

She continues, "Since you two may have found something that could benefit the State of South Carolina, we, along with Homeland Security, are willing to pay you a finder's fee of ten million dollars and the State of South Carolina will hire you as consultants to see what you can find at the location."

As I turn to look at TC, he is already smiling.

I turn back to the governor. "Where do we sign?"

Chapter 49: The Hearing

The Senate Sub-Committee Hearing convenes. Senator Tim Mullins of Ohio is the chairman. The sub-committee is looking into allegations from an anonymous source that Senator R. Gene Brazile has been taking bribes and kickbacks. That same anonymous source also named Gary Sherman, president of Derrick Oil, as a possible person of interest, for making illegal bribes to the senator.

Senator Mullins is a die-hard conservative Republican and he has never cared much for Senator Brazile. Mullins is sixty years old, almost bald, and a little bit on the chubby side. He wears thick lens glasses and dresses like Colombo, but don't be fooled, he is about as dumb as a fox.

Since this is only a hearing, Senator Brazile does not have to appear but he does watch the proceedings from his office.

Gary Sherman is sitting at the witness table with his attorney, Chris White, waiting for the procedures to begin. Senator Mullins bangs his gavel to start the hearing. The senator introduces the other members of the sub-committee and begins by telling Mr. Sherman that this is not a trial but he was sworn in and is expected to tell the truth.

The senator begins, "Mr. Sherman, I do not want to waste a lot of time and the taxpayers money with a long, drawn-out hearing, so I am going to get right to the point. Are you acquainted in any way with Senator R. Gene Brazile of North Carolina?"

"Only that he is a senator from North Carolina."

"Let me rephrase the question, Mr. Sherman. Do you personally know Senator Brazile?"

"No, senator, I do not personally know Senator Brazile."

"Mr. Sherman, have you ever spoken on the phone to Senator Brazile?"

Gary Sherman looks directly at the senator and smiles, "No senator, I have never spoken on the phone with Senator Brazile."

"Mr. Sherman, have you ever given money to Senator Brazile's re-election campaign fund?"

"No, senator, I have never given any contribution, money or otherwise, to Senator Brazile."

"Mr. Sherman, do you know that Senator Brazile is the chairman of the committee which will decide on oil and gas drilling off the coast of the Carolinas?"

"Yes, senator, I do know that."

"And you did not try to influence or lobby the senator for a positive vote on offshore drilling?"

"No, senator, I did not."

"Why not, Mr. Sherman? You stand to lose a lot of money if offshore drilling is voted down."

"I believe that the government and the taxpayers are looking for energy independence and want offshore drilling. I figure it is a done deal or I would never have invested in the leases."

Senator Mullins leans back in his chair, looks directly at Gary Sherman, and shakes his head, "Mr. Sherman, you should have been a politician instead of running an oil company. You have more bull crap than a Christmas turkey."

"Thank you, senator, I'll take that as a compliment."

"Mr. Sherman, do you know Dean Rutland?"

"No, senator, I do not know Dean Rutland."

"Mr. Sherman," and this time Senator Mullins smiles while peering over the top of his glasses, "I have phone records here showing that Mr. Rutland placed several calls to you in the last six months."

Gary Sherman leans over and speaks to his attorney and then smiles back at the senator, "Senator you asked me if I knew Dean Rutland, not if I had ever spoken to him."

"Again, let me rephrase the question, Mr. Sherman. What is your relationship with Dean Rutland?"

"Dean Rutland called my office several times trying to get me to contribute to Senator Brazile's re-election campaign fund. If I was not there to accept the call, as a professional courtesy, I always returned his call."

"And did you ever contribute or give money to Mr. Rutland?"

"No, senator, I did not because I knew that would be a blatant conflict of interest since the senator is the chairman of the committee making the decisions on offshore drilling."

"Mr. Sherman, you just keep getting better and better. Are you sure you're not running for office somewhere?"

"No, senator, I am not. I am the type of person who likes to get things done, not just talk about them. I would make a poor politician."

Gary Sherman's attorney lightly touches his arm as if to say, *shut up Gary, you're moving onto thin ice.*

Senator Mullins' smile turns to a frown but he does not let Gary Sherman's comments rattle him. He continues with his questioning, "Mr. Sherman, do you have any idea where Dean Rutland is?"

"No, senator I do not, is he missing?"

A buzzer goes off and Senator Mullins relinquishes the floor to the next senator for questions.

Gary Sherman is smiling inside because he knows very well that Dean Rutland is missing and unavailable for questioning. In fact, Gary Sherman was the anonymous caller who caused this sub-committee to meet today. He also knows that all of his transactions with Dean were in cash and there is no way to track cash. He just isn't sure if any of the money ever got to Senator Brazile or his re-election campaign fund. He figures this hearing is the best way, other than money, to get into Senator Brazile's back pocket. The senator will owe him big time for this.

ॐॐ

Senator R. Gene Brazile is livid as he watches the proceedings from his office. Not only did Dean Rutland not show up one day and seemed to disappear from the face of the earth, but he is pretty sure he was taking money from Gary Sherman.

Mr. Sherman is saving the senator's ass but he is going to want something in return at some point in time. One thing is for sure, he does not think any of Gary Sherman's money was ever funneled to him, but he does not want anyone looking into his personal business and accidently find out about his *earmark* money.

He figures Dean probably kept all of the money himself and is living on a desert island somewhere in the South Pacific, probably with the senator's secretary, Connie Smith.

They may think the senator has forgotten about them, but he has not. They are on the top of his to do list.

Chapter 50: Dean Rutland

Dean Rutland has been in the captivating, quant, historic town of Todos Santos, Mexico, for almost six weeks. He is renting a very nice oceanfront condo and plans to eventually buy a house here and retire. Todos Santos is almost an hour away from Cabo San Lucas, but worlds away from the bustle of Cabo. He vacationed here several years ago because being a big fan of the musical group, The Eagles, he wanted to visit the Hotel California, which is located in Todos Santos. The small town boasts of art galleries and courtyard cafes set along pleasant streets with traditional colonial architecture. It also provides excellent surfing and pristine beaches for sunbathing. He spent most of his previous vacation watching and dating those sun worshipers.

When things started to warm up around Senator Brazile's office, he felt it was time to leave. He didn't have time to sell the house and condo so he leased both properties to a rental company. All of the income will go to a numbered bank account in Peru. He owned both properties outright so he only has to make property tax payments from his Peru account.

He brought with him almost seven hundred thousand dollars and he will be receiving five thousand a month from the rental company. It doesn't cost much to live well in Mexico. Most of the cash came from Gary Sherman at Derrick Drilling. When Gary finds out Dean has skipped town, he will not be a happy camper.

Dean wonders what happened to his on-again, off-again girlfriend Connie Smith. She just went missing one day and no one has any idea what happened to her, not even the senator. Her disappearance, along with the news that Barry Green, from SIL, had been killed by Mickke D, helped him make his decision to leave town. Too many people were dying and disappearing. Mickke D was too close to figuring out the whole thing. It was the right time to leave.

Dean is on his way to his favorite courtyard café for coffee. It is located along Ocean Drive not too far from his condo. It is a quaint little shop with fully shaded outdoor seating. As he enters the coffee shop he notices the midday air has warmed; the sun bright in a cloudless sky. It is going to be another hot day in paradise.

He orders a latte at the counter and goes outside to sit in the shade and watch the tourists go by. He always enjoyed doing the same thing in airports, but that was when he was working. Now he is just enjoying the good life.

He notices a very nice-looking woman in her mid thirties sit down at the table next to his. She is dressed in a silk blouse, khaki shorts, a large straw hat, sunglasses, and the most important feature; she is not wearing a wedding ring. She seems to be searching for something in her over-sized straw purse. She is not having much luck finding whatever she has lost.

Being the gentleman that he is, Dean gets up and asks her if there is a problem. She takes off her sunglasses and smiles. Her blue eyes are expressive and warm. She tells Dean she can't find her car keys and she is afraid she has locked them in her car.

Again, being the gentleman that he is, Dean offers to go with her to see if indeed the keys are in her car. As they are walking, the young woman introduces herself, "Oh, how rude of me, my name is Kathy."

"Hi, Kathy, I'm Dean, very nice to meet you."

The car, a very shiny new Lexus, is parked in a little used alley just off the main street. Kathy walks over to the driver's side of the car and Dean goes to the passenger side.

Kathy peers inside and smiles, "There they are, cross your fingers."

She pulls on the door latch and Dean hears a click. "Thank goodness, I forgot to lock it."

Actually, she hit the clicker on her second set of keys as they turned the corner into the alley. She sits down in the driver's seat and starts the car. She removes her large straw hat and reveals short, pixie like, blonde hair. The color of her hair causes her blue eyes to appear even bluer. She pushes a button and the passenger window rolls down. Dean puts his hands on the window, leans in and smiles at her.

"Dean I really want to thank you for walking me back to my car. You are such a gentleman."

She looks into the rear view mirror and side mirror. She opens her purse and puts her hand inside.

"Oh, no Kathy, you don't owe me anything. It was my pleasure. Your phone number will be more than adequate payment."

His eyes light up with anticipation but then Kathy pulls a 9mm Glock 29 with a silencer from her large purse. "Dean, I owe you much more than a phone number. Liz says to send you her love."

Dean can see the repulsion in her eyes. The anticipation in his eyes is replaced with rushing fear, pain, desperation, and then darkness as she fires one shot. He is dead before he hits the ground. She rolls up the passenger window and drives off.

Chapter 51: The Second Hearing

It has been almost four weeks since Gary Sherman testified before Senator Mullins' sub-committee. He is back sitting in the same chair at the same table. Attorney Chris White is back as well and questions why his client has been called back to testify.

Senator Mullins answers his question. "We have obtained some new information and evidence, counselor. We would just like to set the record straight. Mr. Sherman, please consider yourself still under oath."

"Of course, senator, but I think this is a complete waste of the taxpayers money."

"I see you are still running for office Mr. Sherman."

Gary smiles but does not respond.

"Mr. Sherman, do you still stand by your previous testimony?"

"Yes, senator, I do."

"Mr. Sherman, did you know that Dean Rutland has been found?"

All of a sudden, Gary begins to get a sick feeling in his stomach. "No, senator I did not know that. Has he been on vacation?"

"No, Mr. Sherman, Mr. Rutland is dead. He was murdered or I guess you could say he was assassinated."

Gary Sherman's stomach problem starts to ease. If Dean is dead, he can't testify against him.

"I am sorry to hear that senator, but what does that have to do with me?"

The senator smiles from over the rims of his glasses and continues, "He was found in Todos Santos, a little town about an hour from Cabo San Lucas, Mexico, with a gunshot wound to the head. The local authorities found several hundred thousand dollars in his condo and local bank accounts."

"Sounds to me as if he planned well for his retirement," Gary replies.

"Did any of that money come from you, Mr. Sherman?"

"I told you senator, I do not know Dean Rutland and I have never funneled any money to him or Senator Brazile."

Senator Mullins feels like he has a big old carp on the end of his fishing pole and he is slowly reeling him to the side of the boat.

"Mr. Sherman, since Mr. Rutland's death, the police have done an extensive investigation. During that investigation, they found a key to a mailbox at a private location. Do you have any idea what they discovered in that box?"

"No, senator but I have a funny feeling you are going to tell me."

"Yes, Mr. Sherman, I am. They found a letter detailing everything that went on between you and Dean Rutland. Should I continue?"

Gary Sherman's stomach problem returns. He leans back in his chair, smiles, and does not answer the question.

"Mr. Sherman, right now I cannot prove that you killed Dean Rutland. However, I do have you for lying under oath to a Senate sub-committee, possibly paying to have Mr. Trever Byers killed, and trying to bribe a United States senator. I wonder if you'll continue to be a wise-ass in prison."

Gary Sherman looks over at his attorney, who seems stunned by the turn of events and says, "Well, Chris, are you going to do anything?"

Senator Mullins motions and two U.S. Marshals walk over to the witness table. They tell Gary to stand up. They handcuff his hands behind his back.

As he is leaving the room, he looks back at his attorney and says again, "Damn it, Chris, are you going to do anything? What do I pay you for?"

Gary Sherman and the U.S. Marshals disappear into a hallway. Senator Mullins smiles again and bangs his gavel. "This sub-committee is adjourned."

Chapter 52: Connie Smith

Connie Smith is sitting on the beach on Grand Cayman Island. She is enjoying the sun and sipping a glass of white wine.

She retired as a schoolteacher after twenty years and since she had started at age twenty-two, she was still young when she went to work for Senator Brazile.

She had been married at age twenty-four and that lasted about seven years. She decided that marriage was not for her and decided to move on. They had no children so parting ways was not a big problem for her.

The senator made several moves on her when she first started but Connie made it very clear to him that she did not mix business with pleasure. The senator did not really mind, Connie was a good and efficient employee so he just moved on to the next young woman.

The senator was right; Connie was a real stickler for perfection in the office. She noticed everything and looked at everything even if it was on or in the senator's desk. She kept a diary of daily happenings, activities, phone calls, visitors, political functions, and she knew all about the money in the senator's desk safe. She found the combination to the safe on his desk one day when he had to rush off to cast his vote. She also knew where the spare key was for the other lock on the desk.

Once a week she took the diary notes and transcribed them into a three-ring notebook while the events were still fresh in her mind. She figured someday all of the information in her notebook would be useful to her.

Yes, Connie knew where all of the skeletons were buried and where all of the illegal campaign funds and bribes were kept. Then one day she decided to retire, rent a condo on Grand Cayman, and enjoy the beach life. She knew the senator usually only checked his desk safe once a week so she figured she would have at least six days to get the money and get out of town before he discovered what had happened.

She took the money one day and filled the empty gym bag with rolled up newspapers just in case he happened to look and not open the bag. She told the senator she needed to visit a sick relative and that she would be back in about a week. She had her bags packed and she had rigged a raincoat with several new, large, inside Velcro pockets so that between the pockets and a large money belt, she could carry the entire $800,000.00 with her on the plane. If any of her friends had seen her, they would have thought she had put on a lot of weight. She walked right through the metal detector and right onto the plane. She didn't breathe until she sat down in her seat after stowing her carry-on bag in the overhead storage compartment. She took off her coat but kept it on her lap.

Like Dean Rutland, she also had taken out a life insurance policy. She wrote a letter to Senator Brazile and left it in the gym bag. She told him exactly what she had done and why he would keep his mouth shut.

She strongly suggested that he should not try to locate her. She would name names, places, events and phone calls. She had enough on the senator to ruin his political life, his social life and his marriage.

If there were to be an investigation, the senator could and probably would end up in jail. You might say Connie had the senator by the short hairs.

Connie really doesn't feel bad about what she has done; she took money that didn't belong to the senator anyway. It was illegal money, tainted money, which is not traceable. So who is hurt? The senator still has his job, his position, his marriage, and he is not in jail. Life is good. She figures it is just bonus money to her from the senator for her being a devoted employee all those years.

At least that is her story and she is sticking to it.

૪૭

Liz Woodkark is sitting in her office in Washington when her private, secure phone line lights up.

"Hey, Liz, how are you? I got the message that you called."

"Yes I did. Have you found anything negative on that Mickke D guy?"

"No, not really. I don't see him as a threat but if I do find out anything that changes my mind, I will be happy to go ahead and eliminate him myself."

Liz replies sternly, "Not without my okay, we may be able to use him later. And get over being pissed off at him just because he found Trever Byers' killer before you did."

"You got it, boss lady."

"Oh and by the way, how did you do in that golf tournament in Myrtle Beach?" She asks.

"Not very well," replies Stan (the man) Hutchinson.

EPILOGUE

A lot has happened in the past six months. First, I found out that Barry (the person who was going to kill me) left a will naming me as sole beneficiary of SIL. It seems he owned the company lock, stock, and barrel. Ted and Bill were only hired employees. The will stated that I was the only one he would ever trust to carry on the business. Go figure.

Second, TC and I split 10 million bucks from the Feds and South Carolina for our terrorists intervention off the coast of Pawleys Island. The Feds figured out the cargo ship was controlled by Iranian terrorists and the shit hit the fan in the Middle East. Iran closed down its nuclear program in exchange for an agreement that we would not retaliate for the attack on our shore line. TC and I are getting ready to head up the underwater search team to find out if our discovered wreck is for real.

TC did send a nice check back to Freddy's family in Brazil. He also found a relative of Rusty McRichards and sent her a nice check.

I closed SIL's office in Culpepper and I got rid of the illegal business entities at SIL, the organ farming, and the arms buying and shipping deals. I also changed the name to Grand Strand Investigations (GSI) and moved the business to North Myrtle Beach.

I sold the helicopter and I did not replace the first plane Paul blew up. I figured I did not need personal airplanes.

I bought the building where my real estate and landscaping business was located and completely refurbished the entire building. Jean and Bob decided not to stay. They moved their plumbing business closer to their home out on Route 9.

I hired my neighbor Jimmy to run GSI for me out of the new building.

I found Mark Yale back in Ohio and I talked him and his wife Jannie into moving to the beach. Now Mark is running the landscape business. I oversee the entire corporation, Mickke D Enterprises, LLC. I run the real estate end of the business out of the same small office that Paul tried to burn down.

Everything is moving along well. Jimmy has a contract with Senator Brazile to find one of his ex-employees. He pretty much told us that since he is our client that we are bound to secrecy. I guess he wants us on his side this time.

Mark is busy with the landscape business and real estate has finally picked up again. I have pretty much retired from teaching golf although I do give an occasional lesson to some old students.

I have no idea where Bill is and even if I did, I would keep it to myself. He saved my butt and I still owe him, and when and if he ever calls to collect, I will be there to pay up.

Detective Sam Concile at least smiles when I run into her and she has actually sent Jimmy some referrals for GSI.

My three ex-wives have become very friendly since they discovered I am well off but I have kept my distance. Two of them live in the area and I think they have weekly meetings to discuss ideas on how to get their hands on some of my good fortune.

Steve (the sign man) Griggs finished second in the World Am in a three-hole playoff with Dane Mienhart's wife Karen from down at Possum Trot. It was her first time to play in the tournament and she won. You go girl!

Steve ended up marrying one of his playing partners from the World Am, a young woman named Pat Lawyer. She has persuaded him to give up gambling and raise a family.

I had a call about a month ago from Blue's owner Terri. The place they are living in Murrells Inlet is not working out for Blue. It is a very small house with a very small yard. Terri wanted to know if I could take him for a while, until she can find a larger place to rent. I guess I owe Blue that much, so I said yes and now he lives with me. Of course, just for a while. *Yeah right.*

Blue has really helped my love life. If you ever want to pick up women, just take your big, friendly, chic-magnet dog for a walk on the beach. It is like shooting fish in a barrel. I have been dating one of my fish for several months now and I think this could be serious. Her name is Beverly and she is a well-built blond with gorgeous long legs who just adores Blue.

The only problem is that Beverly is a cat person and I am not sure if Blue will be willing to share me with two cats, Seby and Bernard. I guess we will just have to wait and see.

I hired Beverly to be my receptionist for the entire building on Sea Mountain Highway. She and Mark's wife Jannie hit it off right away. They became good friends as if they had known each other forever. Go figure.

My demons have disappeared for now. I mentally acknowledged to myself, the past can't be changed, only forgiven and forgotten.

Made in the USA
Charleston, SC
23 July 2014